Dale Mayer

Maddy's Floor

Book 3

Psychic Visions

MADDY'S FLOOR
Dale Mayer
Valley Publishing
Copyright © 2012

ISBN: 1927461006
ISBN-13: 9781927461006

DEDICATION

This book is dedicated to my four children who always believed in me and my storytelling abilities.
Thank you!

ACKNOWLEDGMENTS

Maddy's Floor wouldn't have been possible without the support of my friends and family. Many hands helped with proofreading, editing, and beta reading to make this book come together. Special thanks to Amy Atwell and my editor Pat Thomas. I thank you all.

MONDAY

When you believed in the goodness of life, why did darkness always nudge up against you – test you – try to make you change your mind?

Late afternoon sunshine poured through the window of The Haven casting warm rays across Madeleine Wagner's spacious office on the top floor of the long-term care facility. The early part of August had been hot and humid. Now, entering the last week, the dead heat had cooled to a comfortable temperature.

She stared at the paperwork stacked high on one side of her desk, then at a smaller mountain on the other. Groaning, she leaned back and rubbed her throbbing temple. *Why had she wanted to become a doctor anyway?* Although, today her career choice wasn't the problem; it was her other skills. The skills no one mentioned but everyone knew about. Dr. Madeline…was not only a brilliant doctor, but a medical intuitive.

And her unorthodox skills were the reason Dr. Johnson, from the second floor, had asked her to look at Eric Colgan. He wanted Maddy to try to find out why Eric's condition was deteriorating so rapidly – for no apparent reason – when all his tests were coming back negative.

She'd gotten her first inkling something wasn't right while Dr. Johnson had been explaining the case. Then he'd sent her an email with more details. As she read, a weird twinge settled at the base of her neck. A sensation something was wrong. That feeling had grown until just the sight of her colleague's email brought goose bumps on her arms.

She'd immediately printed the page off, dug out a new folder and buried it under a dozen others.

It made no difference.

It pulled at her. Sitting there.

Waiting.

She sat up straight and forced herself to continue through the large stack of paperwork, until the pull refused to be ignored.

Crap.

She pushed the open file off to the side and dragged the email out. Maybe she should take a quick peek. See if there was anything she could do, and if not, then she'd pass the case back – quickly. She wasn't able to help everyone.

She quickly accessed Eric's file on her computer. With his information displayed in front of her, she eased back from the heavy mahogany desk and mentally distanced herself from her emotions. She took several deep breaths to calm her energy. On the next breath, she opened her inner eye and focused on Eric's energy. Almost instantly, the outline of a young man's body formed; it stood upright in the center of the office, as clear as if he actually stood before her.

Sometimes the person appeared in street clothes, as if they'd just walked into her office, and she'd see the energy moving through them and over them. Other times she saw only a vague shape pulsing with colors. This time Maddy saw both the physical and the energetic forms of Eric.

Now the shell of Eric's body teemed with a swirling darkness as energy poured outward in hundreds of dark red and purple ribbons. Hugging the outside edge, his aura hung lanky and dark, missing the vitality of someone in good health and good spirits.

Colors swelled and receded in a grotesque dance. Stretching away from the body, they faded outward, filling the small office. Maddy rose and circled the desk to get a better view of this apparition. She reared back slightly and blinked several times. The energy still twisted and stretched in its macabre dance. She rocked slightly on the balls of her feet. She'd never seen anything like this.

Angry energy had one appearance. Hatred had another. But this...this defied description.

Maddy needed more information. Letting the vision dissolve, she walked back to her desk and laid one hand flat on top of the printed email.

Eric's energy reached out and grabbed her by the throat. She coughed and choked – tears filled her eyes. She snatched her hand back and bolted to the far end of the room.

Christ.

Maddy paced around the small office trying to calm herself. Another 'first.' In the middle of the room she stopped, her hand on her chest. She took three deep breaths, and frowned. His energy was incredibly strong.

Maddy's mind stalled...reconsidered.

Was it *his* energy? She'd assumed it was his, but did she know that for sure? Not really.

Frustrated, she returned to her chair to flip through the online information. Changing tactics, and with her finely tuned control locked in place, she released a small amount of energy outward in Eric's direction.

It normally took a moment or two to see the pattern, feel the pain and locate the regions of distress in an unhealthy body. Not this time. This time, tidal waves of anger washed over her. Whatever had happened to this young man, she knew he hadn't come to terms with it.

That didn't surprise her. Few people came to terms with imminent death, whether it was their own or that of friends and family. Anger was an understandable reaction to learning you had less than three months to live. But what she'd experienced just now was so much more than anger.

Maddy hugged herself to ward off the unearthly cold now permeating the room. She tried to focus on Eric's physical condition, but emotional trauma blasted at her, disturbing her balance. This man was beyond angry. He'd moved into panic. Confusion and pain agitated his space. His outrage – palpable.

So was his terror.

Tapping into her inner eye, she brought up the same energy vision as before. The aura had thinned until it was snug against his body. Leaning forward, she studied the color patterns, searching for the origin. Energy swarmed throughout the different layers of the young man's body, refusing to stay contained. It was as if the shell were too small to hold it all. The colors darkened, the energy slowed – as if heavy – engorged.

Static energy filled the small room, strong enough to cause loose strands of her hair to quiver.

The image was painful to observe. It reminded her of the aftermath of a feeding frenzy. One energy feasted on the other. Then it hit her. Clearly.

There wasn't a single energy spinning endlessly inside this body – there were two.

Two separate and distinct energies fought a battle within his body as he stood before her.

Stunned, Maddy tried to locate and identify the two distinct energies. One energy, pale and indistinct, sat low and snuggled close to the center of the body. She frowned, recognizing the signs. This energy was weak, dying.

A wave of black swept down the front of the body so fast, Maddy barely saw the paler energy cringe beneath. The wave had depth, density almost. Instinctively, she stretched out her hand, tracing the slow pale ribbon closest to the middle of the image. Her hand went right through the strip.

She gasped as she understood this was in real time. Whatever battle was playing out in the young man's body, it was happening somewhere in The Haven…now. She moved back to the computer and checked the location of Eric's bed – number 242. He was almost directly below her.

As she watched, the energy waves to the right of his body zipped off somewhere out of her vision, speeding forward. The force was so extreme, it snagged the other ribbons, dragging them along in its wake.

A weird noise filled the room. *Laughter?* She spun around...searching. The room was empty.

Then a voice, so malevolent, so angry, that it was almost tangible, whispered through her mind's eye. *Just try to stop me.*

Was it possible?

Maddy jumped to her feet as the energy waves winked out of existence. Panic set in. The mocking laughter swelled to encompass her entire office. She raced out but still the faint laughter snaked through her psyche as she ran down the stairs to the second floor. Urgency fired her long legs as she tracked the faint thread of energy back to its source. She had to stop this – whatever *this* was.

She swerved to avoid a cluster of young people hugging in the hallway. Up ahead, a laundry cart rumbled down the main aisle, clogging it even further. She blasted through the crowd, heading for Eric's ward.

She had to be wrong – to be right would open up something unthinkable.

A horrible suspicion filled her mind, one too bizarre to believe – even for her. And suddenly she knew she was going to be too late.

Surely, no one was capable of doing this.

The laughter cut off as she came to a shuddering stop at the doorway to Eric's ward. The room was filled with frantic activity. A trauma team crowded around the first bed. A crash cart sat between two beds. The other patients in the ward watched on in fearful silence. Maddy stood at the open doorway, unable to see which patient the team worked on.

Confused, she tried to stay out of the way as the chaos heightened around her. Outside, people mingled in the halls. Nurses bustled in and left, and throughout it all, the team worked diligently.

Maddy opened her inner vision only to slam it closed again. Colors, images and sounds crashed into her mind from the chaotic emotions and the overwhelming number of energy systems of those around her. She doubled over with pain from the onslaught.

One nurse raced to her side to help, but Maddy waved her away before stepping back into the hallway to regain her sense of balance.

Several beds lined the hallway. An older woman, her bed in the middle of the others, slept through the commotion. A sheet barely hid her bony frame, decimated by disease. A grayish cast covered her thin, almost translucent skin. Maddy's heart ached for the poor woman. There were several beds with patients that looked in similar condition. A normal state for this half of The Haven that operated as a long-term care home.

Maddy heard Dr. Samuel finally call it, requesting a time of death. She stepped into the room in time to see him tug the sheet over the patient's face. A moment of respectful silence ensued. Maddy quickly sent out a prayer for the family of the unknown man. Death was an all-too-common event here at The Haven. This was the last placement for most patients.

The staff filed out, wheeling some of the equipment with them. The doctor closed the curtain around the bed, smiled at her quietly and left.

Taking advantage of the sudden calm in the room, Maddy walked into the room, nodded politely at the shocked patients whose eyes followed her every move. Then she checked the bed numbers. She stopped in front of the closed curtain and pulled it back slightly.

Bed 242. *Eric Colgan.*

Stunned, Maddy stumbled back to the hallway, taking a last, long look at the white-curtained area. Her heart raced and her brain stalled. Confusion and fear churned together.

What had just happened?

She stared aimlessly down the hallway, unsure how to process the event. Her glance fell on the same elderly woman in the bed in the hallway.

Maddy blinked. Surely, the old woman's gaunt frame hadn't thickened slightly? Her bony ribs seemed less pointed. That couldn't be right. Surely physical changes like that weren't possible? It had to be her imagination. Or possibly it was a different woman instead. There'd been several lined up in the hallway before.

Maddy peered down the corridor. One bed was being wheeled down toward the next ward, with another old woman propped up on the pillows. Maddy breathed a sigh of relief. That had to be the woman she'd seen before. Still, she couldn't resist a last glance at the first woman still positioned in front of her.

Damned if she didn't closely resemble the woman she'd seen earlier – when she'd first reached Eric's room.

Except…this woman's gray-tinged skin now sported a peaceful pink glow that made Maddy's stomach cramp and her heart seize. The old woman opened her eyes and stared at Maddy in surprise, a quick sly smile coming to her face.

Shocked, Maddy stared back as fine tremors of disbelief wracked her spine.

She had been too late.

But too late for what? What had just happened?

TUESDAY

The sun shone on the brick sidewalk leading to the front door of The Haven. It was late. Maddy's morning schedule was already off – on a day she could little afford it. Not with yesterday's bizarre happenings twisting in her mind. She'd had a horrible night. She'd worried well past midnight before managing to nab a few hours of sleep

What she needed was a good dose of adrenaline to toss off her lethargy and kick-start her morning. The many floors of the building gave her a perfect opportunity. The meeting she had this morning was on the main floor beside the physio center and pharmacy. The first and second floors offered open wards and major storage; laundry and morgue were on sub levels. The small hospital serviced the community's needs as well as their own. Her special healing project occupied the top floor, known as Maddy's floor. Her floor.

Walking to the tall narrow stairwell inside the massive stone building, she glanced around to see if anyone was close by. Nope. As usual, she was alone. Another good thing about the cage elevators – people loved them and that left the stairwell free for her to run. Slipping off her heels and flexing her bare feet on the rubber stair edge, she mentally counted to three then bolted upwards. She'd been running these stairs since she'd started at The Haven five years ago. Only twice had she met anyone in her mad dash.

She loved to run. The power she felt as her long legs took the stairs two at a time was addictive. She whipped around the first, then the second corner where the double doors to the next floor remained quiet and closed. Just the way she liked them.

Onward and upward, gaining speed, she felt laughter bubbling up. She had a reputation for being prim, proper and a bit staid. She hadn't cultivated that image, but it did give her a professional persona that made people listen, and in the medical world that counted. If only her coworkers could see her now.

The next landing flashed by. She laughed as she sped faster and faster. Most people tired out as they climbed. Not Maddy – the vertical climb energized her. The next landing went by in a blur. Maddy hardly noticed. Being so focused on the end goal, she pounded ever upward.

And ran into a wall.

"What the hell?"

Maddy stumbled, scrambling to stay upright even as hands reached out to steady her.

"Whoa, easy there."

Gasping for breath and waiting for her balance to reassert itself, Maddy struggled with the shock of hitting what appeared to be a linebacker in a charcoal suit. She stared, stunned at the oversized stranger before her. Then she frowned.

Maybe not a stranger – there was something familiar about him.

"Are you okay?" Concerned pools of blue steel stared down at her.

Part of her brain heard and understood his words. However, the rest of her understood something was seriously off-kilter. She recognized him, yet she was sure she'd never met him before. There's no way she'd have forgotten this man.

Maddy took a step back, blowing out a breath, and managed a light laugh. "Thanks. That was close."

"Do you always run like you're being chased?"

"I was laughing so it was pretty obvious I wasn't in trouble." She gave him a cheeky grin. "And yes, I do like to race up and down these stairs." His gaze dropped to the floor. Maddy glanced down and wiggled her toes self-consciously. Heat climbed her cheeks. Hurriedly she slipped her heels on again.

"Bare feet?"

"Bare feet or heels. I run in both." Maddy tossed her head, her jet-black, shoulder-length hair flipping around her face as she stared him in the eye.

The stranger's eyes widened. "Hardly the safest or healthiest way to start your day."

Her back stiffened. She hated criticism, especially from people who didn't know her enough to be an expert. "Better than a donut."

The stranger's hands fisted on his hips and his forehead creased as he scowled at her. "How'd you know I was a cop?"

Surprised, she arched a brow. "I didn't." She smirked, feeling on a more equal footing. "Maybe that's your guilty conscience talking, Officer."

"Detective."

Maddy acknowledged his title with a nod. "So why is a detective hiding out in the stairwell of The Haven?"

He snorted. "I'm hardly hiding, and I definitely was not expecting to be mowed down. I'm visiting my aunt and checking on my uncle's application to transfer in."

"Ahh, I can understand that. Good luck." She checked her watch. So much for making up lost time. "If you'll excuse me, I have to run." She grimaced at the automatic turn of phrase.

"Right. Back to full speed, I presume." He stepped aside.

Maddy walked up the last flight of stairs at a more sedate pace. She couldn't resist looking over the railing for one last glimpse of the stranger, disappearing below.

Drew continued down the last few stairs, his mind consumed with his 'run-in' with the intriguing mystery woman. She'd worn no nametag, had on no jacket to identify her role in this mausoleum, but her height was a definite clue that would help him find out who she was. He should have come right out and asked her, except he'd been lust-struck by the sight of the six-foot Amazon running barefoot in such a wild fashion up the stairs. And that flash of red and black lace peeking through the buttoned-up blouse – yeah, mega sexy.

How odd. He was usually drawn to petite women. Then again, he also went for the helpless take-care-of-me-because-I-can't-do-it-myself type.

He snorted at his folly. Drew glanced up the stairwell. His mystery woman had vanished.

Though tempted to chase her down for her name and number, he held back. In an all-out race, she'd probably leave him eating her dust.

Still his fingers flexed as if remembering what had slipped through their grasp.

Drew walked down the remaining flights, his mind locked on her. Could she be the elusive Dr. Madeleine Wagner? He'd pictured her as a stiff professional with high-buttoned shirts and thick-rimmed glasses that hid a deep intelligence, not a barefoot, lingerie-loving wild woman flinging herself around the stairwell with complete abandon. How was he to reconcile the two halves to the whole?

If she were Dr. Maddy.

Aunt Doris had been here for close to a year. In that time, Drew had come to respect the staff and the facility. Uncle John, with his rapidly declining health, should be happy during his last few months here – if he could get in. Then again, his uncle was another wild card. He demanded and expected everyone else to hop to it – even though he'd retired a few years ago. Of course, he'd been forced to retire and that twisted his view of 'retirement.' John McNeil would still play the role of the 'chief of police' until the last breath left his body.

Uncle John had run roughshod over everyone all his life and he wasn't about to stop now. If the old guy could arrange life to suit him better, he'd do it.

Drew reached the busy parking lot. His uncle was a challenge, but he was family and that had to count for something.

***

Maddy reached her office with barely enough time to clean up, calm down and grab her notes before her appointment. Today was important. The board meeting needed to go her way. Though she was progressive in her thinking, she was settled in many parts of her life...and change, for her, wasn't something that happened easily. Maddy wanted to stay exactly where she was – on the top floor – with her patient roster exactly as it was. She'd written the Board a nice letter explaining her reasons...that she understood their budget problems, but that if she had to take on more patients it would not be possible to maintain the quality of care each deserved.

Still, if it came down to the bottom line, she'd rather accept more patients than spend hours working on another floor. The latter would divide her energy and compromise the project – hence today's meeting. Tossing a grin as she passed Gerona, one of her senior nurses who marshaled the front nurses' station, Maddy strode to the elevators. Impatiently she pushed the down button – no stairs now. She'd already burned through the last of her time and energy, worrying.

The elevator descended, slow as a snake on a frosty day. She leaned against the back wall and tried to focus on anything other than the meeting ahead. Glancing down at her navy suit, she checked to make sure her outfit looked as appropriately somber as when she'd put it on this morning. Normally, she loved color. Today was all about conforming, at least on the surface. A grin slid out. A prize piece of her Victoria's Secret collection comprised the under layer. Maddy wiggled. No one knew. Except Visa!

Though Maddy was tall that didn't stop males from being interested in her, yet it did slim the numbers down some. Maddy considered that a blessing. If someone drop-dead gorgeous, with that extra something, walked across her path and thought she'd make a great playmate – well then, he'd be in for a happy surprise when he found out about her secret passion. Maddy loved to play – only she didn't do short-term.

It didn't bother her that she'd been alone for over a year now. Someone would show up eventually.

The elevator dinged.

Straightening, she brushed her jacket off and strode forward to face the lion's den, aka Gerard Lionel, The Haven's badass CEO.

***

Gerard stretched, easing his arms upward to erase the kink in his back. A bad night and a lousy morning gave his spine a feeling of being pounded to conform to other people's wishes. He was only thirty-nine, what was life going to be like by the time he hit fifty? He and the other five board members present were once again trying to cut the budget and keep The Haven viable and operational, an almost impossible feat in today's economic crisis.

"Have you considered trimming supplies? Surely, we can reduce this heavy laundry bill. Look at the expenditures on paper towel and tissues." Peggy Wilson, the most annoying, penny-pinching accountant Gerard had ever met, thumbed through the pages she held. "The budget cuts have to come from somewhere."

Gerard groaned silently. Not this again. This was a long-term care facility, for Christ's sake. "We trimmed that area of the budget a year ago. The staff is struggling to maintain this figure as it is. We can't cut things that could affect the spread of infection. You know that. By rights, we should be adding fifty thousand to this figure."

Peggy pouted, her stern countenance almost cracking with the movement. He knew she didn't like being thwarted.

"I do understand that. What is the answer then? We can hardly cut the wages of doctors or other staffers. As lucky as they are to have jobs, we're the ones lucky to have them here."

Gerard put down his pencil and sank back in his chair. "And I know that. We're going to have to raise the fees again and increase doctors' workloads instead of filling open job vacancies. There's really no other option at this point."

And there wasn't. Gerard knew that. He'd been to this point before, at other facilities as well as this one. The past year had been tough on all of them. Theirs wasn't a unique problem and neither was the solution. Yet telling Maddy she'd have to spend some hours each day working on the floor below was not something he was looking forward to. She might consider the alternative worse.

He knew he had to follow the dictates of the Board of Directors. He knew he was the boss below that. He knew she was bound by his decisions, and none of it mattered one bit. Dr. Maddy was…well…she was Dr. Maddy. Special and unique, with skills he'd never be able to replace. Without her, they'd lose a large percentage of their residents, and the huge donations for her project – something they could ill afford.

She'd worked on the top floor for close to five years, and had been running it for the last three. Sure, Dr. Cunningham ran it with her, but his presence fooled no one. Still, with over thirty years of impressive experience he'd lent his name and reputation to the project. But, it was called Maddy's floor for a reason.

In addition to the special project she ran there, her light, her presence, just the person she was radiated something special. When she turned that light onto 'her' patients, they blossomed, improved, and in some cases, they even healed. Her personality or her 'skills' – whatever you called it – was a common thread of discussion in the lunchroom and meetings, but always behind her back. She had a gift that caused everyone to want to reach out and touch her – if just for a moment – to know that miracle healing was possible.

Gerard shook his head at the fanciful thought. These thoughts dominated every time he watched her work, and lately, every time he thought about her. Not good.

"What about extending the day clinic hours?" Peggy suggested. "Open up for more private consultations, have the doctors do an additional half-day a week…or something?"

"That's possible, but the best thing to do is involve the doctors in this issue. In its resolution too. They're all intelligent and aware of the problem. Ask them what they see as options," suggested Dr. Jack Norton, seated beside Peggy. He rarely spoke and when he did, people listened. Jack knew his stuff.

Gerard considered the possibility. "We'd have to set up a meeting, which they won't like as they're strapped for time now. However, if we bring them in to discuss the problem, together we might brainstorm some solutions, or present a few options for them to consider."

"Don't give them too many options. That's asking for trouble." Peggy jotted notes down on her yellow legal pad. "One or two at the most and see what they think. There's a lot of brain power in that group and it's their future as well. It wouldn't hurt to give them a say."

A knock at the door interrupted the thread of conversation. Sandra Cafferty, Gerard's administrative assistant, opened the door and pushed in a coffee cart. "Coffee, everyone. Gerard, Dr. Maddy has arrived."

Gerard nodded and picked up his pencil again. Maddy's visit should be short, and probably not sweet. He needed her to accept the new patient and she wasn't going to like it – at all. Not that he could blame her, but The Haven needed to take in more patients as soon as possible to stay afloat. Even this patient.

"Good to see we can still afford a decent cup of java, hey Gerard?" Moneyman and Chief Financial Officer, Alex Cooper, stood and walked over to the trolley and doctored a cup for himself.

"Let's not joke about such a serious issue," Gerard replied. He'd cut what was necessary, but the team needed to focus on creating a bigger income stream, not just making temporary fixes to the expense drain. He rose and walked over to pour himself a coffee. Bringing it back to his place, he said, "If everyone's ready, let's bring Dr. Maddy in and deal with that issue so we can get back to the rest of the agenda. Sandra, please."

Sandra walked out, leaving the door open.

Maddy's presence filled the door seconds later. It was as if an air of lightness entered with her. "Good morning, everyone. So good to see you."

Even taciturn Jack had to smile at her. "Come on in, Maddy. Grab a coffee and take a seat. This shouldn't take long."

Maddy hurried over to the cart, quickly poured herself a coffee and glanced around the room. "Does everyone have coffee?"

Peggy lifted her gaze from her files, her brows beetled together. "Oh, I'd love a cup. Black. Thank you."

With a sunny smile, Maddy poured the second cup and placed it down in front of Peggy before taking a seat.

Gerard waited until he had her attention. "Now, the new wing, although it's not officially open yet, is causing a stir." Shuffling papers, Gerard, pulled out the one he required. "We have a long list of people waiting for beds."

Maddy remained quiet, her dark chocolate eyes watching his every move. That was a little unnerving, even after all these years. "As you know, there will be twelve extra beds on your floor. Theoretically, two or three of those could be filled now and the rest later."

He raised his gaze to Maddy.

Her eyes never wavered. "It won't be as quiet or as peaceful for them if the space isn't completely finished. There is still equipment to be installed and the finishing touches done to match the rest of the floor. You know the effect atmosphere has on healing."

En masse, the board members dropped their eyes to the various papers in front of them. Gerard studied the bent heads, knowing they were all thinking the same thing. This was a long-term care facility. People came here to die, not to heal. Unless you were on Dr. Maddy's floor. Then weird things happened. Good, but weird, and everyone who was sick wanted to be on Maddy's floor. Hence, part of the current problem.

"Right. Unfortunately, that's not negotiable right now. The budget requires cash. Either we ask you to take over shifts on other floors, or we bring in the new patients early. Four residents means four more sets of fees, and we need that funding at the moment."

Maddy had tensed initially, yet now seemed to ease. He studied her face to see if she understood. So focused on patients and healing, many doctors didn't get the basics of dollars and cents.

She inclined her head. "That'll be fine. The patients will take several days to adjust anyway. The noise will be part of that."

Gerard let out a small sigh of relief then plunged onward.

"On the waiting list for your floor are, of course, many current residents, some you referred yourself." He looked up at her. "The waiting list for new patients is longer. We're in the screening process now and have two good possibilities." He frowned.

This floor stuff bothered him. A care facility should be open to all, and it was, except this issue of requests for Maddy's floor had grown beyond him and beyond the facility. People offered an incredible sum to have a bed for their loved one on Maddy's floor and sometimes refusing wasn't an option, particularly when the applicant fit the stringent requirements – like the one they were considering now. And Maddy wouldn't like this scenario one bit.

He forged on.

"Dr. Lenning has requested one of those beds."

Every person at the table stilled.

Dr. Lenning was not Maddy's favorite person. Not by a long shot. In fact, it was safe to assume she'd buck this choice any way she could. Gerard studied her calm face, wondering at the utter stillness of it.

Finally she spoke. "And why would Adam want to be a patient on my floor?" Her voice, so quiet, so calm, raised the bent heads. Everyone looked at each other before staring at Maddy.

Gerard cleared his throat. This is where it got tricky. "He says that he'd like to experience your healing magic firsthand."

One cool eyebrow rose, heat flaring briefly in her huge eyes. "Magic. Rubbish." Her gaze was clear and serene. "We all know these people are here to spend their last months as comfortably as possible. I repeat – why would he want anything to do with me now...at this critical stage of his illness? His feelings toward me are well-known. He tried to discredit me, to have my license revoked. So why my floor, now?"

"He may have had a change of heart, my dear. Dying men do, you know." Peggy offered an unusual insight. Gerard would have to remember to thank her later.

Maddy's gaze never wavered, a hint of suspicion remained. No one could tell what she was thinking. Finally, after a long pause, she said, "As I presume you've already made your decision, a discussion on this is moot."

Damn it. Gerard hated the burning frustration eating away at him. He dared her to pass up the size of the check he'd received to let their former doctor have one of the new beds. Morals and preferences aside, he had bills to pay, and Maddy needed to do her part.

"And the other patient?" she inquired gently.

"We're considering Dr. Robertson's request for Felicia McIntosh's transfer." Gerard had already approved transferring the seven-year-old from the local children's hospital as a boon to help Maddy deal with Lenning's impending arrival. Not to mention that any child would have outstanding results with Maddy's particular skills. For that reason alone, they tried to find a place for most children who applied. He watched the reactions flit across her fine-boned features. Instead of a beam of joy, her face softened, gentled and warmed. He actually felt like he'd received a pat of approval on his head.

"I'm sure she'll like that."

"As for the next bed to be ready, we're considering former police chief, John McNeal."

Maddy nodded, her features smooth and unworried. "I'm sure you'll make the right decision on that one." She drank the last of her coffee. "Was there anything else?"

"Not at the moment. Just know that we won't be hiring any additional staff. I'm afraid these extra beds will be added to the current workload without any budget additions. We'll still be within the state guidelines – barely."

Maddy stilled yet again – unnaturally so. Everyone watched without being overt.

When she inclined her head a second time, the occupants of the board room sighed with relief.

"That's fine. My team can manage – at least for a while. Thanks for letting me know."

In one smooth elegant arc, Maddy stood, replaced her cup on the trolley and strode from the room.

The board members once again looked at each other.

"That went well, don't you think?" Gerard relaxed his tight shoulders.

Peggy snickered. "Like hell."

Then Jack raised the real issue. "And why *would* Adam want to be under her care when he tried to have her license revoked? *Has* he had a change of heart?"

Ben, the marketing director, who had yet to speak, added, "Or is he going after her again?"

***

Maddy made it back into the gilt cage elevator before her composure dissipated. Her stomach rolled in horrific waves of unease and yes, fear. Dr. Lenning. The world must really hate her right now to toss him her way.

Maddy worked to achieve her best all the time.

Sometimes she failed. Dr. Lenning was proof of that.

It wasn't that Maddy was a goody two-shoes, as some of the other staff believed. She knew firsthand what difference her emotional balance made on the patients' energy around her. Anyone involved in energy work understood the impact negativity had on others.

Maddy leaned back against the wall, her hands against her belly. Two deep breaths later, she could almost straighten her spine. A third did the trick and with the fourth, some of the tension lifted off her shoulders.

So, Dr. Lenning wanted a bed on her floor and, of course, the Board buckled under his demands. He'd make their lives a living hell otherwise. He might also have tossed his checkbook around and bought his way in. The man wasn't as rich as King Midas, but close.

Maddy frowned. She had a hard time with the constant budget cuts. Money was often short and now it was critically so. It wasn't only in her sector. This lousy economy affected everyone.

The elevator slowed its upward climb before coming to a stop. The gated doors opened, letting her exit. Maddy strolled to her office, maintaining her calm as if her world hadn't just collapsed.

"Good morning, Dr. Maddy."

Maddy smiled at the nurse pushing a medicine cart down the hallway. In general, everyone on her floor was happy with their jobs and the people they worked with. Maddy strove to keep it that way. It took finesse and compromise. However, they'd pulled together and had created something special here. Everyone on her floor knew that a delicate balance was required to keep this floor functioning at a higher energy level than the others. Her staff fought any suggestion that they transfer out – as hard as the patients fought to get in. Maddy didn't take all the credit, yet she understood the synergy on her floor. It was important that new arrivals not disturb the delicate balance.

Dr. Lenning already had. It was about damage control until everything could truly be harmonious again.

Instead of disappearing into her office as she'd hoped, Maddy walked down to look at the area under construction. She'd prefer to wait until the workers had finished before moving new patients in, but that was out of her hands. Besides, the renovation was mostly complete. The inspector had been through and the fire marshal was due today. There were a few little finishing touches, and they waited for some medical equipment to arrive and be installed, but the rest was cosmetic. Everything that had been ordered for twelve new patients was coming in piecemeal. She hoped all this would be over before the first new patient arrived, but knowing Gerard, that wasn't likely to happen.

In truth, the renovations weren't the biggest problem. It was expanding the healing energy from the main area into the new area. With new people coming in over the next month, she didn't know how to make that happen without destroying the strong healing cocoon that the patients in the main part of the floor were enjoying.

Maddy considered the problem. Dr. Lenning would move in here – down at the far end. He couldn't complain about the location because he'd have a little more privacy there, plus a window overlooking the treed area behind the facility. The advantage of that location, from Maddy's point of view was his physical distance from the other patients who were actively working on their healing…and to be honest, the distance he'd be from her office was even better.

The more she considered the issue, the more she searched to distance herself from him and the problem of him. A light went on.

With a sharp nod, Maddy smiled. Dr. Paul Cunningham could take on Dr. Lenning. He'd agreed to take on a couple of the new beds so this would be perfect. He would do this just to help Maddy. He'd been a stalwart supporter of her and her project, and someone she'd come to depend on. He didn't put in as many hours on her floor as she did, but he spent many more over at the hospital side of The Haven where Maddy's presence was minimal. She preferred it this way but with extra patients coming in, she'd need him more than ever. They'd work that out.

On the plus side, Dr. Cunningham found it more difficult to deal with children. Maybe due to his grandfatherly age? Maddy, on the other hand, saw the potential of a young person's ability to heal, regardless of the disease wasting their body away. Felicia would be Maddy's patient and she was delighted to have her. *Perfect.* Everything would work out and calm would be restored.

Maddy strode back to the welcoming warmth of the main area. At her office, she emailed Dr. Cunningham on the upcoming changes and her suggestions for the first two patients. The other two patients would be determined at a later date.

With that email sent, she felt a sense of relief. Adam Lenning might be on her floor, only he wouldn't be under her care.

✱✱✱

The nurse walked into the ward, a smile on her face. Sissy watched her approach.

"Good morning, Sissy, how are you feeling today?"

"I'm Occupant of Bed 232, not Sissy."

With an age of patience in her voice, the nurse asked, "Why do you insist on calling yourself something so impersonal?"

"It's what I am. How is that impersonal? Besides, the doctor says it has to do with my disassociation disorder or some such thing."

With a smile, the nurse left her alone with her thoughts, all of which centered on the knowledge that yesterday's session had relieved the soreness on her left hip, and what a difference. She shuffled slightly in her bed, pulling the thin sheets up to her chin. Thankfully, there should be no more tests for another couple of weeks. She hated being taken out of her room. Look what happened yesterday. She'd spent hours in the hallway, in an assembly line of the lost and forgotten, until someone had remembered why she was there.

It hurt to be treated as if she didn't count as much as that kid dying across the hallway. Of course, she counted. More than they could imagine. Now why hadn't they accepted her request to transfer upstairs? She wasn't unstable mentally, no matter what people whispered about her. She'd heard them talk. So what if she talked to herself? So what if she called herself Occupant of Bed 232? Everyone should be allowed to make fun of themselves. There was little enough joy in her life.

And so what if damn near everyone in The Haven had applied for a transfer to Maddy's floor? Why didn't they just move the whole floor up there one at a time as beds became available? That was the fair thing to do. She snickered. Better yet, move Dr. Maddy down.

Besides, she'd been here for ages. She should get priority over the new arrivals. Let them put in their time like she had. She didn't want many more months like this – even with her private healing sessions.

Although, she did feel much better today.

***

Confined to his bed at Summerset Home, dying from some stupid disease that none of the damn doctors could identify, former chief of police, John McNeil stretched out his full length. The foreign sounds of machinery droned endlessly at his side. They weren't attached to him, thank God though his days were numbered. He knew that. The doctors and nurses could continue down their same bullshit-lined path, but he'd been a straight shooter all his life. He wasn't about to change now.

He did miss his work, though. The process of dying surprised him – it was plain boring. He needed stimulation. Watching bedpans being changed, tubes being adjusted and charts being marked didn't quite do it for him. Surely, dying hadn't made him useless.

The concept made him so mad, he wanted to growl. His body might be rotting before his very eyes, yet he'd be damned if he'd let his mind do the same. And it was almost dinnertime – good thing. Too bad the food sucked. At least he'd had his bath already. He shuddered. Who wanted to be treated like a goddamned baby at his age?

Thankfully, his nephew was on his way. There had to be some case he could offer advice.

***

Drew was pissed. The meeting had run late again. "About damn time," he muttered, exiting the station and heading to his black Ford F250. Checking his watch, he realized he was already twenty minutes behind. His uncle had pre-chewed lectures ready to spit out at the least excuse, and by now he'd be spewing them at anyone who'd stop by long enough to listen. Particularly as it was after dinner, so he could lambaste them about the lousy food.

Unlocking his truck, Drew hopped in and started the engine then pulled out of the lot. At least he could update his uncle on his application to enter The Haven. Drew spoke with Gerard Lionel during this morning's visit. Good news. Now Drew would be able to visit both family members at the same time. There was still some uncertainty as to which floor Uncle John would be placed.

Drew knew John had his heart set on Maddy's floor. There was no guarantee that he'd get that boon though. Twenty years of law enforcement didn't guarantee a spot in the 'angels' wing.' Drew snorted. Angels' wing. Who came up with this shit? On the other hand, he'd found there was more than a little to like about the head angel, having verified she was his running goddess.

The Haven had a reputation for caring for their patients. That's all. Nothing more.

Regardless of what rumors abounded, the only thing that happened at The Haven was that people eventually died.

Not him. No way. He'd rather get killed on the job than let one cancer cell into his body. Christ, all he'd done for the last decade was watch members of his family waste away to nothing. He'd eat a bullet first.

The access ramp to the highway loomed ahead. Threading the truck into the traffic, he checked his watch and groaned. At least the meeting that had kept him late had ended with good news. His transfer to the Cold Case Squad had been approved. Now maybe he could make a difference.

That was another move that would piss off his uncle – big time. Tough shit. Not everyone wanted to be the chief of police – especially him.

And following in his uncle's footsteps had never been in his plans. Regardless of what others thought.

***

The visitors to Maddy's floor had gone. The lights had been lowered. The nurses were going through the special ritual to cleanse the day's energy from the floor to facilitate healing overnight. A routine Maddy had established right from the beginning. She had enough different energies to deal with without having to work around residual energy of grieving relatives.

Stiletto heels clicked on the bare marble floor, the echoes bouncing in the dimly lit hallway. Maddy strode from doorway to doorway, checking each sleeping occupant before moving on to the next.

This wasn't part of her job description. This was part of her self-assigned Maddy duties. Besides, it had been a tough day after a tough night, and she needed this. Her patients were family. She loved the journey called life and her beliefs allowed that death was not a crushing end.

The next room was Belle's. This eighty-nine-year-old wisecracker extolled the virtues of living life to the fullest. At every chance, she eschewed healthy eating and the rest of that 'mumbo jumbo,' as she loved to call it. Maddy leaned against the divider between the patients' open areas and chuckled at the shot glass, half full of golden whiskey. Belle's favorite replacement for sleeping pills went totally against regulations, making her doubly happy. Tonight, Belle slept deeply, her energy rippling along her prone body in soft soothing waves, revitalizing her body for tomorrow.

That's the way it should be.

Too bad most people didn't get to experience the same joy and level of balance. So many people took their stress and troubles to bed with them, manifesting their negativity into bad dreams as a result.

Maddy could see patients' energies easier when they slept – when they weren't trying to hide their secrets or control their futures. She'd learned that fear, pain and stress caused energy to drain from a person's body.

Maddy hesitated outside Belle's room. As a patient, Belle wasn't the easiest to deal with. Maddy knew Belle wanted to make peace with those she was leaving behind. She had more than a few relationship wounds to heal. As a healthy vibrant woman, she had been an unapologetic hell-raiser. Maddy had been trying to give her time to deal – but the end of the road was coming.

She entered Belle's room where it was very quiet. For all Belle's peaceful sleep, she was bleeding energy from her lower chakras like a hemophiliac bleeds blood.

Maddy continued her rounds, the soft staccato of her heels tapped out a comforting rhythm. On Maddy's floor, the different patient areas offered privacy without the four walls and doors that one would expect. Several people on her floor had passed on over the years, although fewer every year and so few in the last several months that people had begun to notice.

Maddy didn't delude herself to think that she had unique, fantastic healing abilities that offered the fountain of youth. She chuckled softly. At least not yet. However, she knew that her patients tapped into warm loving energy to deal with their life issues and this often resulted in a prolonged life and healthier last years. In a couple of cases, the people had actually gone home with a new chance at life.

She ignored the whispers behind her back, the curious looks from nurses as they did their rounds, and the subtle criticisms from the rest of the medical team. If she let their doubts in, they'd affect the healing. All actions had an equal reaction – and negative action always caused a bigger reaction.

She hadn't gotten yesterday's weird two-energy incident and the death of a patient off her mind and then there was the board meeting and their bombshell about Dr. Lenning's placement on her floor. She shuddered. Those things alone were enough to rattle anyone's cage.

Consciously shoving away the memory, in favor of deliberate calm had worked throughout most of the day, only to bounce back to problems whenever her schedule eased and she had time to think. Really think.

Jansen Svaar's room came next. With the renovations, Jansen's bed had been shifted. He was not quite in the new area, but not as cozy as he'd been before.

Jansen hadn't minded. The big Swede had enjoyed every one of his seventy-eight years and wasn't ready to jump off yet. Big and robust in his prime, his physical body had withered to one battling diabetes that defied control, and cancer that defied remission. Yet, he was still here and looking so much better than when he arrived. Even his thick head of hair had returned with rich brown color. His last tests had come back with very positive indicators. So much so, Jansen wanted to stop his treatments. According to him, he was all better. If it were possible to heal by his word alone, then he'd see it done.

Maddy grinned as she recalled the many conversations they'd shared in the past.

At the entrance to his doorway, she stopped to survey his bed.

Something was wrong.

Purple energy hovered over Jansen; a thick blanket of colored haze covered his midsection. Frowning, Maddy studied the odd essence. Energy had a signature – like DNA, the energy was unique to each person. It just wasn't as easy to identify.

She'd worked with him long enough to know it wasn't his aura.

The smoky blanket moved.

Who or what did the energy represent? Her gaze swept the rest of the room before striding forward. The activity over Jansen did not shy away; it increased. She narrowed her gaze. The eerie silence of the room magnified the unearthly scene before her.

It wasn't what she'd experienced the night before, racing through the hallway into chaos. She expected noises of some kind. Not this hushed silence, as if sound would shatter the intensity of whatever was going on. She frowned. A struggle of some kind was going on.

She shook her head, panic stirring inside. Could energy fight with itself? With someone else's energy? Is that what happened to Eric? She studied the energy again. This time she saw it. The blanket of malevolence was moving over the bed and occupant, spreading and growing every minute.

Underneath, Jansen was suffocating.

His energy, tiny and thin, struggled to remain separate and distinct from the purple amoeba-like entity sucking the life force from him.

Fear shot through her. This couldn't happen again. Maddy raced to the bedside. "Stop," she cried out hoarsely, not wanting to disturb the other patients. "Leave him alone."

The purple energy quivered in place but did not dissipate.

Maddy wafted her hands over Jansen's body. Her fingers slipped into and through the mist, neither feeling it nor dispersing it. She fed her own energy into Jansen's heart chakra, giving him her strength and will to hold on. At the same time, she closed her eyes and surrounded herself and, by the extension of her hand on his, Jansen's body with white light. The old answer to keeping oneself safe and balanced.

The energy shifted, cooled.

She opened her eyes to find the energy still wiggling in place, the purple haze malicious in appearance. Then slowly, like fog blowing in the wind, the haze thinned before sending tendrils into the darkness.

Maddy reached out and checked Jansen's pulse. Her medical training took over on the physical level as her medical intuitive training took over on the energy field. She observed the thread-like cord of light stretching far out of Jansen's body, gently pulsating in a reassuring rhythm. Maddy coaxed his system to relax a little more, then to wake up gently.

"Dr. Maddy?" His paper-thin lids opened to reveal rheumy blue eyes blinking in surprise.

"Yes, it's me, Jansen." Maddy studied his face. "How do you feel?" He appeared fine, normal but surprised.

"Christ, I don't know. I had the most horrible dream." He coughed slightly and shifted position in the bed, tugging at his covers as if chilled.

"Oh?" Maddy kept her voice calm and soothing. "What was it about?"

"Like someone was pulling my soul from my body, one inch at a time." Fear filled the old man's eyes. His thin hands grasped hers nervously. "I don't know what the hell it was, but I felt on a precipice between life and death. It was like meeting Peter at the pearly gates himself, and him not being too happy to see me."

"Shhh." Maddy stroked his hands, noting with clinical detachment that his liver spots had begun to fade. "It was just a dream. Not to worry. It's over. I'm here, and you're safe. Go back to sleep."

Relief washed over his face. "Thanks, Doc. Don't know what I'd do without you."

Shifting sideways, Jansen closed his eyes and fell back to sleep.

Maddy walked to the doorway, turned around and glanced back.

No sign of the purple grim reaper. Jansen was safe.

For now.

WEDNESDAY

The Haven buzzed with activity. They had several hundred residents and more than that amount of staff. Without Gerard, the place would have imploded years ago. Maddy massaged her temples in an effort to draw out the tension.

She wondered if she'd missed a growing thread of discontent. One that had started or fed the horrible negativity – or, dare she say it, evil – that she'd observed over Jansen last night. She couldn't even begin to understand the source of the hellish energy that contributed to Eric's death, either.

After going home last night, she'd tried to contact several of the other medical intuitives she'd met over the years. She only managed to touch base with two. Neither had seen or heard of anything like that deep purple-black blanket of energy. A crime may have been committed in Eric's case, although what it was or how it was perpetrated was beyond her. Too bad she couldn't go to the police.

That handsome detective she'd barreled into on the stairway bloomed in her mind, making her pulse quicken. Damn if that man hadn't made her hormones sit up and sing. She'd obviously been single too long. Maddy didn't do one-nighters, but right now her body was pushing her to reconsider the concept. That the detective wasn't impervious to her, helped keep his smile alive in her mind and the 'what ifs' dancing through her body. The warm light of approval she'd seen in his eyes had been hard to ignore. She should have asked his name. Hell, she should have asked for his phone number. She could only hope his uncle would make it onto her floor so he'd become a regular visitor.

31

She walked out to collect the stack of papers waiting in her intray.

"Dr. Maddy. The ambulance has arrived with Dr. Lenning."

Silence descended on the nurses' station. All movement stopped. Furtive glances came her way. Everyone knew about their new patient, and the impact it could have on Maddy.

Maddy nodded as if she'd been expecting the news. Gerard was nothing if not fast.

"Right. Let Dr. Cunningham know, will you Nancy? Dr. Lenning is his patient. Dr. Lenning's to be put into the new area, in bed 349. I'm presuming the bed is in place. If not, we'll need to get one brought up immediately."

"It arrived an hour ago. Except, uhm, Dr. Cunningham isn't in yet."

"Isn't he?" Already on her way to her office, Maddy spun around to stare at Nancy, her head nurse and confidante – not to mention best friend – who had been there almost as long as Maddy. A frown creased her brow. "Where is he?"

"He phoned in to say he'd been called to surgery unexpectedly." The two women looked at the clock.

"Ten o'clock." Maddy tapped her toes, thinking rapidly. She'd do a lot to avoid meeting Dr. Lenning, but she wouldn't be able to avoid that forever.

Shrugging as if it didn't matter, Maddy said, "You know what to do. Get our new patient comfortable and check his vitals. His information should have come with him. If it's there, bring it down to me and I'll see what we're looking at. If it's online, send me the link. I'll speak with Dr. Cunningham when he gets in."

After scooping up the stack of paperwork from her box, Maddy headed to her office for a little down time before facing the one man who'd managed to teach her quite a lot about fear. She walked the short hallway, feeling the eyes focused on her back, the whispers in her wake. Let them talk. Maddy only hoped they wouldn't indulge in a gossip fest. Gossiping destroyed a peaceful balance faster than anything.

Knowing this didn't stop it, however. People were human and reacting was instinctive. It's when the gossip didn't stop that it became a problem.

She dropped the paperwork on the corner of her desk and walked to her window to stare out at the courtyard. Having to deal with Dr. Lenning was not going to ruin her day. She wouldn't let it. Gerard knew what he was doing, and if he said this was a necessary step, even given her history with the good doctor, then she'd accept that and try to make it work. She was a professional.

One difficult patient, a dying one at that, wasn't worth making a major life-altering change. Not now. She'd put so much time and effort into this floor, and she could hardly abandon it. To do that would tear her soul apart.

Grimly, she reached for the paperwork on her desk. She had work to do. Making the new patient comfortable required at least an hour, possibly two. With any luck, Dr. Cunningham would show up by then.

✳✳✳

Dying was a bitch and Dr. Lenning had sworn off bitches years ago. Until now. The trouble with dying was it gave him too much time to think. He'd been more than satisfied with his life until he found out he was losing it. He'd lost the best thing in his life when he'd lost the love of his life, Mark, five years ago. Even now, his heart ached at the memories. He'd loved and been well loved in return.

Four years ago, he'd lived a normal life – at least for him.

Then he'd seen Maddy and he'd lost the one sure thing he knew about himself – his sexuality. She had changed that. Her slim, lithe, vibrant femaleness had challenged his beliefs. She'd made him doubt himself and the choices he'd made. Made him

33

wonder if he'd been fooling himself all these years. He'd hated feeling like he was betraying Mark. He tossed his head back and forth. He wouldn't be disloyal to Mark or his memory. He couldn't. But these feelings...

He detested the emotions Maddy had stirred up, the glow he felt when he was around her. He wanted Maddy and he *hated* her for that. He'd wanted her removed from The Haven. He had even gone so far as submitting a fifty-page document to the medical board hoping to kill her medical career. Only she'd had some powerful people on her side. So he'd spent the last four years alternating between a need so crippling he shook with it, and a hatred so violent he vibrated because of it.

Maddy's never-ending legs rose in his mind. Christ, he couldn't get her out of his thoughts. Knowing that made him angrier. He closed his eyes and shuddered. These feelings were worse than he'd experienced during puberty. He'd never had a woman and now, bedridden and dying, the chances were good he never would. That left him in endless torment. Teenage fantasies tortured him with excruciating 'what ifs.'

Why now, when he had no time to explore that side of life? Why her? And why had he demanded to be on her floor where this exquisite torment would be that much worse?

Even as he asked the questions, he knew the answers. He was desperate, that's why. Not that he understood her New Age bullshit, but dying made him more open, more willing to look at other options. He hoped she did have some magical skill that would save him. He wanted to believe.

His education and experience said there were no second chances for anyone.

Plus, he couldn't resist an opportunity to get close to her.

"Stupid bastard. Why didn't you do something about this before? Why didn't you grab some pills and finish this once and forever?" But he hadn't. As long as there was one more day to live, one more chance of a life, one more hope of seeing Maddy again, he'd take it.

He grimaced. God, he was weak. The woman wouldn't give him the time of day. Not now. Not after he'd tried his damnedest to get her out of his life, his profession, his space – to where he'd never have to see her again. Then cancer had ground his life to a halt. Now he needed the special healing powers she was rumored to have. The same ones he'd used to try to run her out of the medical association.

She hated him.

He couldn't blame her.

He hated himself.

A heavy knock on her door interrupted Maddy from her drug interaction research. "Come in," she called out.

The door opened tentatively. Gerard poked his head around the corner. "Maddy? Sorry to bother you. I just checked to see how Dr. Lenning was faring. He's not in a great mood."

Maddy raised a brow in surprise. Things couldn't be that bad. No one had come to tell her about any problems. With a discreet check on her watch, she realized only an hour had gone by. The patient would barely be in bed and checked over. Stifling a sigh, she leaned back to give Gerard her full attention.

"Not surprising. He's dying and any attempt to make him more comfortable requires more drugs, which leaves him moving up and down on the moody scale." She sighed and added gently. "It is normal and expected – regardless of whether we like it or not."

Gerard grabbed the spare chair, swiveled it around and sat on it backwards to face her. Slightly older than her, Gerard had garnered a lot of respect in the years he'd been here. "He says he hasn't seen you yet."

Maddy willed her patience to suck it up. "No, he hasn't." She glanced at the time on her computer. "It's early yet. I doubt the floor nurse has even completed her assessment. Dr. Lenning knows the length of time it takes to complete admission. There are deadlines to meet and we will meet them."

She held up her hand to forestall Gerard's next words. "Yes, I will go and welcome him to The Haven if Dr. Cunningham doesn't arrive in the next hour. I do want to see his paperwork first, however."

"Fair enough. I'll stop by before I go downstairs and let him know you'll be along in a little bit." He stood, flipped the chair back around the right way, and stepped to the door. "I want to tell you that I appreciate your cooperation on this. We all know that he isn't the ideal patient for this floor, but his money is good and our need is great."

Maddy smiled at Gerard who was doing his usual, putting money first. He exemplified tunnel vision. "I don't have a problem with either point. However, his presence on my floor is definitely not required. The rest of The Haven is just as great a facility. The staff is equally qualified." She stretched her arms forward, clasping her hands together and rested them on her desk as she had in grade school. "To have insisted on my floor doesn't mean he gets *me*."

"No, it certainly doesn't. You're carrying a large caseload as it is. However, this morning, if you would step in for Dr. Cunningham, we'd appreciate it."

"Absolutely." She firmed her jaw. "But should he cause any unrest or deliberately attempt to sabotage my floor, my people or my project, I will ship him downstairs. And I don`t care about how much money he spent to get here. Do *you* understand?"

Maddy watched as surprise lit Gerard's eyes, followed by a tinge of anger and then finally his tensed shoulders relaxed and he nodded. "I suppose that's no different than for any other patient we take in."

His cell phone rang. Sliding it from his pocket, he looked at the number and grimaced. " I need to take this call." With a quick salute to her, he left.

He hadn't been gone ten minutes when Nancy arrived, rolling her eyes. "The new patient is settled in and complaining loudly." She held out a fat binder to Maddy. "This is his. He might squawk loudly, but I doubt he's going to die tonight or tomorrow. When you're done going over it, we'll enter his information online."

The binder sat on her desk. Maddy gazed at it as if it were a viper ready to strike. The Haven was more advanced technologically than many other facilities. She'd forgotten how much easier it was to have everything online.

How much longer until Dr. Cunningham arrived? She reached for her cell phone. He answered almost immediately. "Hi Maddy, the roof must have fallen in for you to need me."

"Maybe it has." She leaned back in her chair, relieved to have reached him. "Dr. Lenning transferred in this morning."

He chuckled. "So the pain in the ass is there, is he? I have to admit, I hoped he'd change his mind at the last minute." Paul coughed and cleared his throat.

Maddy waited until he was quiet. "No, he's here and would like to see his doctor."

"Par for the course. Well, buck up. This is one we have to have whether we like it or not."

She knew and understood that. But she still wanted him in to deal with the new patient. "That's why I'm calling you. When are you coming in?"

"I'm still going to be another hour here, so do me a favor. Give him the welcome speech, or the warning speech in his case, and tell him I'll be there soon to go over his medical information and current treatment. You have to face him sometime and this way he can't fault you for your lack of professionalism. I promise I'll be over soon."

And that was as good as it was going to get.

Maddy closed the binder on her desk, and stood. She'd grab a coffee, put on her most professional smile and be civil. She could do this. She had to. Maintaining the healing balance on her floor depended on it.

***

John shifted positions, hating the throb that raced down the outside of his right leg. Damn useless body. Piling the sheet at his waist, he shifted his cell phone so he'd hear better.

"Gerard, I want to confirm that my transfer's gone through." John strained to listen to the voice on the other end of the phone. "Wanted to say thanks. I've been waiting to get onto Maddy's floor for a while now, but it's not like beds open up there. Good thing that new wing was being developed. And that I donated to it, huh?" He laughed until a cough caught him out. "Damn chest. Can't stand all this coughing."

He reached for his glasses atop the small bedside table. "Speak up, boy. I know you're busy, however I want to know when the transfer will happen. I've waited all morning for news, and nary a peep out of your people. Haven't got all year, you know." He chuckled at his own joke as he pulled his day planner to his side.

"I gather Drew spoke with you."

"Yup, he did. Now I've got my calendar out. So when can we make this happen? I have lab tests this morning…the dietician's coming midafternoon – I'm happy to miss her. Lord, if I have any more fiber in my cereal I'm going to start to moo with the damn cows. I know there are a couple of other appointments here somewhere. Give me a minute…" He studied the handwritten notes that kept his daily activities organized. What a pitiful way to live. He knew the ward clerk kept it all straight, but he needed to keep track of it himself. A matter of pride. He wasn't that decrepit.

"What's that?" He'd missed Gerard's last comment. Damn the man, why wouldn't he speak up? Christ, the guy was big yet had the voice of a woman. He was probably a damn fairy;

wouldn't surprise him, knowing his mother and the antics she'd been up to way back when. In his day, that wasn't talked about, but now, Christ, these men wore pink shirts to advertise the fact. What the hell was happening to the world?

"The logistics of the move aren't your concern. We have people who will take care of that. But I don't have the room assignments sorted out yet."

"Yeah, whatever. I don't really care about that. It'd be nice to look out over the back woods, though. I'd like a spot of nature to remind me of better days. Didn't I hear something about balconies in some of those rooms?" He rubbed his grizzled chin. "That'd be mighty fine."

Gerard sighed. A deep, long-suffering sigh that made John roll his eyes. "I know. However, the balconies are designed to be for everyone, as are the sitting rooms. There aren't closed bedrooms John. There's privacy, only not the same as four walls and a door would provide." He hastily backed up. "That's *if* you're getting onto Maddy's floor."

"What?" John roared. "Of course I am. You said so yourself. What are you trying to pull here?"

"John, I said your transfer to The Haven had been approved. I didn't say you were guaranteed a spot on Maddy's floor."

Panicked, John's face burned, his heart slammed inside his chest and it was all he could do to catch the next breath – the fear was so bad. He had to get onto that floor. It was his only chance. "Don't play games with me, Gerard. Maddy's floor *is* The Haven and that's the only place I want to be."

"I can't just give one to you without going over all applications and making an unbiased decision, John. The beds are at a premium. More than that, there are strict requirements to gain entrance to the third floor. Requirements you don't necessarily fit. We have a stringent interview and selection process, for that reason."

Unbridled anger rose in John's chest at Gerard's words. His left hand pressed against the sudden constriction as he tried to breathe. The bloody bastard. "Why you little prick! This has nothing to do with the entrance requirements – this is all about money, isn't it? You want more to place me on Maddy's Floor. Haven't I paid enough? Or maybe it's you who hasn't paid enough. I thought we'd put the past behind us, but if you don't get me onto Maddy's Floor, the past is going to rear its ugly head and bite you in the ass."

Silence.

In an odd voice, Gerard asked, "Are you blackmailing me?"

"Hell, no. Nor am I threatening you. This is a goddamn promise." This couldn't happen, not now. He had so little time left. With so much panic surging through him, he almost dropped the cell phone. His breath came out in anguished gasps. "Don't you understand? I *have* to be on Maddy's Floor," he cried. "What makes someone else more important?"

"Well, for one, they've been waiting much longer than you. Some of the other patients have been waiting for over a year now. From their perspective, you should be on a lower floor and they should move up one at a time. You have to understand, John. I don't have a few applications, I have several hundred. Not everyone will qualify, but we have to consider them."

John sank back down into his wrinkled bed, tears welling up at the corner of his eyes. Not fair. So close and yet so far. He pulled up the corner of his sheet and wiped his eyes. Giving himself a hard mental shake, he tried to see the situation clearly. He understood that requirements had to be met, a set of criteria had to be established and followed. He knew that for these twelve beds to be filled, hundreds had to be rejected. He was a lawman. He understood justice. He'd played fair and square all his life ...and he'd bent the rules just once.

Now he needed the beneficiary of that one slip to bend the rules for him.

Gerard's voice turned brusque. "Listen, John, I know we go way back. I'll take another look and see what I can do."

John didn't dare speak. Sixty-six-year-old men didn't cry. Shit, real men didn't cry. He was being a wuss. He could blackmail the bastard into getting what he wanted. However, he also had money. Maybe he should sweeten the pot. Sniffling hard and coughing as if to clear his throat, John said, "Let me know if there is any equipment you're short of down there. I might be able to help."

There was silence for a moment before Gerard answered. "Will do. Give me a day or two to check some figures. Then I'll get back to you."

"A day or two is fine. Don't wait too long."

The meaning was clear. John meant to get what he wanted. And he'd pay his way if he must, but get it he would. One way or another.

✳✳✳

Gerard stared across his large executive office. His gaze landed on the huge oil painting on the far wall. He didn't bother to bring it into focus. What was he going to do now?

He didn't have much choice with the bed assignment issues. And in this case, he was good with that. Still, wouldn't it be nice if people took to their beds and were happy? But no, just like little children with desk assignments in school, everyone thought having a bed somewhere else – in some cases, anywhere else – would be better.

The hospital policy stated they were not to cater to the petty demands of patients and doctors. Fat chance of following that policy to the letter. Still, if making minor changes appeased the parties involved, then The Haven tried to accommodate all reasonable requests.

Then there was the problem of John's thinly veiled blackmail threat. He shuddered. However, if John were willing to pay a little more, then he'd pass his application through the Board no problem. With the budget shortfall they were currently experiencing, anyone who could pay would pay, whether the Board liked the system or not. This wasn't the time to raise the moral issues of better care for the wealthy. The doctors on the other floors were extremely capable. The Haven was known for the quality of care for all patients, not just those on Maddy's floor.

Damn that man anyway. The same persistence that had made him a hell of a cop made him a hell of a lousy patient. Choices were limited. Bills had to be paid and patients needed care. Yada, yada, yada. That Maddy wouldn't be happy over this decision was a given. What choice did he have? He hoped John's life expectancy was incorrect, because that would be a sticking point. But if he did get John there without her knowing about it, then she'd find a way to make it work, she always did. Manipulative? Yes.

Desperate? Oh yes.

Well, there was no point in waiting. Grabbing up the correct application file from the top of his overflowing in basket, he picked up the desk phone. "John, I have good news for you."

***

John ended his call and immediately placed a second one. His emotions were still on a roller coaster. "Drew, I got onto Maddy's floor. It took a bit of finagling, but I did it."

"Wow," Drew's tired voice perked up.

That damn kid worked too hard. He'd have made a hell of a police chief.

"That's great news. Did he give you a date yet?"

"Nope. They have to finish the rest of the wing. I told him I'd move in with exposed lumber as long I made it out of here, but he just laughed and said it wasn't that bad. Apparently they've moved one new patient in already, however, the rest of the medical equipment and supplies will take a day or two."

Drew said, "Please tell me you didn't offer to pay for equipment..."

John's smile beamed across the room at the three other patients shamelessly listening in on his call. "What's the point of having money if it doesn't help you?"

Drew was silent for a moment. "I think that's called bribery."

"Bribery, smibery. Who cares what it's called as long as it works? Gerard needs donations and I need a bed. That's called a *trade*." He wanted to get up and dance around the room. This was going to work. He just knew the famous Dr. Maddy would fix him.

"Hmmm. At least I'll be able to see both you and Aunt Doris at the same time."

John coughed. "That's the best part. I'm getting on Dr. Maddy's floor, but I doubt she is. She's going to be pissed."

"You have the money, *trade* her way up there, too."

What? Like hell. John couldn't help the harrumph that slid out. "She can pay her own damn way. Christ, the sibling bond doesn't stretch that far. Especially a step-sibling. She's a pain in the ass with all her ordering about. Do you think I want to listen to that to the end of my days? Like hell." He shifted in his bed, pulling the blankets up higher on his shoulders. This damn place was either cold or hot. There never seemed to be a happy medium. Cheap buggers, all of them. All they ever wanted was money.

Well, he'd spend his the way he wanted to. And he'd leave it to whomever he wanted and that person sure as hell wasn't his stepsister. He winced as his guilty conscience poked him. "Besides, look at her mental deterioration. It's not like she'd appreciate the difference in the floors. Why waste the money?"

Drew's long-suffering sigh, the one John had heard a million times before, sounded through the phone. "Whatever makes you happy. You do know you can't take it with you?"

"Hell, I know that. Otherwise I'd have kicked off and taken it with me years ago, before this old body decided to break down. Now I'll spend it when I want to and how I want to. Have to go. The dinner cart is coming."

John hung up on his nephew. Damn do-gooder. How the hell had Drew gotten so strong on family? Besides Doris wasn't really family. And she'd spent all her money on her loose lifestyle. Why should he pay for her care now? Drew was the only one worth helping, but if Drew kept bugging John to be nice to Doris, Drew wasn't going to get anything.

Just like Doris.

***

Drew put away his cell. Why the hell couldn't those two get along? Didn't he have enough trouble on his hands without running interference between his aunt and his uncle? Jesus. For two bedridden people they caused a pack of trouble. Like he needed that, today of all days – his first day on his new job.

He stood in the doorway and surveyed his new space as part of the Cold Case Squad office space. He'd visited before, but now this was *his* office. The large open room featured windows down one long wall that opened out to the back parking lot. Bulletin and white boards filled the other walls. Some were filled with notes and pictures and others remained empty, waiting for cases. *Stacks* of boxes, file numbers written on one end, filled the back wall. In the middle of the room were several large empty tables and two desks sat toward the back of the room. Open and friendly looking. He liked it already.

"Drew, welcome. Glad to have you here, finally."

Wilson Carter walked toward him, arm outstretched. They'd worked together for years, then apart for the last two when Wilson had transferred to this unit. He'd worked on Drew, slowly, inevitably persuading him to join the Cold Case department. Drew hoped to find that sense of job satisfaction here that eluded him in his former position.

Solving old cases with forgotten victims and helping out the families that had been waiting for closure since forever, should give that to him.

He shook Wilson's hand and listened as his old friend gave him an overview of the work area and the cases in progress. "Wow, it seems like we have some work to do."

"Ya think?"

Drew grinned, feeling a weight slide off his shoulders. "And I'm damn glad to be here." He glanced at the one wall beside the doorway that held several kids' pictures. "Where do we start?"

"We have several cases that have been reopened. It's going to take you some time to get up to speed on everything so I suggest you start with one. Go over it so you can become familiar with it, and then go on to the next. However..." He walked over to study the board in question. "This isn't really one of them. Although, when we have a lull or spare time, feel free to look deeper. But unless you come up with some concrete lead – well, it's not in the budget. We have to use the limited man hours where we can make a difference."

Drew stepped closer to the old photos on the wall. Six of them, boys and girls, one black and one of mixed race, Mexican maybe. The others were Caucasians. The fresh happy faces tore at his heart. If they were on the wall, they were victims. Victims he'd come here to help. He read the brief notes interspersing the old photos.

Glancing over at Wilson, he said, "I'll find time to go over this case though, even if it's in my spare time. I remember my uncle telling me about this one. Fascinating stuff."

Wilson nodded. "And very odd."

***

Doris glared at the small black cell phone. Her hand trembled so hard, she could barely hold the receiver to her ear. Her perfect asshole of a brother was gloating. Again. *Jerk.* In truth, he wasn't really her brother. Her mother had married his father when they were young enough to share their parents and old enough to hate having to do so. A difference she'd come to appreciate over the years. She tugged ruthlessly at the blankets, pulling them higher on her chest.

"You got a bed on Maddy's floor? I don't believe you." And she didn't. Her application had been in for months – if not years. Who could remember? The days rolled into one hellish moment after another. "How did you get accepted before I did?"

"Money. Something I have a lot of and you don't."

John's joy made her sick. How dare he bribe his way in? And gloat about it. No siree, she wasn't letting this slide. The Haven would pay for this insult.

With the new wing opening, she'd hoped her application would finally be accepted. So far, only a couple of new patients had heard about their transfer requests. If she trusted the gossip, there were another ten beds or so still to fill. Patients had been in a frenzy trying to get transfer requests in as fast as possible, only they needed their doctor's approval too. Surely, one of those beds had her name on it?

She closed her phone while her brother was mid-sentence. There was only so much gloating she could handle. Besides, the second floor of The Haven was chaos. Doris watched the organized mess continue, as it did at this time of day every day. There was no weekend off from being poked, prodded and asked silly questions, with answers noted on the clipboard for all to see. Who in the world cared if she'd had her fiber and whether it was working or not? Peace was a prized commodity. Still it was better than the being in the morgue. Doris shook her head, her busy fingers pleating the sheets on her chest.

She studied the others in her ward. She'd had the same three neighbors for the last six months or so. No one left here except in a coffin. They should paint the walls black to prepare everyone for that certainty. Instead, someone had painted a happy yellow color on the walls. Yuck.

Still she'd been here close to a year. If John would give his head a shake, he'd understand that she was the one who deserved to be on Dr. Maddy's floor – not him. She didn't mind if he joined later – after he'd done his time on the other floors.

The higher the floor here, the closer to God. At least that was the rumor. She could believe it. The few times, she'd been privileged to see Dr. Maddy, she'd given off such a peaceful serenity it made Doris want to reach out and touch her. So young and so beautiful... Doris just knew she'd been graced by God.

That her stepbrother should get to Maddy's floor before her was intolerable. Settling back into bed, Doris pondered her next move.

Something had to be done.

Maddy, carrying her big ceramic mug, clipped down the open hallway at an astonishing speed. She wanted this over as quickly as possible. She had to curb the negativity and the fastest way to deal with that was to face the issue. Smiling at the patients as she walked past, her steps slowed as she reached the new wing.

"Dr. Lenning." She turned her groomed smile on her new arrival. Only by drawing on her years of experience did she keep her shock at his appearance from showing. The tall arrogant doctor who had made her life hell had turned into a shrunken and obviously very ill man – a shell of his former self.

"Welcome to The Haven."

His response?

A glare.

She raised an eyebrow and waited him out. Everyone knew the only way to beat an aggressive dog was to make sure he knew who was boss. Maddy had no intention of backing down to anyone on her floor – especially him.

Keeping her professionalism firmly in place, she let him see the amusement in her gaze. If he wanted to pout, let him. She'd dealt effectively with similar patients before. To that end, she walked forward and straightened his sheet, tucking it up to his shoulders, shifting his little table closer so he'd be able to reach his water. Lifting his glass, she asked, "Would you like a drink? I'm sure your mouth must be dry from the air in here."

His glare deepened.

She smiled as if he were an obstinate child. "No? Okay, maybe you'll feel like it later." She replaced the glass and stepped back. As if by rote, she rambled off the traditional greeting. "Welcome to The Haven. Here your comfort, your health and your state of mind are important to us. Our guarantee, our promise to you, is to make your visit as happy as can be. We'll give you the best medical care we can and hope you enjoy the rest of your stay here with us."

As she finished, she grinned down at him. "That's the professional version. Now for my version. I'm not sure what brought you to my floor or why; however I take my responsibilities and my residents' care seriously. I will do everything I can to maintain a loving and peaceful state among the residents and staff. As harmony is a prime goal, those that find 'being nice' on a regular basis too challenging will be moved to a different floor immediately. This floor is for those who are interested in improving their quality of life for however long they have one to enjoy."

His glare, had it been lasered, would have left her in tiny pieces strewn across the floor. Maddy didn't care. For the first time, the reality sank in. So what if the high and mighty Dr. Lenning had made her life hell before? This man was dying. He was incapable of getting up off that bed and attacking her again. His words would never have the same impact they'd had before, and knowing this was his last stop before death's door put the control firmly in her hands.

She relaxed. She didn't need to fear him. She could sympathize with his situation.

It was a long way from compassion and love but it was equally far from fear and hate.

For her, life was all about balance.

She smiled at the silent patient and continued. "Your doctor, Dr. Paul Cunningham, will be here this afternoon. You know the drill. He'll review your information then make his way here to go over your treatment options with you."

Shock lit his eyes. "What?"

"Oh, didn't you know? My caseload is full. Dr. Cunningham, however, who has been reducing his load for the last year, has agreed to take on your case. So you are in good hands."

She stepped back, her heels clicking on the hardwood. "Now if you'll excuse me, I have other patients I must see." With a final nod in his direction, she repeated her greeting, this time with real feeling. "Welcome to The Haven."

THURSDAY

Halfway to work the next morning, a light misting rain started, soaking Maddy. Typical coastal weather – although technically Portland wasn't on the coast. What a day to decide she needed fresh air. Just as she resigned herself to getting drenched, a car honked and pulled up beside her. Maddy turned and recognized Gerard driving his charcoal beamer. She smiled with relief.

As she slid into the front seat, her suit jacket started to steam and her hair started to curl. She clipped in her seatbelt. "What a mess."

He pulled back into traffic, his movements sure and confident like the CEO he was. "You will walk."

"I know," she said ruefully. "Most of the time, it's fine. Then there're days like today."

He shot her an admiring glance. "Even soaking wet and imitating a duck, you're damned gorgeous."

Maddy laughed. Gerard had been making backhanded compliments to her for years. She refused to take them seriously. It went against her personal policy. Dating coworkers was bad business. Messy. She didn't do messy. "Thanks, I think."

"I'll be sorting applications today to fill that bed as soon as possible."

She frowned, a knot forming inside. She had no empty beds "What bed?"

He frowned at her. "Didn't Dr. Cunningham call you?"

Alarm triggered her nervous stomach, making it want to empty on the spot. "No. What did I miss?" Maddy pulled out her cell phone. She checked but there were no messages and no missed calls.

She frowned. Dr. Cunningham was usually good at staying in touch as a professional courtesy. If something had happened to one of her patients, he'd have called her.

"Jansen Svaar passed away last night."

Maddy stared at him, uncomprehendingly. That wasn't possible. "What?"

Gerard kept an eye on the traffic before darting a quick glance at her. "Apparently he died in his sleep. He was found by the nurse around three this morning."

That didn't feel right. In fact, it felt incredibly wrong. She chewed on the inside of her lip as she turned the information over in her head. Jansen had not been on death's door. She knew that. She'd have known if anything were going on. In fact, she'd scanned his system two days ago, after that weird visitation that had scared her so badly. Everything had been fine. Strong and healthy.

She didn't have all the answers to life and death. In fact, the more she learned, it seemed the less she knew. Particularly with energy work. And people died all the time - except, the last death on her floor had been eight months ago. Eight months was a long time for terminally ill patients. And she wouldn't have taken Jansen Svaar for the next candidate; far from it.

Jansen shouldn't have died.

And Dr. Cunningham should have informed her.

Gerard pulled the car into the underground parking lot. Disturbed, Maddy strode with him to the elevators.

"I'll speak with Dr. Miko. See what she has to say about his death." The in-house pathologist hated mysteries and could usually be counted on to come up with the answers Maddy wanted.

He nodded. "Remember Maddy, people die. Especially here."

Maddy tilted her lips slightly. She knew Jansen's bed would be filled within hours.

She understood, although she didn't particularly like it.

An hour later she closed the door to her office, relieved. She needed a few moments of peace…to adjust. A few minutes to mourn the loss of someone who'd been a joy to have on her floor. She couldn't believe how personally devastating she found Jansen's death. He'd been doing so well.

A knock sounded on her door.

"Come in," she called out, trying to compartmentalize her feelings and lock them down until she had space and time to sort through them.

A tall imposing man stood in her doorway. "I'm looking for Dr. Madeleine Wagner."

Maddy's gaze widened at the dignified stranger in her doorway. "Yes, that's me. What can I do for you?"

He smiled, walked forward, held out his hand. "Nice to finally meet you. I'm Dr. Chandler of Madison House. I'd like to speak with you, if you have a couple minutes to spare."

She stood up, smiling at one of the most respected surgeons and researchers on this side of the country. "It's a pleasure to meet you, Dr. Chandler. Please, have a seat." She motioned toward the seating arrangement out on the covered deck. The earlier rain had stopped, letting the sun peek out. "May I offer you some coffee?"

At his surprised nod, she fussed at her machine for a few minutes, then picked up the two cups and joined him outside.

She sat across from him. "Now, what can I do for you, Dr. Chandler?"

Several files sat open on Gerard's desk, applications under consideration. Another bed had just opened up on Maddy's floor. Perfect. Who had money and who would be willing to pay handsomely for a chance to move up in life?

His office phone rang. Damn, now what?

"Hello. Oh, hi, John." Gerard rolled his eyes and sank deeper into his high-backed wing chair. "How are you doing?"

"Getting impatient. When is my transfer going through?"

"Soon. I haven't gotten the forms from your doctor yet. Being in a different facility means there's a mess of paperwork to complete."

"If that's the only thing holding you up, I'll take care of it." John's tone made it clear there'd be hell to pay if his doctor didn't move on the issue – and fast.

Gerard smirked. Better to have John target someone else for a change. "Go easy on him. He's probably swamped with work. And it's likely to be his nurse taking care of the paperwork. You may want to check before you snap at him."

John's snort blasted through the phone. "Like hell. It'll get done today."

Gerard pinched the bridge of his nose and did something he rarely did – he excused himself. "John, I'm rushing to a meeting. I'm sorry but I have to run."

"Right. No problem. I have someone else to chase now. Have a good one."

Gerard stared at the phone as he replaced it. Given a new target, John sounded positively perky. That man must have made his department hell for any lollygaggers. Still, he was off Gerard's tail for a bit. Thank God.

Sandra walked into Gerard's office, a large stack of opened letters in her arms. "How bad is it today?" he asked.

"It's an interesting mix. The bulk of them are applications, requests for applications and questions about The Haven, all of which are good things." She dropped the stack in front of him. "And they give me confidence that I'll still have a job at the end of the year."

"Yeah," he growled, "but you may have to take a pay cut."

"Not going to happen, so don't go there." She turned to leave. Before she reached the door she turned back as if she'd forgotten something. "Although, speaking of pay cuts and the employment issues in today's world, I thought I saw Dr. Chandler walking the halls this morning, heading upstairs."

Gerard glanced up at her, his mind already immersed in the morning's mail. "Who?"

"Dr. Chandler. You know the physician with that leading-edge-technology-stuff from Madison House."

Gerard's eyes widened. "What?"

She looked over her glasses at him and frowned. "Is that a big deal?" The glint in her eyes said she knew it was.

He pushed his chair back and stood. "Do you know why he was here or where he was going?"

"Nope. Haven't a clue." She pushed her glasses up the bridge of her nose and walked toward the door again.

Jesus, Sandra had been here since forever. Nothing much happened here she didn't know. Damn it. He sat back down and tried to refocus on the morning mail. He didn't see the words on the page. What the hell would the head of the most expensive, most prestigious hospital want with anyone upstairs?

Upstairs? His head snapped up.

Maddy.

Oh, Christ.

Drew pulled his scratchpad closer. He had several pages full of notes so far, but he was a long way from done. He hadn't been able to resist a closer look at the kids' cases – on his own time. Wilson had explained that wall was a reminder page, a memorial so to speak, rather than a current case.

He remembered more the deeper he delved into the case. His uncle had spoken about the raging argument among the members of his department as to whether it was a criminal case – or a case at all. He couldn't resist trying to find out. The mystery behind it was addictive. He'd stayed late last night to catch up on the details.

In all six cases, the cause of death had been listed as inconclusive. No evidence left behind and no links between the children – none that anyone had found, at least. He picked up the folder and flicked through old detectives' notes, results and timelines. The first victim, Sissy Colburn, had been sitting at her kitchen table doing homework when she'd fallen to the floor dead. The last victim, Stephen Hansen, was found in the backyard of his home, fully dressed, backpack hanging off one shoulder and a half a chocolate bar in his hand. Dead. As if his last breath had just left his body and he'd collapsed on the spot.

Odd. For some unknown reason, all six healthy kids had just dropped dead, under what seemed ordinary circumstances.

Even odder was the tiny bruise on the base of the spine on all six kids. The doctors had no explanation, the autopsy hadn't shown a cause for them, and none of the parents knew anything that would indicate how each bruise had occurred.

The intriguing thing was that each victim had the same bruise. Six victims within a four-month span of time. No similar cases could be found before or after, according to Wilson's research.

He studied the old photos. The bruises looked insignificant, like an everyday small bruise.

The hairs on the back of his head rose. Spooky stuff.

Could he contribute anything to the case? Was there anything, any evidence that could be processed again with today's technology?

He set the boxes, four of them, off to one side and sorted through the swabs and clothing samples. It took the rest of the afternoon to determine that the detectives on the case had been thorough. Their notes spoke of their frustration with the lack of evidence.

Many cops expressed their doubts that a crime had even occurred, suggesting these were medical deaths – sad, but not their problem.

Then there was the evidence box full of diaries. Small, feminine diaries chronicled the years prior and the twenty years after the death of Darcy Durnham, the second victim of the six. According to Wilson, the father, Scott Durnham, had started dropping the diaries off a good ten years ago after the writer, Darcy's mother, passed away, in the hopes the police could find something helpful in them. Wilson had put them in order to find that there was no diary for the period covering Darcy's death. He'd expressed doubts that it had existed, but Drew figured it probably just hadn't shown up yet. Compulsive writing like Darcy's mother had demonstrated with her diaries rarely stopped one day to the next…and started again just as abruptly.

Scott showed up once in a while through the years when he found another one in the house. As always, it was logged in and added to the pile. So far, Wilson hadn't found anything of value in them.

Now it was Drew's turn.

Not an easy job.

Bed 232 smiled. No, not bed 232, she'd be Sissy today. She did feel so much better. She shifted slightly in bed. Mornings were always better. 'Good drugs,' the docs would say.

The long-term care aide stepped up to her bedside. "How are you feeling, my dear?" Bending over, she searched Sissy's gaze for a long moment as if trying to see who she really was. Satisfied, she pulled back with a decisive nod. "My goodness, Sissy, your color is so much better today. You're positively blushing. Is this a special day for you?"

Sissy eyed her slyly. "Maybe. One never can tell. I'd like to have breakfast out of bed this morning."

"Well, you certainly do look nice today. That's great that you are feeling well enough to get dressed. Shall we choose something special to wear? And how about your makeup, would you like some lipstick on today?" The aide bounced around the room, chattering happily and pulling out various pieces of clothing. "Let's try the pink sweater, and if you're feeling up to it, how about slacks?"

Sissy gave a graceful nod in thanks. "Pants and a sweater sound lovely, and maybe the Summer Blush lipstick to match."

Collecting the clothing, the aide walked over and laid everything on the bed. "Here we go."

With a fat smile, Sissy said, "Thanks." It had been awhile since she'd been in such good spirits. There was nothing like getting out of bed first thing in the morning to make life brighter and the day more positive. She could get used to this.

Of course, the buzz of excitement helped.

A new bed on Dr. Maddy's floor had opened. A flurry of excitement drifted through Sissy's ward. She sniffed. Like any of the old biddies in her ward had a chance at that rare lottery. She watched and listened as they all dreamed about moving up to that floor. As if that would change their lives. They weren't doing anything to help themselves. Hadn't they understood this whole concept? A bed had opened up because someone had died. *Died.* As in people died upstairs just as easily as downstairs. Stupid twits. Didn't they think at all?

A transfer upstairs for them would be a waste.

They weren't like her. She needed to do some serious thinking about the next step in her healing process. Sometimes, the days went by so fast, she had trouble keeping up. Probably her medication. Her old doctor had kept her so drugged out, no wonder she'd had trouble adjusting to the world around her.

It was his fault, not hers.

But he'd paid for that one.

***

Adam Lenning lay still, frozen in his bed as the first morning light warmed his corner of the world. The nurses hadn't noticed anything out of the ordinary. He'd closed his eyes to appear asleep. It had fooled them but there was no fooling himself.

He had seen something…wrong. Horribly wrong.

Yet, he couldn't say exactly what he'd seen.

The patient in the next bed had died last night. Adam knew the exact time. He'd been woken in the night by the cold. After growing up in Alaska, he understood cold. This part of Oregon did get chilly, except it was late summer, not the dead of winter. Last night, well, he'd have sworn the temperature on the floor was below freezing. Surely the furnace had quit unexpectedly? Although, given the time of year, there shouldn't have been the need for it in the first place. This eluded logic.

He'd tried to snag the blanket at the foot of his bed to spread it over himself, only the shivers that wracked his frame had made that virtually impossible. It's when he'd been lying there, shivering, that he'd noticed the shadows through the curtains surrounding Jansen's bed at the end of the open area.

Unlike the rest of The Haven, where you could barely walk for the people, Maddy's floor wasn't crowded. This floor didn't have private rooms, but each person had privacy through partial walls and curtains, making the areas individual, homey, yet accessible in an emergency.

He liked it. The place offered companionship and medical care without cloistering each person in their own room for hours on end. There was room to walk and be social and yet, there was privacy.

Footsteps approached, the sound mingling with the gentle whisper of a small cart rolling forward. A cheerful voice called out, "How are you doing, Dr. Lenning?"

"Cold," he muttered, his teeth chattering uncontrollably. "So cold."

The nurse frowned and immediately pulled out a thermometer from the medicine cart. She checked his temperature, before returning to a small computer on the cart to make a notation on the file. "I'll be right back."

She took her cart back down the hallway. It seemed to take forever before she returned, but then she wrapped his shaking body in heated blankets. She put a second one over his shoulder and neck.

"Ohhh," he moaned, sinking into the welcomed heat. He turned his face into the blanket, feeling the warmth on his cheeks and against his eyes.

"It's okay. Let's give your body a chance to warm up. I'll come back in a couple of minutes."

The nurse disappeared again.

He didn't care. For the first time in hours, heat was seeping into his old bones.

Warm and feeling safe, he succumbed to fatigue and his eyes drooped closed. His sense of balance reasserted itself. He almost believed he'd imagined the whole thing.

Almost.

Maddy moved through the morning, trying to ignore the sense of foreboding hanging over her head. Not an easy thing. Something had warped through her world, leaving a trail of unease and confusion in its wake and she didn't know what it was or where it had come from. What she did know is that she couldn't let fear or unrest take over her thoughts.

Moving through the floor, she checked on each of her patients.

At Beth's bedside, she spent a few minutes with the sixty-four-year-old woman. The patient had a zest for life that Maddy admired. Today, that spirit had disappeared. Beth lay curled up in a ball, the covers pulled to her neck. Tiny already, she looked like a child now.

"Bad night, Beth?"

Beth shuddered, her pink scalp showing through her sparse white hair. "Horrible. I had nightmares about death and dying. Nasty stuff." She lifted her liver-spotted hand and reached out for Maddy. Though she tried to smile her lips had a tired droop.

Maddy sat on the side of her bed. She noted the pallor of the woman's skin and the tremors shaking her hand.

It was obvious, Beth, along with every other one of her patients, had been disturbed last night.

"Well, it's a new day, Beth, and that terrible night is over, sent into the annals of history with every other bad day in your life."

Beth attempted a bigger smile. It failed. "I don't know, Dr. Maddy. It scared me pretty good."

Maddy studied the position of Beth's bed. Looked around, wondered. Was it possible? Jansen's bed was at the far end of the floor. Beth shouldn't have seen anything, yet she'd obviously felt it. No surprise there.

"Beth, what was the dream about? Maybe if you tell me about it, you'll be able to let it go."

The old woman's trembling increased. "I don't think so. It seemed like death was sitting on my bed, watching me, waiting for me. There was no lightness or angels. Only darkness and ice." She gasped for breath, a thin film of sweat breaking on her forehead. "I can't think about it! I know my time is coming and soon. I'm petrified that death will be like my dream." Her eyes filled with tears. "Dr. Maddy, I'm scared."

Not good. Beth's attitude toward her own health and death management had been spot on since Maddy had first met her. This dream had really sent her for a spin. Maddy pulled out a small bottle of Rescue Remedy, a homeopathic tincture, and gave the old woman several drops under her tongue. The natural remedy was used by many paramedics for shock and trauma of all kinds. Maddy had found it worked well for frights too. And being all-natural, it didn't mess with patients' energy or medications.

Satisfied, once Beth rested comfortably, Maddy stepped over to her next patient. And found a repeat of the same story. Frowning, Maddy made her way through the floor, finding variations of the same theme. The negative energy ripple had a bigger effect than she'd thought possible.

As Maddy approached the new wing, Dr. Lenning called her over.

She frowned as she saw him bundled up, his head swathed in warm blankets. "Bad night?"

"Terrible, just terrible," he whispered. "Thank heavens this place is equipped with blanket warmers. So, what happened, Dr. Maddy? Did the furnace quit overnight?"

That surprised her. None of the other patients had complained of a debilitating coldness. Chills, yes, but not to this level. Although his reaction reminded her how she'd felt when she'd first seen Eric's energy. "No. There were no reported problems or dips in the temperatures. Apparently, several people did have a weird night, though."

"Honestly, it feels like I've had less than an hour's sleep."

Maddy frowned. "Any change in your medications?" She stepped closer, pulling up his file on her tablet. He wasn't taking anything unusual.

"Oh, it isn't my drugs. No, I woke up and thought I saw something going on over at that bed." He pulled a frail hand far enough free of the blanket to point at Jansen's old bed.

Maddy spun around, realizing that from this position, Adam would have had a good view of Jansen's area. Staring down at him, she also understood that Dr. Lenning really was a helpless old man now. Why had she given him so much power over her emotional well-being? Shaking free of the thought, she sat at the edge of the bed. "What did you think you saw?"

"When I watched the curtain, it appeared as though someone attached a rope to Jansen's body and was pulling him up toward the ceiling. He didn't lift clear off the bed, his back arched up and down several times. Then it was like someone cut him free and he collapsed back down again. It was almost like someone was trying to pull his shadow from his body." His hands folded the corner of his sheet over and over in precise uniformly sized folds, but his eyes darted up to see her reaction.

Maddy's spine locked in place at his first words. Oh no. She needed to call Stefan, her friend, mentor and fellow energy worker – and fast. Though worried, she did her best to placate Adam.

"I'm not sure what to say. I can't imagine Jansen being able to do that on his own and there's certainly no evidence to suggest anyone else was here with that physical strength. Jansen, like everyone else here, came to enjoy the last days he had. It was just his time to go." She gave a casual shrug, patting his hand. "Take it easy and rest." With a gentle smile, she turned and walked back toward the nurses' station.

"Dr. Maddy, was there a full moon last night? I swear everyone is acting weird today," Amelia asked. Several of the other nurses gathered alongside the long-time nurse to hear Maddy's answer.

Maddy shook her head. "I have no idea." She reached for the schedule. "Who was on last night?"

Amelia handed over the staff roster. "Amber. So far today, I've heard that last night was the result of everything from a bad planetary alignment to the new government's spending."

The nurses chuckled. Over the years, these nurses had heard it all. And sometimes even they were surprised by the comments and actions of patients and their visitors.

"Susan mentioned patient concerns in the meeting this morning. I wrote it down." Nancy held up her notepad.

Maddy stepped over to read the note over Nancy's shoulder. "The thermostat registered normal temperatures; however, all patients were hollering about feeling cold. She says staff were kept running with requests for sleeping aids, water and hot blankets. *Hmmm.*"

"I know that hmmm. What are you thinking?" Nancy twisted to look at Maddy. Her gaze narrowed on Maddy's face. "Is this all related to Jansen's death."

"Maybe."

Nancy frowned, leaning in closer so as not to be overheard. "How?"

Maddy glanced around as the nurses resumed their other duties, then lowered her voice. "It's hard to say. However, energy is energy and whether it is used to heal or to kill, everyone will feel it or experience it in a different way."

"We've had deaths here before without everyone freaking out."

"I know. This does concern me. I can only assume at the moment that as the healing energy here increases, everyone becomes more sensitive to changes in that energy."

Nancy walked to the coffee maker. "So this may not be a bad thing?"

"Let's say I'm not panicking over it yet. If it happens again, we'll have to look at minimizing the impact on those left behind."

"Can we do that?" Nancy was wise. Her years of working with Maddy had made her intuition more open and she was more receptive to new concepts. That they were best friends and confidants didn't hurt, either.

Maddy smiled. "To some extent." Something else occurred to her. "I wonder if patients on the other floors were affected."

"We can ask."

With a gentle squeeze on Nancy's shoulder, Maddy said, "Ask one or two of the nurses on the other floors, will you please? Find out if anyone there had similar reactions. Or was it localized to our floor?"

***

Dr. Roberta Miko sat at her overflowing desk, dwarfed by the stacks of papers and files circling her. The rest of the office looked the same. Tuning it out, she debated the issue for hours in her head. There'd been no reason to believe Jansen Svaar's death was suspicious, not with his history of Stage II mesothelioma and diabetes. He had been exposed to asbestos during his decades-long work in the shipyards. Chemotherapy and radiation had slowed the progression of the lung tumors for just about a year. Then the cancer had advanced. When he had moved into The Haven, his prognosis had been for less than seven months. He couldn't care for himself and had slid to skin and bone. That had been close to ten months ago.

She frowned. So, what had happened in the meantime? She walked over to the cooler and pulled out the drawer where the body was stored. Lifting the sheet, she gave the body a slow perusal. This man showed a healthy weight with good skin tone and elasticity. At first glance, he appeared to have been doing fine. These signs of health meant nothing except that they were in direct opposition to the condition he'd been in when he'd arrived at The Haven.

Something at The Haven had worked for him. Maddy again. Roberta hadn't been sent many of Dr. Maddy's patients down here, a fact she'd pondered more and more as time went by. When Maddy's patients arrived at The Haven, they were no healthier than the rest. Roberta cocked her head to one side, and considered possibilities. She didn't know how bed assignments were arranged here. Maybe those on Maddy's floor had to fulfill requirements different from those of other patients. Something she'd look into.

She'd heard the rumors. She didn't have a basis to believe or disbelieve them. *Except...* She stared down at the interesting case before her. *What a perfect opportunity to learn more.*

FRIDAY

Maddy closed the door after the last of the nurses left and allowed her shoulders to slump. The daily meeting had cleared the air on several issues. Dr. Cunningham had shown up late as usual.

Her stomach grumbled. She'd missed lunch again. The small fridge contained the usual stash of yogurt and veggies, only she needed more today. Her eyes studied the stack of files on her desk. As much as she'd love an hour away, her workload also beckoned.

Her cell phone rang.

Maddy recognized the number and picked up. "Dr. Miko, hi."

The pathologist spared no greeting. "Look, I don't know what to tell you. Jansen Svaar's cancer was in remission. So whatever magic you were doing up there was working. There were several tumors of varying sizes in his lungs. However, there was no evidence they were growing or contributed to his death. I'm waiting on the tox screen so I have nothing specific at the moment. The only thing I can tell you is that I can't give you a direct cause of death at this point. And I have to tell you that I don't like that much, either. In fact, this one is liable to bug the hell out of me." By the end of her tirade, Roberta's voice was almost snapping with annoyance.

Maddy didn't like the information, either, but it wasn't as if it were the first time or indeed, unexpected. She said gently, "And sometimes, people just die. Jansen was seventy-eight. He'd lived a good life and he died a good death." At least she hoped he had.

Maddy had seen plenty of deaths that science didn't explain. Still, with any death, she always saw a blockage or a major energy system gone awry, or the energy cords thin and worn out. The body ready to go. Very rarely, did a person go to bed and disconnect their one link to their body – their own energy cord.

And when death did happen in this way, instead of being a horribly sad event, it was usually a peaceful passing.

But Jansen's death didn't feel the same. Her misgivings stemmed from her sense of guilt over that purple-black energy she'd seen hovering over him – that same energy she had yet to identify. In hindsight, she realized she shouldn't have left him alone. Yet it was impossible for her to be everywhere all the time.

"Maddy, are you still there? What's wrong?"

Staring down at the phone in her hand, Maddy shook her head – hard. Lord, Dr. Miko was going to think she'd lost it.

"I'm here. Sorry. Lost in thought." She coughed several times, clearing her throat. "Roberta, were there any bruises to indicate perhaps he'd fallen or other signs of trauma that we may not have noticed? Anything out of the ordinary?"

"No. Except for…" A slight silence filled the line. "A small bruise at the base of his spine. But there was no puncture or damage to the spinal column or even the muscle tissues. It appears to be a superficial mark."

Maddy snatched up a notepad and jotted down the coroner's words. "Could you send me a copy of the autopsy report, please? Oh, by the way, that bruise, what size is it?"

"About that of a quarter, maybe slightly larger. As there was little else to put into the report, I have measured it out and documented it along with a photo should anything arise later."

"Right. Let's hope the mystery can be solved one day."

"So many never are."

"Isn't that the truth?" Maddy sighed. "Thanks for the call."

After she signed off, Maddy stared out the window. A bruise might mean anything, except in that location, it made her uneasy. Settled in behind the base of the spine in a spot most people referred to as the root chakra, or root energy center, lay the Kundalini energy. This powerful energy lay dormant at the base of the spine in everyone. It was less developed in children, but still an incredible energy source. *If* someone outside that body could access it... And that was a big *if*.

It also related to the crown chakra, another powerful energy center, at the top of the skull.

She'd forgotten to ask Dr. Miko if she'd checked Jansen's head. Should she call her back? Or let it go as a slim-to-none chance that Jansen had a matching one at the top of his skull?

Shit. She had to know. Maddy quickly dialed.

"Roberta, sorry. Did you happen to notice a matching bruise on Jansen's head?"

"Hmmm. Checking the report now. At the base or the crown?"

"Crown. It would probably be around the same size as the other one." Maddy couldn't help chewing her bottom lip nervously as she waited.

"I don't have anything written down. Let me go check."

Maddy listened as Roberta placed the phone on the desk with a clunk, followed by soft-soled steps and a heavy metal slide. Her impatience grew, the longer she waited. What could be taking so long? Surely it was a simple matter to check? Then she remembered Jansen's hair. That man had a full head of stiff, wiry stuff. He'd always liked it long. In fact, he'd been quite particular about keeping it just right.

"Maddy?" Roberta's voice sounded odd, confused even. "I'm not sure. You might be right. I'm going to take a closer look and call you back."

Maddy's heart sank.

She'd hoped she'd been wrong.

***

Doris held her notepad firmly in one shaking hand and tried to finish the letter to the Board. No way was she going to lie down here while her brother used underhanded tricks to get his way. That man thought way too much of himself. That he'd been able to buy the spot she'd been waiting for on the famed third floor, was intolerable.

She cast a furtive glance at Sissy in the bed beside her. She hadn't been able to stop studying her all morning. How odd. She looked better every day. How did that happen? As Doris had steadily declined, that woman appeared to have steadily improved. In the last few months, the improvement had been noticeable.

Sissy wasn't friendly. She had that better-than-everyone attitude, so it wasn't as if Doris could up and ask her what she'd been doing. As it was, the two rarely spoke.

Who called their daughter 'Sissy' anyway? Doris had met one other person with that name, a child she'd taught piano lessons to way back when. The poor girl had died a mysterious death, as Doris recalled.

Doris kept her head down, tugging her focus back to the half-written letter in front of her. Surely, Sissy shouldn't be here on this floor anymore, at least not much longer. She didn't know what drugs she'd been getting, but Doris wanted some of the same for herself.

She'd have to ask her doctor. Maybe he'd prescribe the same thing. She stole a second look. Damn, that woman looked good. She offered Sissy a tentative smile and received a lukewarm response.

Doris returned to draft her letter, happier. Maybe they could be friends. Most of her other ones had died.

Time to meet her new patient.

Maddy barely kept her bouncing step in control as she walked down the hallway to meet her newest arrival. She smirked at Nancy's eye roll. "What? I'm happy. We get so few children in here. Felicia's arrival is a huge deal." Hospice care differed from location to location across the country. Yet Maddy knew from experience that children responded better to her energy work than any of her other patients. Children didn't come here normally – it was considered an adult care facility. But the hospital was open to everyone and sometimes, on rare occasions, a child moved into The Haven. Often their family fought to have them here. They always came to Maddy's floor.

Maddy came upon Belle, as she visited with her latest great grandson. Contentment whispered through her aging energy. Belle had come a long way these last few weeks. It was good to see her adjusting.

"Except the arrival of this child means she's deathly ill and there's not much great about that," Nancy reminded her.

"And that's why she needs to be here. Maybe we can turn things around." Maddy refused to let her joy dim with negative thinking. She wished she could work only with children. Her healing skills could do so much more with them. Unfortunately, the medical establishment was a long way from acceptance on that issue.

They passed the nurses' center, where two of her staff worked tirelessly, their energy calm and relaxed. That was so important here. People liked to believe they were independent of each other, but everything they felt and thought affected those around them. Children were particularly susceptible. The good news was the children also had the ability to heal – almost overnight.

The last two children had been released in steadily improving health. Paul Dermont had cancer that refused to respond to treatment. After his transfer to this floor, his cancer had gone into spontaneous remission within months of his arrival. Sending Paul home had been a highlight of Maddy's year.

Nancy smiled, her features softening. "Let's hope so. Felicia could use it. It's a good thing Dr. Robertson is on your side."

They shifted to walking single file, as two orderlies moved carts down the hallway. Maddy smiled at Horace, who'd been working here for decades. He was a favorite among the patients – always had a smile for each one.

Momentarily distracted, Maddy tried to pull the threads of their conversation together. Where were they? Right, Dr. Robertson. "How true. Unfortunately, it took him a lot of years to get there."

Convincing doctors at the beginning had been tough. Many misunderstood and viewed her work with dismay or distrust. They wanted proof. Something she could only provide after working with a patient – and she couldn't do that if they didn't invite her in on a case. Now, after seven years, she worked with two specialists and several doctors at the local children's hospital.

Felicia's medical history would be an interesting read. Maddy knew a bit about her condition, but not her full history. She'd have a conference with Dr. Robertson to discuss treatment options and to set up a pain management program.

Maybe Felicia would be lucky and experience something magical here, too.

Felecia was moving into Jansen's spot, a circumstance that had given Maddy pause, until she realized that had also been Paul's bed and he'd gone home to continue his recovery. Jansen's death was an anomaly. It had to be. Nothing else made sense. Maddy insisted Jansen's bed be moved back to its original position, tucked securely inside the protective energy. That didn't guarantee the child's safety, but it would help – and it made Maddy feel better.

The increased noise level said they'd almost reached the right bed. Gerona was there, paperwork in hand, to sign off on Felicia's arrival.

"Dr. Maddy, it's good to see you again." A tall, silver-haired man in a white lab coat hovered protectively beside Felicia's bed, holding out his hand to two interns. Dr. Robertson shook the two men's hands and thanked them for taking good care of Felicia.

One man grinned and waved at Felicia while the other chucked her under the chin before leaving. "You be good. This is the luckiest move of your life. Let's hope the next one will take you home... So behave yourself."

Maddy shook Dr. Robertson's hand. "Why am I not surprised to see you here with her? Did you follow the ambulance in?" she ribbed him gently. Felicia had been Dr. Robertson's patient since her birth. She was also his most heartbreaking case. Terminally ill children were hard on everyone – especially the children.

The sheet-covered body moved, a sock-covered foot slid out, then the toes wiggled. Maddy grinned. God, she loved children. As she reached to snag a toe or two, the sheet slid down and Felicia's head popped up. Shaved and bruised looking, yet the little girl wore a gamin smile that melted all who saw her.

"Hi, Dr. Maddy," she piped in the optimistic singsong voice of a child. And that was one of the reasons Maddy wanted her here. Her life force was strong, regardless of the brainstem glioma threatening to kill her and the unsuccessful radiation and chemotherapy that had made her life hell. Her spirit shone bright and free. That gave her a fighting chance.

"Hey, pumpkin. How are you doing?"

Doernbecher Children's Hospital had given her great care. However, it was Dr. Robertson's push that brought Felicia to Maddy. Paul, the patient who went home, was also his patient. There was nothing like success with one case to bring hope to another.

Maddy studied Felicia's energy field. Low, thin and pale, yet still strong. The core pulsed with possibilities. Maddy had watched her from the sidelines this last year and as each treatment failed, Dr. Robertson and the parents had become a little more desperate. She'd undergone surgery once, only the growth had returned. At that point, Dr. Robertson had thrown his hands up and asked for her help.

Medical practice required permission. Maddy had it now. Felicia was hers. Hopefully, it wasn't too late. Maddy immediately reached for a brighter thought to overcome the negative one. Lord, she'd been doing that a lot lately.

"I'm good. The ambulance ride was fun. Do you have television here?" Felicia twisted her head from side to side, checking out her new home.

Maddy threw her head back and laughed. "Of course, do you think all these patients would stay if we didn't?"

Felicia giggled. "Maybe if you served chocolate ice cream."

Dr. Robertson reached out and lightly tapped her bald head. "Not everyone is as addicted to chocolate ice cream as you are, young lady."

"Then they don't have taste buds." Her eyes opened wide at several posters on the walls that depicted animals and kids playing sports. That would be Nancy's doing most likely. They'd be able to decorate the area more fully now that Felicia was here. There was rarely time before patients arrived.

Opposite was a large window that allowed the midmorning sun to sneak in. A super-sized balcony sat outside huge double doors halfway to the next bed, sectioned off by partial walls and curtains.

Maddy smiled at her patient's curiosity. A good sign. Activity bustled around them as nurses stepped up to complete the transfer of paperwork and equipment, and warm blankets arrived to take off the chill that had been induced by the move and any uncertainty the girl felt over the changes in her life.

"Mom said she'd be here." Felicia glanced around for her mother – the first glimmer of nervousness showed in her eyes.

"If she said she'd be here, then she'll be here. This place is huge. She's probably lost like we would have been if not for your terrific ambulance guys," Dr. Robertson said with a smile.

With a nod and a wink at the tiny addition to her floor, Maddy led the way to her office. Once inside, she offered Dr. Robertson a coffee from her espresso machine.

"Only you'd have a coffee station in your office." He shook his head, accepted the cup of Italian coffee from her and sat down in the leather seat opposite her desk. "I may have to reconsider my career options. Look at this place. High class indeed."

"The Board indulges me." Maddy shrugged. She'd also taken over from Dr. Newell, who'd been fastidious about his office furniture. She actually preferred light-colored wood furnishings like cedar or oak, but asking for a complete furniture switch had been prohibitive and unnecessary. She'd rather have the funds go to patient care.

"So what are we doing for Felicia now?" That turned the discussion back to business and they sat down to discuss the next step in Felicia's medical journey, hopefully one that would lead to an improved outcome.

Drew relaxed at his desk, enjoying the new office. So few people. So much space. So little noise. He finally felt like he was adjusting to his new caseload as well as his space. They had a lot of freedom to work here, but it was hard to re-evaluate old cases to find a new angle, find a way forward with the old evidence. He had to wrap his mind around a lot of information. Technology had changed this field tremendously, allowing them to retest old samples, provided they hadn't deteriorated. DNA samples were a huge boon.

The dead kids though, with their faces staring down at him from the wall, had affected him. Their unexplained deaths were a puzzle with no way forward. That hadn't stopped him from trying. He'd left a message with a contact in the FBI Behavioral Unit this morning, hoping to run some info through the MO databank. There'd been no return call at this point. Chances are there wouldn't be one.

Portland didn't have a similar database and he'd already run the bruise pattern through the Oregon State Police Law Enforcement Data Computer or LEDS system, with its limited MO files. No luck yet. Next were InfoNet and its system that allowed him to email anyone on the LEDS system. Maybe he'd get lucky and find someone who had seen this particular bruise pattern.

Then there were the journals. Sigh. He'd flicked through a couple, only he hadn't been able to find anything except the painful ramblings of an older woman. He'd put them in chronological order, yet hadn't devoted much time to them. He figured he might get through a diary a day. That would still take him a month or two, but at least he'd know that he'd done what he could in that regard.

He was about to reach for his coffee cup when the phone rang. Dr. Miko, the pathologist at The Haven. Interesting.

***

Maddy collected the flowers delivered for Felicia and carried them down the hall. Painted bright and cheery with lavenders and turquoises, her area looked like any normal child's bedroom, complete with a bookshelf and a toy bin.

Felicia was awake and appeared to be playing with her Nintendo video game. Her hands and fingers were painfully thin as she manipulated the small buttons. Handheld computer toys were a great way to pass the time. As her condition was terminal and she was debilitated to the point she couldn't live a 'normal' life, Felicia had teachers visit for various lessons and she attended school online with her laptop. Her mother visited her each day to help with the homework.

"Hi, Dr. Maddy. Are those for me?" Her young face brightened at the gorgeous sunflowers in Maddy's arms. "Wow, those are beautiful. Who are they from?"

Maddy grinned as she placed the bouquet on the bookshelf. Pulling out the card, she handed it to Felicia. While the girl exclaimed about the flowers, Maddy opened her tablet to Felicia's file. Hmmm, Felicia's appetite was down. Not unusual given the transfer, but that couldn't be allowed to continue. Felicia needed her strength. Healing would only happen if the body had energy to spare.

She studied the drugs listed. The cocktail was daunting, particularly considering that nothing was working. Her radiation treatments had been discontinued and the traditional way forward appeared to be the only option – help her make peace with the future.

After her rounds this morning, Maddy planned to go into her office and do a full energy scan on her youngest patient – something Maddy needed peace and quiet to do. She'd like to do one here at Felicia's bedside while she slept. However, until the place returned to normal from the repairs and new arrivals, she'd do her scans remotely. Switching her vision, she checked Felicia's energy. It pulsed slowly and was snug against the tiny body. White with soft lavender ripples, but the pulses had a tenacity to them that gave Maddy hope. Still, the energy was low and fainter than Maddy would like.

There was no time to lose.

"Felicia, I have to go and run a bunch of tests. When I'm done, we'll talk again." With a bright smile, and a brief touch of her hand to Felicia's cheek, Maddy left and strode down to her office. At the nurses' station she stopped for her messages and told the staff she'd be working and not to disturb her.

They understood, at least to some degree.

Few understood the world of a medical intuitive. For Maddy, her special awareness was a natural complement to her medicine and as instinctive as breathing.

She closed her office door, drew the heavy curtains together and turned off her phones. She walked over to the wall beside her door, pushed the visitor's chair back and away and cleared a space where she could sit on the floor. She could do this standing or sitting; however, as yoga was her preferred method to unwind, she usually chose to relax into one of the many poses her body loved so well.

After unbuttoning her jacket and kicking off her heels, Maddy gracefully sank to the floor to sit cross-legged. She sighed deeply, rotating her neck and releasing the tension in her system. Tension was resistance. She knew that, and slowly eased her body into a state of relaxation and self-awareness.

Feeling a familiar calming detachment, Maddy went to work.

Using a technique called remote viewing, Maddy focused on Felicia until her awareness was right at her bedside where she 'saw' Felicia's body. It was almost as good as being there in person. She shifted her focus to Felicia's energy systems. Every physical body had a road map of energy like highways rippling across it, servicing all the main body systems. Maddy saw the energy flows and drains, as they moved to address worry, stress, past events or even joy.

Most people in The Haven had little energy dedicated to the good things in life. If they had, they wouldn't be as sick. The human body created and tapped into so much more energy than people understood. Instead of reaching for the energy so readily available, people 'used up' their stock of this resource with the little irritating things in life, leaving their systems short for healing. They could get more anytime, but rarely did. Most people, if asked, would say they didn't know where or how to get more energy.

Maddy had perfected another technique for use on her terminal patients. She moved from one end of the body to the other, seeing thin slices of the body similar to a CT scan, which allowed Maddy to flick through one area to another.

Starting at the toes, Maddy studied Felicia, making note of any issues on the way through the layers of the child's body. Energy buzzed or slugged its way through Felicia's circulatory system, shining with light, and in some areas, with a dark, purplish slow energy.

Working steadily, she familiarized herself with the ebb and flow of Felicia's life force, her health, her condition and her illness. The back of the child's neck and the lower portion of her head had a dead black pulsating look to it. This was the problem. She'd known that much already though. The question was, what fed this tumor's insatiable growth? Usually a growth of this type came when blockages prevented the normal spread of energy, causing new pathways to form around it.

Distancing herself slightly, Maddy studied the meridian lines tracing movement of energy the length of the child's body. Several blockages existed: one below her right knee, one on the left side of her chest. Slicing the layers lengthwise, Maddy scanned the holograph, studying the images from top to bottom. One definite problem centered in the large intestine, with a complete energy blockage in the forefront of her spine. Interesting.

Maddy didn't know what to do with this information yet, but she now had an idea of the severity of Felicia's condition. Complete blockages caused energy pathways to rework, regrow and reform. In Felicia's case, they spread out in tiny webs searching for other pathways to take care of the problem. Felicia's body was a spider web of tiny networks.

All illnesses and diseases affected the body's nervous systems and developed tension. As she had used one method to read the energy, Maddy used a companion method to soothe the ruffled energy of Felicia's aura, easing the tension rippling through the child's body into a smoothly flowing stream. Then Maddy went to work on one meridian, the one running up the front of Felicia's leg and chest where a minor blockage was forming.

The blockage disappeared under Maddy's ministration, surprising her with the speed of its disappearance. She knew better than to do too much at one time. Pulling back, she smiled as the clean meridian energy glowed brighter.

Maddy's energy levels dropped. She checked the hallway clock. Two hours already. No wonder, her reserves were long gone, her body dehydrated. Time to pull back.

The progress she'd made wasn't much, yet it was a start.

***

Drew walked into the pathology rooms at The Haven. Dr. Miko's odd tone of voice had made him drop everything to race over.

"Dr. Miko?" He scanned the gleaming stainless steel room. The joys of a private hospital – they got the best of everything. At the far end of the room, an assistant washed down an autopsy table, the hose forcing the bloody water down the gleaming drain.

"Over here." The strident voice came from behind him, to the left. He spun around. The tiny dynamo in green scrubs strode toward him, her close-cut peppered hair snug against her skull. A frown marred her face. "You didn't gown up," she snapped and led the way through to the offices. "I don't like people in my rooms."

Chastised, and with good reason, Drew remembered her rules too late. "Sorry, I couldn't find you and thought—"

"And thought I might be working and so you'd take a quick glance around. Like that changes anything." She pushed her thick-rimmed, black glasses up her nose and narrowed her gaze at him. "Do I know you?"

Drew hastily shoved his hand forward. "Detective Drew McNeil."

"McNeil? John McNeil's nephew?" She ignored his hand.

Drew tucked his hand back into his pocket. "Yes, that's correct."

"Right. He's a tough man. It must have been hard growing up with him. You don't have to be like him, you know."

Surprised at the personal comment, Drew stalled with a response, finally saying, "He's a good man."

"I didn't say he wasn't. What are you doing here?"

"You called me about a possible connection to an old case?"

Her face instantly sobered. "Right, no way to forget that nightmare." She took a deep breath before reciting, "I was new in the profession back then. That case is one I've never forgotten. Six children, all with no apparent cause of death. A small bruise was found at the base of their spines. No other marks, no DNA, no sign of violence – no proof of anything one way or another."

"What? You know the case?" Excitement jolted his gut. Did she have something helpful to offer? He'd love to make headway on this case. "It's one of our most mysterious cold cases."

Finely etched pain lined her face, and she nodded. "Those poor children. It was a terrible time back then – for all of us. I'd only been out of school a couple years and had seen nothing like it. I'm not sure if what I called you about today helps or hinders, or if it is even related to that investigation." Dr. Miko stared down at the floor, her brow creased in concentration.

When she raised her eyes she stared directly at him. "One of the recently deceased residents from Dr. Maddy's floor has a weird bruise at the base of his spine similar to those of the children who died years ago." Her gaze went to the double doors leading to the drawers holding the deceased. "I don't have any measurements to compare," she muttered in a soft voice to herself.

"Similar? How?"

"It's small, about the size of a quarter at the base of the spine. The bruising is different in appearance. I'm working from memory here. But from my recollection, it's not as tight or as neat a circle, and it's darker, I think. Maybe you can find the pictures so we can compare."

She showed him the photos she'd taken of Jansen Svaar's body, pointing to the second one. "See here. The edges are not clearly defined. The surface was not raised either. There was no rippling in the skin, as if a weapon had been forced against the skin. In fact, the bruising is light colored and soft, not harsh or deep. It doesn't penetrate the muscle layer below."

"Anything else?" Hope and fear kept his voice tight, controlled.

"Just that although he was sick, he was in remission. He just up and died. That's very common for his age and health group. This man *was* seventy-eight years old."

Drew sat back as she fired the facts at him. He sifted through what she'd said and what she hadn't. "I'm presuming you never found what caused the bruise?"

"No, I'm sorry. This may not be related at all since there's nothing else that's similar about them. If I remember correctly, those children were in their prime and healthy – very healthy." She leaned back, studying his face. "But that bruise…each had one…I just don't know."

Drew nodded, adding, "They all had families and were well-loved, all were found alone and there was no visible trauma to their bodies."

She stood up, giving her head a shake. "Until Dr. Maddy called, I hadn't thought about those kids for years. Then I found the one odd mark and she asked me to check for the second one – a matching, fainter bruise at the top of his head. It's hard to see because of the patient's full head of hair. However, it's there, nonetheless."

Drew didn't remember seeing anything about two bruises on these kids in the report. "And these kids, did they have the same bruising at the top of the head?" He held his breath. Waited for the answer.

"I don't know," she admitted softly. "If they did, I didn't see them. The bruise on this patient's spine is darker and more pronounced. The one on his head is softer and much harder to see. I wouldn't have noticed if Dr. Maddy hadn't asked me to search for it. The bruises on the kids' spines were already pale. If they had lighter, matching ones on the crowns of their heads, they would have been difficult, if not impossible to see."

"So it's possible that they did. Why did Dr. Maddy ask you about the second bruise?"

"I don't know." Dr. Miko's brow knitted in concentration. "She wasn't happy with my answer, either." She glanced at her phone. "Maybe she should come down so we can ask her."

***

Maddy strode down the hallway toward Dr. Lenning. He lay huddled under his blankets. Maddy approached warily. He'd had two bad nights in a row. If he'd managed to go to sleep, she didn't want to wake him. The reno workers had been in and out but only to finish the little things. The area wasn't done, per se, however, it was coming along nicely.

Still, Dr. Lenning's area seemed lonely, lost in the bigger room without more patients to fill it with bustle and cheer. He was only fifteen-odd feet from the next patient, yet because of the open bareness, it appeared to be much farther.

As she approached his bed, he snuffled slightly. Maddy paused and shifted position to see if his eyes were open. No. He slept.

She frowned. He looked like hell. His color matched the white sheet he lay on; worse was the flaccidity of his face, as if he'd aged a decade overnight. Bad nights often made people appear older. Only in this case, he looked ancient. She'd have to check his file to see if Dr. Cunningham had changed his medications, but she'd didn't think he had. She decided to come back and visit with him later, when he was awake. See what, if anything, had changed in his life.

As much as she hadn't wanted it, he was here, and he needed care. It was her job to make him as comfortable as possible.

Checking her watch, she walked toward her next patient. Her cell phone went off. Dr. Miko.

Answering it, Maddy changed direction back to the privacy of her office.

"Hi, what's up?"

"Can you pop down for a moment?" Dr. Miko's voice, while always serious, had a stern overtone.

Maddy frowned. "I'll be there in a few minutes." Maddy walked back to the nurses' station, told them where she was heading then walked over to the stairwell. That's exactly what she needed – a run.

The stairwell was empty as usual. Maddy stood at the top and looked down, considering. Making a quick decision, Maddy slipped off her blue heels. As her bare feet hit the cement, chills of anticipation raced up her legs.

Grinning, and her heels hanging on two fingers, Maddy broke into a flat-out sprint and raced down the stairwell. The second floor landing, the first floor landing, all the way to the first of the lower levels. Hitting the brakes at the bottom, Maddy paused to gather her breath.

Exhilaration pulsed in her blood. Her shoulder-length bob swayed with her heaving breaths. It took another long moment of deep breathing before she slipped her heels back on.

The double doors opened easily as she walked toward Dr. Miko's office – a hoarder's paradise. Usually there was one chair available. Maddy turned toward it, then stopped. Her eyebrows rose in surprise and a swarm of butterflies took flight in her stomach. The detective she'd met in the stairwell several days ago stood in front of her. Again.

What was he doing here?

He smiled. "Hello, Dr. Maddy. How nice to see you again."

"Detective." Damn, that man had something. Her hormones started to do a hula dance. What was with that? Maddy shook her head to clear her mind. "What's going on?"

Roberta waved toward a chair. "Take a seat."

Maddy chuckled. "I'd love to. Where?"

Dr. Miko frowned, her gaze going from one piece of furniture to another. "Just move those." She pointed to one chair stacked high with books.

"Take mine." Drew stepped forward to clear off the spare chair.

Maddy smiled her thanks and sat down in his place as the detective emptied and pulled over his seat. "What's up?"

"I see you've already met Detective Drew McNeil."

Drew? So that was his name. Maddy sank back. She smiled inside. It suited him. "Yes, briefly."

Roberta reached for a folder and opened it. "I called him regarding a possible connection between Jansen's case and several old cases."

"What? Jansen? A criminal case?" Maddy leaned forward, her gaze going between the two. What on earth was Roberta talking about? "What did you find out?"

Dr. Miko frowned as she stared down at the papers in her hand. "I was working with the medical examiner at the time of the earlier cases." She glanced up at Maddy. "They're cases that have haunted me over the years. Six dead children who showed no apparent cause of death, no signs of violence and no explanations could be found for their deaths. They just, well…died. At the time, the politicians were saying a crime hadn't been committed because there was no evidence to support foul play." She grimaced. "Then again, nothing pointed to why the children died, either."

That was depressing, yet what did it have to do with her? Maddy waited for Roberta to continue. "And…?"

"The cases back then had one thing linking them together." Drew's gaze hardened as he looked from one woman to the other. "Each child had one small bruise at the base of their spines. Similar to the one found on Jansen."

Maddy's eyes opened wide. She stared at Drew in surprise before switching her gaze back to Dr. Miko. "That's...odd. What caused them?"

"No idea."

Fear rose in Maddy's chest. "I don't understand. Are you saying Jansen was murdered?"

"No, not at all. All I'm saying is that there are similarities with this body and with those from thirty-odd years ago. I'd love to understand what caused the bruising." Roberta folded her hands. "It may be nothing. However, if it turns out to be something, I wanted to make sure you were both in the know."

"What a horrible thought." Maddy's mind couldn't grasp the connection. She crossed her arms, holding them tight to her chest. Maybe her mind didn't *want* to see a connection. "Six kids? Boys or girls?"

Drew stepped in. "Both. No understandable reason for any of their deaths. It was a sad time – for everyone. No one knew how to handle it. Most people were divided as to whether a crime had even been committed. Like all cold cases, it's haunted many people."

"Can anything be found after all this time?"

Roberta looked at Drew, who tapped his fingers on the wooden arm of his chair. "Let's hope so."

Maddy stood, her knees a little shaky at the thought of a murderer operating at The Haven. The whole concept had a surreal overtone to it. "Well, thanks for letting me know." She smiled at Drew. "If there's anything I can do to help, call me."

He faced her. "I will need some information from you. Such as a list of all the visitors Jansen Svaar had while he was at The Haven."

"There's no formal list of visitors, but I'm sure we can come up with something for you. Give me your card, and I can email the names to you."

As Drew handed over his card Maddy couldn't help but notice the compelling energy he exuded so naturally. It was hard not to appreciate self-confidence and strength.

Maddy narrowly avoided knocking over a stack of books, and wound her way carefully out of the office. "Thanks, Dr. Miko. If you learn anything else, please let me know."

Drew held the door for her but stood in her way. "Dr. Miko forgot to ask something. Why did you ask her to check Jansen's crown for a matching bruise?"

Surprise lit her features. "Oh. That's because they're the two main energy entrances and exits from the body. The crown and the base of the spine."

He blinked and stepped back.

With a small smile, she walked to the stairwell, her mind full of implications from these new developments. As much as she'd like to discuss them further with Drew, she wasn't sure how much she should tell him. Her world was a touch unbelievable to those not involved in energy work. Striding down the hall quickly, she couldn't help a quick glance behind her.

He stood in the middle of the hallway, his hands fisted on his hips, staring at her. Maddy chuckled, gave him a small wave and entered the elevator, making good her escape. Her mind was more than a little overwhelmed, her emotions already somber. Already scared.

A murderer? At The Haven?

SATURDAY

Maddy strolled down the street. Her mind consumed with the issues going on at work. She'd slept in on her day off, had lost herself in hours of research and then spent hours checking on her patients, even though it was her day off. It had been late by the time she'd gotten away.

Now, walking home, the evening sky was a cool gray and dry, not that there was any guarantee it would stay that way. Living in the greater Portland area, windy, wet and gray were the norm. One needed to appreciate nights like this.

Her favorite Italian restaurant was a couple of blocks past her apartment. She'd be a few minutes early, but would enjoy waiting by the fire at the restaurant with a glass of wine in hand. Family-owned and operated, Lugardo's offered good wholesome food for a decent price. Not that she cared about the price. Maddy had money. She worked hard, was paid well and spent little. Since she worked all the time, there was little opportunity to spend.

Her Visa bill popped into her mind. Right, nothing to spend it on except her lingerie. Bustiers, panties, thongs, garter belts, thigh-high stockings – it didn't matter, she loved them all. She smirked, her hand going instinctively to her waist where the purple thong with tiny white and gold flowers decorating the straps lay hidden beneath her clothing. The matching bustier was a treat. Maddy loved the sensuous feeling of wearing it – so delicate, feminine – and so hidden.

Reaching the front door of the tiny café, she pushed it open and entered another world. Momma Rose greeted her effusively and led her to an intimate table for two, covered with a red-checkered tablecloth, beside the fire.

"Oh my dear, you must be freezing. Come, sit. We will feed you, make you feel much better." As soon as Maddy sat down, Momma Rose took off. She returned within minutes with her tall portly husband. "Bill, Dr. Maddy is here. She's chilled."

Maddy chuckled at the eye-rolling look he gave her. "Good evening, Bill. As you can see, I'm fine. And hungry. Lunch was a long time ago." And it couldn't even be called lunch. She'd scarfed a yogurt cup along with her coffee around two o'clock as she'd waded through a stack of paperwork, a ritual that was becoming all too common in recent days.

Tonight was different. Stefan was joining her. Stefan, her mentor, best friend, fellow energy worker. As well, he was an incredibly talented psychic, with a physical beauty that was just plain unfair – he was a man after all.

"Ohhh no." Momma Rose, who carried a nice layer of padding around her full figure, sounded horrified. "That's not good. You need food. Good food."

Bill winked at her. "Maybe you should start with a glass of good wine. I've got a nice Merlot you should try."

Before she knew it, Maddy had a full glass of wine in her hand and a carafe sitting beside her. The wine had an earthy aroma and a hint of…was that…blackberry? Whatever it was, it made her taste buds sing. Maddy relaxed back into the deep cushioned chair and let the warmth of the fire roll over her.

The door opened. A murmur rose in the small room before dying off into a stunned silence. Maddy grinned. She didn't need to turn around to know that Stefan had arrived. Stunningly gorgeous, his presence caused a ruckus wherever he went. Maddy had known people's jaws to literally drop when he entered a room. And he the nicest guy you'd ever meet.

Thank you.

So he'd been listening for her.

The voice floated through her head, a whisper of warmth and loving energy that made her heart lighten and her smile brighten.

She stared at the fire, enjoying the gold and orange flames doing their wild dance.

Stefan's shadow fell on the table.

"Sit, my dear. Your amazing beauty dwarfs the fire."

He snickered. "Only you talk to me that way." Stefan pulled out the other chair and sat. Reaching across the table, he picked up the carafe of wine, and inhaled the bouquet. "Good choice."

Maddy smiled at the blond Adonis as she took a sip. "Bill's choice."

"Good on Bill."

Momma Rose, continuing to chatter, rushed over to give Stefan a big hug. Finally, Stefan patted her shoulder and had a chance to answer. "I'm fine, Momma Rose. Life's good. Yes, I've been busy. And yes, I'm hungry."

Laughing, Momma Rose took off and returned with a second wine glass. She emptied the carafe into his glass before taking it away with her. She returned within minutes, a full carafe in one hand and a breadbasket piled high with hot buttered garlic bread.

Maddy reached for the steaming piece at the top, biting into it with a moan. "Lord, I'm hungry. It's been a hell of a day."

"It must have been. It takes a lot for you to call out for help."

The reminder that she'd called him and why, slowed her enjoyment of her treat. "I know. Didn't want to put you out. I did suggest that I drive up to your place."

"Not an issue. I've been in the city all day. I'm more than ready for a chance to sit and visit with an old friend." Stefan reached out, his long artist fingers hovering over the basket before making a selection. "Did you order?"

"No. Momma Rosa will bring us whatever she feels we need. Chances are my portion will be enough to feed three."

He grinned. "That's not a bad idea. You're dropping weight again, Maddy. Not good."

Maddy frowned at him. "Surely not. At least not enough to be noticeable."

"Only to someone who knows you well." Stefan studied her face intently. Maddy sipped her wine. She ignored him but couldn't stop the heat from rising up her face. Thankfully, Momma Rose arrived with two steaming plates. As she placed them down in front of them, Maddy giggled. Her plateful could feed a small army.

"Tut, tut." Momma Rose shook a finger at a grinning Stefan. "You make sure Dr. Maddy eats. She's too skinny. She needs a good man to take care of her."

Maddy's eyes widened in shocked amusement.

Stefan's grin deepened.

"You're right. She does need a good man."

Momma Rose beamed at him. "Yes, yes. She works too hard looking after everyone else. No one looks after her."

"We're working on it, Momma Rose. Not to worry. She'll be partnered soon."

Maddy, in the process of taking a sip of wine, choked, spitting wine everywhere as a beaming Mama Rose disappeared into the kitchen. Reaching for a napkin, Maddy gasped for breath then coughed until her eyes watered and her air passages cleared.

Reaching over, Stefan patted her on the back. "Are you okay?"

She glared, at him and gasped, "I was until you opened your mouth."

Stefan sat down, a gentle smirk turned her way. "Are you telling me that with all your energy work and healing ability, you have no idea that your single state is changing?"

Maddy put her napkin down on the table. Her astonishment turned to alarm. "Like you're one to talk. Why don't you have someone special in your life?" She glared at him. "Of course, I don't have any idea. There is one basic element missing here – it's called a man. The man."

A knowing grin swept across his face. "He's a relatively new addition to your life. However, he's there now. You know it, you feel it, and you're denying it." The smile dropped off. "And I do know what is happening in terms of my own private life, but there won't be any movement in that area for several months, or longer. Your time is now."

Maddy stared at one of the most powerful psychics in the modern world and didn't know what to say. Questions crowded her mind, but the biggest one demanded an answer. "Who?" she whispered, urgently, her gaze locked on his face. She needed to know. "Who?"

"I don't know."

Her spine straightened. "What? You can't tantalize me with tidbits. I need to know who." Outrage and disbelief swept through her, only to be replaced by the image of a tall linebacker-of-a-detective and that instinctive recognition she'd noticed when she'd first met him.

Ageless black eyes opened in front of her as Stefan slipped from reality to the seer he was. "He will save your life – at a price. Your healing abilities will be needed, at a level you rarely go."

The fire flared suddenly, then dimmed.

Shivers rippled down her spine. "What?" she whispered urgently. "When?"

"Soon. Too soon. Something in your world has gone wrong. Dangerously wrong." Stefan's voice echoed in an eerie whisper.

"Oh, God." Maddy watched, fascinated. She'd seen him do it time and time again: Stefan returned to himself, almost unaware of the shifting energies as he morphed through realities.

Back to normal. With one eye cocked in her direction, Stefan lifted a fork piled high with spaghetti and a luscious meat sauce. "Problems?"

"No." Maddy smiled. "You shifted for a moment."

His fork stopped in midair. "I what?" His gaze turned inward. "Oh, so I did."

"A little unnerving message, too. Thanks for scaring the bejesus out of me." Maddy took a bite from her plate.

"Some of them are like that."

"Great," she murmured. "That adds to the reason I asked to meet with you."

Stefan ate heartily for a few moments before sitting back and lifting his glass of wine. He took a sip, studying her over the rim of his glass. "Speaking of which, what did you want to discuss?"

Casting a glance around the room to make sure no one else could hear, she leaned closer and said, "Something peculiar is going on." Quickly, she filled him in on the odd events on her floor, starting with the weird purple-black energy she'd found surrounding Eric and Jansen and then she told him about their subsequent deaths, the changes in the energy on the floor, and the new patients. "We both know black energy can be many things, including a toxic environment that over time can cause disease."

"And some people will hook their energy into another person to keep them connected. Look at husbands who are jealous of their wives or mothers that won't let their sons grow up. That can cause the toxic environment." Stefan took another bite of his dinner. "And people who hate each other or try to control others do the same thing."

"But usually unconsciously." It was important to recognize that people didn't know what they were doing to others – in most cases. But when people internalized these negative emotions, it squandered their energy and disease could be the result. She leaned back, her fingers gently rubbing her temples.

"Maintaining balance and conducting healing in this environment was always a challenge, but now...well, it's next to impossible."

Stefan's gaze narrowed on her face. "This energy, did it have any emotion attached to it?"

Maddy frowned and cast her mind back. "It happened so fast. I don't know. If I had to put a name to it, I'd have to say the energy had a feeling of 'need,' single-mindedness, almost a touch of desperation to it."

A grimace whispered across Stefan's face. "I was afraid you were going to say that."

"Why?" Maddy leaned forward. "What is it? I don't get it." Her barely touched plate of spaghetti sat forgotten. "What was it doing there?"

"I can't say for sure. There have been odd instances in history where people had the capability to take, for themselves, the life force of someone with diminished capacity."

A shocked gasp slid from Maddy's lips. "What?" Fearing someone might overhear, she twisted around to make sure no one was listening, then bent forward, whispering, "Do you know what you're saying? The implications?"

"Oh yes, I know exactly what I'm saying." He took another bite of his meal. He motioned for her to eat.

She stared blankly down at her full plate. "It really is possible to steal someone's energy?"

"Not just their energy, Maddy. Their life force."

"Good Lord. That means they actually, willfully kill another person?"

"Right. Theoretically, it's murder."

Maddy struggled to reconcile that the dark purple energy was something that belonged to a person and even worse, that that person murdered Jansen for his life force. "I've heard stories, of course, I hadn't put any credence to them."

"Nothing is impossible at this point. Have I personally seen a case like this? No. Given that you actually witnessed this in a place where you create a special healing energy, it makes me wonder if that healing energy is the attraction. Healing energy has a draw all its own. The Haven is full of dying and desperate people. It's not too far off to suppose that another patient might be doing this, one not lucky enough to be a recipient of your special skills. If they were receiving your healing energy, there'd be no need for them to steal it from someone else."

"No." Maddy shuddered. "Oh, no."

Stefan stared soberly at her. "It's a possibility."

Maddy shuddered violently and reached for her wine glass. Took a healthy drink. "That's terrible. Everyone there is dying."

"Exactly."

Maddy stared at him, confusion clouding her mind. "What? What do you mean?"

"Who would care? Death's expected there, isn't it? People die all the time. After all, that's why they go there. Think about it. Who would notice if a dying patient…died?"

Maddy's stomach roiled. The spaghetti searched for a quick exit. She pushed her chair back and leaned closer to the fire, gasping for calm and balance. Memories crowded her, starting with the crash team that had worked on Eric as she watched, followed by the creepy old woman from the hallway. She'd been so busy, so rushed off her feet, she hadn't had time to follow up on who she was.

Yet, hadn't she had an inkling? She stared at Stefan's calm, unaffected face.

"That's horrible." And unacceptable. Maddy worked with death and dying every day, but she'd never heard of anything so sick.

"Dying people don't have a strong life force, making them easy victims. They can't fight off predators. Add all that healing energy surrounding your patients…well…that's got to be attractive to someone who's desperately trying to heal." He stroked the back of her hand. "What better location for this type of murder to happen than a place full of people who won't be missed and where there are a number of people who are desperate to live – and will do so by any means possible?"

Silence surrounded them. Maddy straightened, staring into the flames, her mind racing in circles, trying to make sense of his words. "How close would this person have to be in order to accomplish such a feat?"

Stefan's brows furrowed. "If we're right and this is another sick person doing this, I don't think he could be very far away – like in another country or city – although if he's powerful and in good health that's possible. Ripples happen in energy levels but too much will actually cause a tear. I believe that's what's happening here. You remember those lessons, right? At a guess, I'd have to say the person either lives or works at The Haven…or is a regular visitor. Could even be someone who goes there on a regular basis for business purposes, like a delivery person." He paused. "Although if the person was connected to the victim in some way, like a family member or a lover, they could do this from further away."

"So." Maddy gulped, took a deep breath and blurted out, "Whoever this person is, he's using The Haven as a feeding ground?"

Stefan grimaced. "As much as I hate the way you put that, I'd have to say yes."

Stefan waited until Maddy's lithe frame disappeared safely indoors before pulling away from the curb. She was a beautiful person inside and out. He felt honored to have her in his life. And he was more worried about her and the situation at The Haven than he'd dared let her see.

Several other powerful psychics and energy workers had already contacted him, wondering what had disturbed the energy field. He hadn't had much to give in the way of answers. It occurred to him, that without trying, he had collected a small group of powerful, aware individuals with unbelievable abilities of their own.

He'd helped several special women, like Sam and Kali, to develop their skills further. Helped them to stop hiding their lights and come out in a position of strength. Both had been blessed or cursed – depending on the viewpoint – with special talents. They'd each blossomed with a little training. He could see wonderful things in their futures. But they, along with several other people, still turned to him for answers.

Ripples in the energy field were normal – tears were not. He'd felt similar problems before, on a smaller scale. These tear-indicators had popped up over the last year at irregular intervals. Then about three months ago, something had changed, worsened. They became different, were off somehow. He wondered if something new, someone new was experimenting. He frowned, changing lanes to access the highway ramp. It almost seemed like the experimental stage was over and that whoever was doing this had put their newfound skills into practice.

Mastery would follow.

He had to find this person and stop them before more innocent people died.

People like Maddy.

He smiled fondly. She was a sweetheart. A giver, not a taker. A lover, even a fighter, but never a betrayer. Maddy's energy was pure and glorious. It had to be for the work she did. Anyone with less couldn't accomplish the good she did – their inner light wouldn't be strong enough.

He had always loved her – as a sister, as a soul-bound friend, as a partner on this journey through both sides of reality. People like Maddy made his life less lonely and more viable. He drew on her strength in times of his own need, as she did on his. She didn't recognize it yet, but the time of her awakening to yet another level of awareness was approaching.

It had to do with the tears in the energy levels. He didn't use the term evil often, not liking the misconceptions that arose immediately in people's minds. This was the first time in a long time that he felt driven to consider what that term meant for him – and for others.

He shifted lanes as he eased into mainstream traffic. The evening light had disappeared behind dark storm clouds. Stefan stared at the unfolding darkness, finding a matching soberness inside. Something nasty was brewing. The energies were stirring and gathering in a most unpleasant way.

The thought had no sooner formed in his mind when his world went black. His fingers convulsed on the steering wheel. The blackness ripped apart and his inner gaze fell on a horrific scene of bedridden people, twisting in agony, their silver cords stretched taut.

As Stefan watched, one silver cord snapped. The man's voice cried out, "Nooooo!" His panicked gaze locked onto Stefan for the briefest instant before the ghostlike entity winked out of existence.

Stefan's awareness slammed back into the vehicle, now crawling along in the wrong lane with traffic snarled around him. Panicked, he quickly pulled off onto the shoulder amid honking horns.

Trembling, Stefan hugged his arms around his chest and bowed his head. *Christ.* He hated receiving visions when he wasn't at home. A major reason he lived in hermit's isolation. Today, he had been forced to travel and had already experienced two of these.

Focused on his breathing, it still took several long moments before he could raise his head and let the tension drain calmly from his system.

He'd seen this type of energy before, when he was a kid. Too young to understand and too unimportant to make anyone else take notice.

Now they'd all get a second chance.

Hell was stopping by for another visit and it appeared its target was The Haven – this time.

Sissy did feel so much better again today. Of course, the hot bubble bath with her favorite sea foam scent had helped. She did so love to indulge herself. Her healing improved every day. She laughed at the other old women in her room. They all whispered behind her back. She didn't care. She *was* getting better. She felt the improvement.

The other sick women weren't getting better. Look at them. They died a little more each day. Silly of them. They should be asking her how she was doing so much better than they were. Maybe they'd get healthier themselves if they practiced some of her tricks. She was here at The Haven, a long-term care facility. No one expected her to be discharged from the place.

So what if she'd been here for almost a year? She planned to walk out of here soon – healthy, happy and capable of dealing with the world outside.

Stupid doctors. What did they know?

Maddy, her hair in a fluffy towel, slipped on a warm robe and stepped into her bedroom. The hot bath had been a relief after the chill she'd experienced since talking with Stefan.

Pulling a silk nightie from her closet, she tossed it on the bed then went to work drying her hair. She sneezed. Hopefully, she wasn't coming down with something. She really couldn't afford that right now.

She needed advice and who better than Janice Shiner? A powerful energy worker, Janice was one of the pioneers of the medical intuitive field. Not a medical doctor herself, she'd come into her abilities through the impending death of her only son.

Janice's determination to save him had flung her into the world of colors, vibrations and transparencies. She'd managed to see inside her son's body to what the doctors had missed. Getting his doctor to listen to her had been a different story. Knowing the child was dying anyway, he'd changed the medication to treat the rapidly encroaching staph infection they'd missed the first time around.

Her son had lived through the experience, and both the doctor and Janice had been forever changed. She'd moved on to work with several other doctors, studying to understand and develop some kind of standardization of her work and to teach others. Out of those students, only a dozen were strong, practicing medical intuitives. Maddy was one of them. She'd been able, not only to see the human body in a unique way, but also manipulate the energy in such a way as to facilitate healing…occasionally with miraculous results.

She picked up the phone and made the call. "Janice, do you have a moment? I've got a possible situation developing and need your help."

"Tell me." Janice never wasted words or sugarcoated anything. Quickly, Maddy explained, adding in some of Stefan's concerns.

"I don't know about the tear stuff, I'm not much into that psychic business as you well know, and I don't buy into any evil stuff when I do energy work. As for this other business…" Janice's voice died off. "I've never seen it myself, although I remember Jimmy, one of my earlier students, telling me years ago, many years ago, about something similar."

"How long ago did this happen?"

"Oh, who knows? Twenty, maybe thirty years ago. It might even have been longer."

"What did he see?" Maddy walked over to her bed and sat down. With her spare hand, she continued to towel dry her hair.

"Something about a deep purple energy and blackness."

Maddy bolted to her feet. "That sounds like what I saw." She paced the small room. "Maybe he saw the same thing."

"Maybe, but who's to say? He didn't say much more. I think it kind of freaked him out, to tell you the truth. I know he wouldn't speak of it again."

"It freaked the hell out of me too." Maddy walked over to the big window, staring out at the blackness beyond her window. "I was hoping you'd say it wasn't anything to worry about or give me a solution to make it disappear. You know, that sort of thing."

Janice's voice took on its usual teacher tone. "Everything is energy. If what you are seeing is a person's energy, then it should be easy to see inside and find out exactly what they are doing. Then you might be able to find a way to stop it."

"And if I can see through it, I should be able to see the source of it." Maddy nodded. That made sense and matched her healing process.

"Right. Now if you don't have any other questions, I'll head to bed." Janice rang off, leaving Maddy feeling calmer and surer of herself. If something was afoot, she did have the skills to get to the bottom of it. That was the trick. She had to be there when it happened. Only she wasn't at The Haven during the night.

SUNDAY

On Sunday, Maddy woke late with more questions than answers.

She needed a better way to see what was happening on her floor. The floor had been deliberately set up with minimal video cameras. She needed to see the feeds from the ones that existed, and better yet, set up a few more. There were too many unsettling issues pulling her away from her work. She needed to focus on healing, on her patients, not all this other stuff. Surely that was for the police to sort out.

Now she was convinced that someone was killing her patients. All of this begged the question, could someone really kill another person by damaging, draining, and absorbing the person's energy, their life force, in some way? According to stories she'd heard, the answer was yes. Yet, why would they do this? What was their need? There was enough energy for every person, for every need. There was no shortage. Ever. The reason behind this was what she didn't understand. And who'd be targeted next.

And as much as she'd like to take the day off, she wanted to keep an eye on her floor. She didn't dare stop her vigilance with this mess going on.

Time to go to work and check on those video feeds.

Drew walked through the main floor of The Haven, heading for the stairs. As he pushed open the fire door to the stairs, he half-hoped he'd see the running wild woman again. Walking up slowly, he listened for any sound that might signal a door opening. No such luck. Then again, it was Sunday, and who knew if Dr. Maddy was on duty or not.

Taking the stairs two at a time, he arrived at his aunt's floor and strode over to speak to her. Doris had been at The Haven for over a year. In the beginning, she'd talked nonstop about coming home. Since her condition had started to deteriorate, she'd switched to speaking more about transferring to Dr. Maddy's floor. According to his uncle, the doctor had said her depression and declining mental state were concerns as well. Medication had helped improve her spirits.

He and John were her entire family, though Drew vaguely remembered talk about her having had a child long ago. He didn't know the whole story as his aunt had only come into his life to help out after his mother died from breast cancer when he was entering high school.

Drew had coped by going a little wild. His dad chased the bottle, or rather, a lot of bottles until his death a good ten years ago.

Walking into her room, Drew waved to a couple of his aunt's friends. He reached her bed and frowned. The bed was empty.

"She's gone to have her bath, she has."

Drew spun around to look at the patient across the floor. Her illness had reduced her frame almost to a rack of bones, but under a mop of pepper-gray hair her smile shone bright and true.

"Has she? Could you please tell her when she gets back that I'm just upstairs? I'll stop in and see her on my way out." Just about to turn away, he stopped and asked, "What kind of a day is she having?"

The heavily wrinkled neighbor grinned. "Not too good today. She was better yesterday."

Drew nodded. Everything was normal then.

Now to see if Dr. Maddy was in. In spite of his calm demeanor, his pulse raced. She fascinated him. He'd heard the rumors. Who hadn't? She'd had some phenomenal results and Drew knew his uncle had twisted someone's arm hard, to get in here. It would be interesting to see how he fared under Dr. Maddy's wing.

At the top floor, he pushed open the double doors and walked through onto Dr. Maddy's floor. Immediately the sensation of peace and love enveloped him. He stood still for a long moment. The tension in his shoulders eased as a long rippling sigh worked its way to freedom.

No wonder his aunt and uncle wanted in. He strode the first few feet into the main hallway, searching for the elusive doctor. The décor had an upbeat yet peaceful vibe to it.

Unlike the rest of The Haven, this floor plan laid out a series of sitting rooms and bedrooms, private yet social, open yet partially closed. Everything was designed for the comfort of a sleeping, healing patient versus the sterile, plastic look of the other floors of the home. Walking a few feet, he casually glanced in at the first bed on the left. He'd been right. There was real bedding and sheets on it. Not the standard issue hospital shit.

Impressed in spite of himself, he searched for the nurses' station.

"Excuse me. Is Dr. Maddy here?"

"I think she's with a patient, right now." The portly nurse wearing the nametag of Gerona, answered him. Her smile actually looked real.

He pulled out his badge to show her. "I do need to speak with her. Could you let her know I'm here, please?"

The smile beamed. "No problem. Take a seat in the waiting room."

"Thanks." He turned around. Waiting room?

"Down the hall and turn left."

He nodded his thanks, then followed the instructions and found himself at the entrance to a bright sunny sitting room that was more inviting than any room in his own house. He wandered over to the double French doors that opened out onto a large open balcony. It overlooked bright, cheerful gardens sprawled out behind The Haven. The seating area was more than generous and although there were a dozen or so straight-backed chairs, the space between the round tables was spacious enough for wheelchairs to maneuver.

He admired the view of the city park off in the distance. This was a nice place. He'd have to remember to congratulate his uncle for whatever devious moves he'd made to get in here. He just hoped those moves were legal.

"Hello, Detective. I understand you're waiting for me."

Drew spun around at the sound of her voice. He couldn't help it, his gaze slid to her feet. Three inch black stilettos. *Be still my beating heart.*

"Detective?"

Snapping his head up, he felt the heat climb his face. "Sorry. I wasn't sure you'd be in. Have you got a few moments?"

Maddy nodded. "I'm not normally in on Sundays. However, with new patients moving in there's a lot to do. Shall we go into my office or would you like to sit out here?"

"Out here would be great."

"Sure." She led the way and pulled out a chair at the farthest table. Turning to face the view, she sat down and crossed her legs.

Damn those long smooth legs. Drew had to forcibly pull his gaze away to stare out over the garden.

"As nice as this is, Detective, I'm assuming this isn't a social visit."

"No." Drew shifted toward her and pulled his notebook out of his pocket. "Thanks for sending the list of people that had visited Jansen Svaar. If you can think of anyone else he saw on a regular basis, please let me know." He narrowed his gaze, frowning at her. "I'm really here because I don't understand the significance of the bruise on the top of his head. You asked Dr. Miko to check for it, you gave me a quick explanation that made no sense, then you took off. So I also need to know if you have any idea how those bruises occurred?"

She was already shaking her head. "No, I don't. They are superficial, so it's not as if they were caused by a blow or from lying on something. Normal energy work doesn't leave marks of any kind. I just don't know."

"Have you ever done any procedure on Jansen that could have resulted on this type of bruising?"

"Absolutely not. Any procedures are well documented and there had been no need for any kind of intervention because he was doing so well. That's the thing, he was healing."

"So his death surprised you?" Drew jotted down a few notes but so far nothing helped.

"Yes and no."

He looked up in surprise.

"You have to realize that everyone here is expected to die sooner than later. Jansen's progress was remarkable yet he had a ways to go for a full recovery."

There was no arguing that.

She surprised him with her next comment. "I understand from Gerard that your uncle will be joining us soon." Her smile brightened. "That will be nice. We have several more beds we're filling over the next few days."

"How about extra staff to help with the extra work?"

Her smile dimmed. "Not going to happen. Budgets, economy and all that." She shrugged those slim shoulders and looked directly into his eyes. "It doesn't really matter. This floor operates separately from the rest of The Haven, so our budgetary needs are separate as well."

"Just how unusual is this floor?" Drew leaned in, his gaze narrowing on her face. Maybe now he could get real answers. "I hear rumors and conjecture, no actual facts. What exactly goes on up here?"

Her face assumed the professional polish of one about to give a prepared speech. He waved her quiet. "No. I don't want the sales pitch. I want to know what *you* do here." He pointed a finger at her. "This floor is named after you. As if you are in charge of something special. I agree it is special. I can see that. I can feel that. I walk through the doors to this floor and it's like coming home. It's warm, peaceful...loving. How? What are you doing to make it so different?"

Maddy sat back and studied him.

Drew stared back.

"It might be a little difficult to explain," she said, cautiously.

"Try me." He watched her huge chocolate eyes deepen as the expressions played across her face. He watched her carefully, hoping she wouldn't lie to him.

"This is off the record and has nothing to do with the case."

Drew pursed his lips and nodded. He snapped his notebook closed and dropped his pen on top. "Fine. Let's hear it."

Maddy leaned forward slightly, glanced toward the door to make sure they were alone, then back at his face. "It's not a deep mystery. However, due to the sensitive nature of the project, we keep it low key to avoid any paranoid backlash."

Interesting choice of words.

"I'm listening."

"I'm a medical intuitive as well as a licensed medical doctor."

Drew's gaze narrowed. Medical intuitive. Did he even know what that was?

She carried on. "As energy is so important to a person's health, we devised a system to maximize a person's healing by utilizing the energy of the person, his surroundings and of those he interacts with to help him to heal. It's like a city system where everything is interdependent and is only as good as the lowest element. In this case, the lowest element is the sick person.

"As each of these people start to heal, then the energy level around them and us becomes invigorated or energized. That then cycles back around for the patients to use for more healing. Most of these patients have been here for at least six months – an average time factor to clean their energy meridians and to open up their ability to utilize what's available so they can progress through their body's various health conditions and heal."

Drew blinked. *Say what?*

"That's why we can't accept just everyone here. And why the next six months will be tough on all of us with so many new patients coming in. The best scenario would be one new patient a month and even that can slow the healing progression for everyone. Adding a new person is adding a lower element every time. The other patients have to adjust to the shift in energy." She sat back. "I have to adjust, too," she admitted.

She spoke as if pondering the chances of having The Haven administrators change their plan. Fat chance. Drew knew 'money' people. If they managed to squeeze an extra dollar out of something, they'd try for two. Not that it would help here. He didn't understand exactly what she'd said and the only thing that had registered was that the people here were healing. *Healing?* These people were dying – weren't they?

The question refused to stay quiet. "When did your last patient die?"

Her mouth drooped. "Until Jansen, it had been just over eight months."

"That long? And how many patients do you have?"

"Over sixty."

"Over sixty and only one death. Holy crap. These people are in seriously bad condition before they come to you, aren't they?"

She nodded. "Yes, they're all terminal. They all need to have a life expectancy of at least six months to join the floor or it damages the energy. Even worse, a death will have a big impact on the other patients, particularly a bad death. Death can be a positive experience for those that have been ill for a long while or it can be a negative experience. Jansen's death affected everyone in a very negative way. We're still working through that."

Drew shook his head. "What's to figure out? Of course, everyone is upset. Someone who appeared to be getting better – something they were all hoping to do – died. And unexpectedly at that."

"It could be that. Or it could be something else." Maddy stared down at the frosted glass table, her finger tracing some invisible pattern. "I don't know."

"That sounds odd coming from a doctor."

She raised her face to the sunlight, a lopsided smile on her face. "Really? Well, I don't know that all doctors are black and white. Besides, like I said, I'm a medical intuitive and a doctor."

"What does that mean? I'm not sure that I've even heard that term before."

She didn't answer immediately. "The term can have a different meaning depending on the level of skill the medical intuitive possesses."

"I don't want to hear about anyone else. How does the term pertain to you?"

"I see the human body in terms of energy. By looking at different angles and layers, sometimes I can see inside the body and check what health issues exist and the possible contributing causes. More than that, I see the energy that flows through the body and where it's blocked."

"Sometimes?" It all sounded bizarre to him. He wasn't sure he liked the idea of someone being able to see under his skin.

"Most of the time."

Drew didn't know what to say. He searched her candid gaze. She was telling him the truth, as she knew it. "To do something like this on a small scale is hard enough, but on a large scale, like the scale of your floor, well...that has to be close to impossible."

"I hope not." She smiled gently. "Otherwise, I've wasted the last few years of my life. And as I plan to expand to help people before they become terminally ill..."

"Has everyone shown an improvement after arriving on your floor?"

"Yes."

"Yes?" He knew he sounded like a parrot repeating himself. He couldn't help it. Her success was unbelievable.

She nodded. "Everyone has improved since they've arrived. Although some have died eventually, we extended their lives and gave them a better quality of life. In the next phase, we'll work toward catching those diagnosed, but not so far along. The results should be faster. I'd be working on it now, but...money, the medical system, people's belief systems, you know. People do get better with good care to begin with and we can help that along."

The implications blew his mind. "You do realize the significance here, don't you? If people on your floor are healing, they could potentially go home again...as in cheat death. Right?"

Maddy pulled back and frowned. "Of course, although that's an odd way to look at it. Several people have gone home, younger ones. With our older ones, we really only expect to extend their lives for a bit."

He shook his head. "You're saying that some of your patients arrived with only six months left to live and walked out of here healthy?"

"On their way to being healthy, yes. We haven't seen instantaneous healing, except with a couple of children. For all the others, we've seen definite turns for the better with continued improvement."

"How many?" He had to know. He wondered if his uncle knew. Shit, of course the old bastard did. That's why he'd fought so hard to get in. And how the hell had he done that anyway?

He'd been given less than six months, not more. According to Maddy, that should have made him ineligible.

"Twenty-one are continuing to improve at home."

"Out of sixty?"

"Roughly. We didn't have quite so many beds before." A confused frown settled on her face as she studied his face. "Why is that so shocking?"

"That's what – more than thirty percent? That's nuts."

"I'm quite proud of it." She flushed. "I know we can do better and we will as time moves on and I can pull the energy into better circulation. The results would also be more impressive if I had more children on my floor. They always seem to do well."

"Always?" Did she have any idea what she was suggesting here? If she did, why wasn't she working at the children's hospital? Oh yeah, because she'd heal everyone and shut down the center, putting hundreds of people out of work. Drew shook his head at his own sarcasm. But still, was she blind to the implications?

"Always – at least so far." Pride beamed from her face and her voice.

And she should be proud. He couldn't get his mind wrapped around the potential. No wonder Gerard worked to get as many patients under her care as possible. The patient-to-doctor ratio sucked, yet considering the doctor involved, not one patient would care.

A horrible thought crossed his mind. It had to be from too many years in law enforcement.

"You do realize what a premium bed space goes for on your floor."

"Actually, I don't. Gerard handles that stuff."

Drew nodded. It went along with what he'd heard from others about Maddy. She was all about her patients. "I wonder how hard it is to get a bed on your floor."

Maddy frowned and shook her head gently, sending her dark hair flipping around her shoulders. "Not hard. After all, it's just an application form."

"How many people know about the new wing on your floor?"

"We've tried to keep it quiet. There's already a huge waiting list. More beds means helping more people, but Gerard doesn't want the news to get out or he'll be inundated with new applications."

"Right. So the real question is – would someone kill off a patient in order to free up a bed so they *could* get on your floor?"

He knew she didn't understand. Confusion clouded her beautiful eyes. Then they widened in horror. "Oh, no."

***

Doris shifted uncomfortably in her hospital bed and tried to adjust her covers to suit. She couldn't remember the last time she'd felt good enough to sit out on one of the many decks and enjoy the sunshine. She stared at her neighbor furtively. She was consumed with the mystery of her. How was she managing to look better every day? Turning to face forward, Doris studied the other two women in her room. They seemed the same as always. A little older, more worn, more tired. Not her neighbor though – she positively glowed.

Sniffing in the schoolteacher way she'd learned years ago, she tried to not care. Still it was hard. She wanted the same healing for herself. She tried so hard to do everything right. She used hand lotion, she drank lots of water, and tried to follow a beauty regime she'd gotten from a magazine years ago, but nothing made a difference. Then, for no apparent reason, her neighbor perked up and appeared better each day – as if she'd found the fountain of youth. And damn, she'd forgotten to ask her doctor about the woman's medications.

Getting on Maddy's floor would help. At least then, she'd get a fighting chance to heal. She shifted again, pulling her blankets up higher. The weather had to be warmer outside than in this room. With another surreptitious glance at her neighbor, she admitted it to herself. Fine, okay. Yes, she was jealous. She wanted to be as good as her neighbor. Surely there wasn't anything wrong with that?

The temperature in Stefan's large home studio was normal, yet sweat rolled off his face. Stripping off a layer wasn't an option. Neither was slowing down. Grimly, he hung on as paint flew in all directions, globules of red splotched on his smock, the canvas before him and the linoleum beneath his feet where it joined puddles of black and blue that had gone before.

Stefan's arm ached. How long had he been painting? His shoulder said it had been hours. Chances were it was less than one.

If he was this exhausted after years of experience he could only imagine how Kali was doing with her psychic paintings. He'd been working with her to develop her skills, and as they were both artists, painting was a natural medium for them to use.

He swabbed the palette with his paintbrush, picking up more red before pounding down on the canvas. He moved to some silent demonic orders. Painting as demanded, refusing to stop – or maybe he was not able to stop – until the demon was exorcised from his mind.

Stefan didn't see what he was painting. Instead, he was gripped by one of the psychic visions that ruled his world. The canvas was there, but he didn't have the vision as a clear image in his mind.

When his arm lifted again, he groaned. He'd need a painkiller after this session. He closed his eyes, letting the energy flow through him. It would anyway. Resistance caused pain. If he relaxed, the pain would ease.

His arm dropped. The force gripping his body drained down to his feet and out through his toes. He shuddered. It was over – for now.

He bent forward, catching his breath from the fury so recently released from his soul. His hands rested on his knees. Finally, he straightened to study his paint-spattered fingers and pants. He frowned. He painted with only one hand. Why were both hands covered in color?

Stepping back, Stefan washed his hands, taking care to thoroughly scrub them. Now to look at the picture – not that he was eager to do so. The picture could be a geometric disaster or it could be a detailed masterpiece. Some of his paintings hung in galleries around the world.

Then there were the paintings that he instinctively knew this one was. Ones that revealed haunted visions that tormented the soul and terrified the mind forever. Mostly they were vicious outpourings of violence.

Gearing himself for what was to come, he turned to view his latest creation, and immediately closed his eyes again. Please not. Slowly, hoping he'd been wrong, he peeked from behind partially closed lids and groaned softly.

Death himself had created this painting.

Still, it gave him a good idea of how he might help Maddy.

Drew was walking down the stairs toward his aunt's ward when his cell phone rang. He frowned at the number. Memorial Hospital, the one attached to The Haven. Not good.

"Hello?"

"Detective Drew McNeil?"

"Yes, that's correct. What can I do for you?"

"We have a patient here who has been asking for you. A Scott Durnham."

Scott, the husband of the diary writer. "I know of him. What happened?"'

"He's suffering from a concussion due to a head injury inflicted as he tried to get in his car."

"Was he alone?" Drew frowned. "Was his vehicle stolen? His wallet? ID?"

"I don't have those details. You'd need to speak with Officer Dale Hansford. He's the one that called for the ambulance to pick up Mr. Durnham."

"Right. I'll do that. Was there a small diary or journal among his personal effects?" It would be too much to hope that Scott had the missing diary on him at the hospital. Not that they'd found anything of interest in the other diaries. But he'd be interested to read the diary written around the time of the boy's death.

He waited. There was a pause and a rustling of papers before she said, "No, only car keys and a mint."

So where was it? Scott had planned to drop it off at the station today. "Fine. I'll follow up with the officer. Is Mr. Durnham going to be okay?"

"He's with the doctor right now. So it's too early to say."

"Thanks, I'm at The Haven already. I'll walk over in a few minutes. I'd like to speak with him, if possible."

Hanging up, Drew called the precinct, looking for the officer.

"Dale Hansford here."

Drew identified himself. "Can you fill me in on the particulars of Scott Durnham's case?"

By the time Drew walked through the front doors of Memorial Hospital, he'd gotten as much information from the officer as was available. He stared at the gleaming corridors, the smell of disinfectant chasing him. Drew realized that regarding work and family, he spent way too many hours in medical centers of one kind or another. After getting directions, he strode down the hallway toward Scott's bed. Dinner was being served, people were eating and in some cases trays were already being collected.

Scott appeared to be sleeping, at peace except for the wrinkles across his forehead. Drew stopped at the foot of his bed. "Mr Durnham? I'm Detective Drew McNeil from the Cold Case Squad."

Scott's eyes flew open, his face creasing in a weak smile. "Detective."

"How are you feeling?"

"Like I had my head bashed in."

Drew grinned at the pissed-off tone. Anger was good. It kept one focused. Giving in was like giving up. Not so good for healing or for catching bad guys though. "Do you remember anything about what happened?"

"Not much. I was getting into my car when pain exploded at the side of my head."

"You didn't see your attacker?"

Scott wrinkled up his face. "Nope. I thought someone called me but when I started to turn around, the lights went out."

"What were you doing there?"

"Having a free breakfast at the seniors' center. Free, my ass. Had to stand in line for almost an hour, put up with shit from everyone else, then got into an argument. I should have stayed home."

"An argument?" Drew stepped closer, pulling up the single chair and sat. "What was that all about?"

"My wife's diary. I had it in my pocket, and that prick, Brent, made a comment about it. Then he followed it by a worse one about my dead son and I lost it. I thought I was done blowing up about all that mess, but apparently not." Scott moodily tugged at the sheets covering his chest.

"No one has seen a diary. It didn't come to the hospital with you, and the detective handling the case didn't see one at the scene."

Scott stared at him. "It was in my jacket pocket when I was in Emergency. I'm sure of that."

With Scott watching, Drew opened the locker beside the bathroom. He gathered up everything and dumped the lot on Scott's bed. Scott pushed himself back up against the pillows to watch.

Drew turned his attention to the jacket. He slipped his hands inside the pockets, first one then the other. "No diary." He laid the jacket within the injured man's reach.

Scott frowned and pulled it toward him, checking for himself.

Drew slowly went through the remaining items. There was no sign of the missing book. "Was it close in size to the others?"

"Exactly like the ones with the little lock on it. This one had blue sparkly things on it."

"Well, it's not here. Did it sit inside the pocket well or stick out? Could it have fallen out?"

"It fit in just fine. I kept my hand on it most of the time anyway." Scott dropped the jacket. "I suppose it's possible that it fell out somewhere. I've gotta find it. I need to ask the nurses." He threw back the bedding and swung his legs around the side. He groaned and grabbed his head.

"Whoa. I'll go. You stay here and rest up. You're no help if you don't get better." Drew helped him back under the covers. "I'll be right back."

"Thanks. I don't want that last one to go missing. I was telling the little Italian nurse about it. It's the one my wife wrote at the time of our son's death. I'd been looking for it for years. I'm finally going through the last of my wife's stuff. She's been gone so long now. I figured it's time I sell the old place." He stared at Drew as he leaned back. "I'd sure like to learn the truth before I die."

"I'm working on it, Scott. We'd all like to know what happened."

"Good to hear." With that, Scott leaned back and closed his eyes.

Drew took that as a good time to leave. He stopped in at the nurses' center first. After showing his identification, he asked about the diary.

"Sorry, I haven't seen it." The nurse pulled up Scott's information on the computer. "There's no notation of it here." She frowned. "He's sure he had it with him?"

"Yes, one of the nurses commented on it in Emergency."

"It didn't arrive here. You can check with them, maybe they're holding it over there." Her polite smile clearly said it wasn't her problem.

Not surprising. Stuff went missing all the time. "Thanks, I'll check there."

The nurse was already talking to someone else. He walked back toward Emergency, wondering if they had a lost and found here. He stopped to ask a nurse. They did, only the trip there proved fruitless.

Back at Emergency, he had to pull his badge in order to learn which nurses had attended Scott. Two nurses were still on shift. "I'd like to speak to them, please." The diary might or might not have important evidence in it but without it, he wouldn't know. He had to trust that Scott's memory hadn't played tricks on him and that he had indeed had the diary in his pocket while here.

A harried looking nurse approached from behind the counter. "You needed to see me?"

She frowned after hearing his problem. "I didn't see the diary myself. Sofie was there with me." She turned around, spotted the woman in question. "Sofie, can you come here for a second?"

The other woman, short and dark haired, walked over. "What's up?"

Drew quickly explained the problem. Sofie's face lit up. "That was such a pretty little book. I haven't seen those in decades. My mother used to write in one. And such a tragic story with it. That poor man."

"It's gone missing. Do you have any idea where it might have ended up?"

Sofie frowned. "No. I put it in the bag with his clothes. That's how I noticed it. We talked a little bit about it, and then I had to go. His personal effects should have traveled to his room with him."

It was Drew's turn to frown. "They did. Without the diary."

He asked a few more questions about who might have seen the diary and if someone had wanted to remove it, when it could have happened. He understood the women didn't like the line of questioning, but they answered readily enough.

The bag had stayed with Scott at all times. In theory, anyone who came by, treated him or moved him had access to the bag. It had no resale value. It might be considered a curiosity worth lifting though. However, as it was inside the closed bag, no one would know the diary was there. It was only important to Scott – and of course himself.

MONDAY

Gerard opened the door to the outer office as quietly as he could. Sandra was at the coffee maker, her back to him. Perfect. Maybe he'd be able to sneak past. His super efficient admin assistant was damn irritating sometimes.

"Good morning."

Gerard stiffened. Damn it. She'd heard him.

"Late, huh?" she said.

"Yeah, bad morning," he said, walking into his office and slammed the door shut.

Sandra opened it almost immediately. "Dr. Chandler called."

"What?" Gerard spun around, his back to the window. Not Chandler again. "What did he want?"

"He didn't say. He asked for Maddy's number." Sandra dropped several pieces of mail on his desk and turned to leave.

Instinctively, Gerard flung out his hand. "Wait. Did you give him her number?"

"Of course. Maddy's a big girl, but even she can't make a decision if she doesn't know the choices."

"Are you nuts?"

She turned and the door slammed behind her, leaving Gerard alone, sputtering in shock. Oh God, he didn't dare lose Maddy. The Haven would spin into a major crisis. Dr. Chandler wasn't allowed to steal her away. No way. "I need a new secretary, for Christ's sake, and maybe a new doctor. Damn it, Sandra, what have you done?" he cried.

From the other side of the door, she called back, "Nothing. Maddy's not likely to leave. As long as you treat her right."

Right. And he'd just added a patient she hated to her floor, cut her budget and increased her patient roster. He clenched the back of his chair. What should he do? Oh Lord, what should he do?

"By the way," Sandra's voice came through the door. "Maddy called. She wants to talk to you."

Oh shit.

His door shoved open and Sandra walked in again. Raising his gaze, anger and frustration warred inside him. He opened his mouth to blast Sandra when he saw the man behind her. Detective Drew McNeil. Damn it. He quickly schooled his features into a polite welcome while eyeing his visitor carefully. Why was he here? Personal or professional?

Gerard walked around his desk and shook hands with Drew. "Drew, nice to see you again. Please have a seat." Gerard sat down. His office phone beeped, and he pushed a button, cutting off the caller.

Catching the detective's questioning look, Gerard grinned sheepishly. "Some idiot did an article on the new wing opening up, now the phones won't quit ringing. People are trying to nab the unclaimed beds."

Focusing on the man across the desk from him, Gerard stretched out his arms and clasped his hands together. "What can I do for you?"

"I need to ask a few questions. It won't take a moment." Drew settled back into his chair and studied Gerard's face. "What do you know about Jansen Svaar's death?"

Raising an eyebrow in surprise, Gerard answered honestly, "Nothing. I only hear if there's a problem."

"And the bed placements?"

"The doctors arrange those to suit the needs of the patients. I have nothing to do with it." Gerard didn't know what the detective was getting at. His next question confused him even more, and started his stomach acids bubbling. Six dead kids from thirty years ago? He frowned. "I knew a couple of them. They went to my school. Everyone who lived here back then would remember those kids. I can't remember any details. Only that no one seemed to know what happened. Why are you asking?"

"Just following up a lead. Now, I understand from Dr. Maddy that, in order to get on her floor, there are stringent requirements in place – a prognosis of greater than six months to live, being one." Drew paused as he searched through his notes, then glanced up, sending Gerard a hard questioning look. "So how did my uncle's application get approved? Apparently, he's been given only three months to live."

Ice filled Gerard's veins. Managing a weak smile, he shuffled the mail on his desk. "Our criteria aren't always so cut and dry. Many elements are discussed before the administrators and medical teams involved determine who is approved." He looked directly at the detective. "Thankfully, it's not my decision alone, or any one person's determination. The waiting list is long and getting longer by the minute." He grimaced at the flashing lights on his phone. "Especially after today."

Gerard had fussed about purchasing more cameras. Maddy had talked him around. Two were being installed as she sat in her office – one to shine on the stairwell and one for the new area. She'd prefer more. This was a place to start though. With the weird energy invading her floor, she wanted to stay here all the time, to move right in so she could watch over everyone. Still, even if she did, she wouldn't be able to watch over everyone all at the same the time.

She'd love to discuss the black energy issue more with Drew. He needed time to adjust before she nailed him with this mess. Once the floor calmed for the night, she planned to do energy readings. She needed to know how far off balance the energy on her floor had shifted after Jansen's death and the arrival of three new patients.

Nancy popped her head in the door. "I'm heading home." She sighed. "Don't stay too late. You need your sleep. Especially with the extra workload."

"How's the newest patient..." Maddy wracked her brain. "John McNeil settling in?"

"The irascible soul is hell on wheels. He's in bed and is ecstatic about being here."

"Good. They make for the best patients." So this was the detective's uncle. That meant she could expect to see Drew soon. Hopefully not until tomorrow. He sent her energy flying, which made it hard to do neutral readings.

Nancy smirked. "This one will be a handful, no matter what."

"I'll go down and say 'hi' in a couple of minutes."

"Good luck. Too bad Dr. Cunningham isn't here… again." With that, she closed the door, leaving Maddy alone with her thoughts.

Dr. Cunningham had popped in briefly. In his early sixties, he spent most of his time working on the hospital side, his first love. She never complained about the workload because bringing another doctor onboard would affect the energy balance of the floor even more. Dr. Cunningham pulled his weight, and left her and her project alone the rest of the time. A perfect system until she became overwhelmed…

Maddy walked down the hallway to check on the cameras. She found the one in the stairway up and functioning. Good. That was one less thing to distract her. She strode down to where the new patient should be. The camera in that area should cover the new wing without affecting the privacy of the patients. Time to welcome John to her floor.

Arriving at his bedside, she smiled at the sight. He had a small, almost shriveled frame with a huge chest that puffed up at the sight of her.

"Good evening, John. Welcome to The Haven."

John's face lit up. For all his apparent joy at the move, it was evident he had found the excitement and the trip arduous. Any move was incredibly stressful on a patient of his age. But what she saw was so much more. Maddy immediately shifted her viewing so she could see his energy more clearly... and frowned. He wasn't just ill and looking for a place for his last year where he could enjoy some quality of life. John was dying — and would soon. Not today, not tomorrow, however, she doubted he'd last more than ten weeks. Her frown deepened. Her floor in The Haven was not a hospice unit, for all the misunderstandings in the public's view. For this floor she only accepted patients much healthier than John. Something had gone wrong in the selection process.

A second death on the floor wasn't going to be easy on the other patients. She pursed her lips. How had his application been accepted?

Frowning, she studied his chart. He was in death management stage. She glanced surreptitiously at his chest area, seeing the gray energy hovering. Yes, his chest was compromised. His shrunken frame wasted. There was some swelling of his hands.

"How's the swelling in your feet?"

She glanced at him as she lifted a corner of the blanket. At his nod, she flipped it back. Both ankles and feet had a tight, purple look to them.

"Is the pain manageable right now? Or do you need something stronger after the move?"

"No," he gasped, "It's okay. I don't know about sleeping tonight, though."

Maddy nodded. "We can give you something for that."

Stepping back, she studied him further. Should she ask or not? "Dr. Cunningham isn't here at this hour, but he'll stop by in the morning. Your transfer came late in the day. I'm sorry. I know that can be hard on individuals. We try to coordinate arrivals to coincide with the doctors' schedules."

"I wasn't going to wait another day. And I don't need a doctor. They can't even say what's wrong with me," he growled, frowning at her. "I need you."

Jolted, Maddy stared at him. "Pardon?"

"I need you and your magic. Don't you go denying it. You're the one responsible for the healing going on around here. I've heard all about it."

As she opened her mouth, he jumped right in. "Hell, half the world's heard about it."

"What?"

"Sure. It's all over the Internet. Checked it out myself." The growl in his voice deepened.

Maddy didn't know what to think. More to the point, did he really think that she was some kind of witch doctor, a miracle healer? That if he could trick his way onto her floor he would be miraculously healed? She had limited success here, helped by the stringent selection process – one that had obviously gone awry with him. There should have been several rounds of interviews, and medical checks, to start. There had been with Dr. Lenning and she'd actually done the testing and intake for Felicia herself.

"I'm not too sure what you've read or heard about me. I am a medical intuitive. That does allow me to see a different level, a different view of the body. Yes, I use energy to heal. And yes, we've had some phenomenal successes, where people have gone home because their condition had improved to that extent."

He nodded with satisfaction. "Right, then. Glad you're not going to give me all the denial bullshit." He settled back into his bed – the pain that had stiffened his face, easing.

"I'm not into denial, but you have a major misunderstanding going on. First off, the only people accepted into the program are those at a certain health level. Anything below that, the patient doesn't have the required strength or health for the healing required."

He blinked a couple of times. "What?" Fear slid across his features.

"I'm saying that your condition has advanced to the point that normally you wouldn't have been accepted here and I'm not sure how you were. Your application should have been declined. I'm sorry."

"How can you tell my condition?" he blustered, puffing his chest. "You haven't read my file."

Maddy's face softened. Just because patients had been told about their condition didn't mean they were ready to accept it. John should be managing his death right now. Instead, he was grasping at straws. He hadn't reached the point of acceptance.

Not unusual, as few people accepted a negative diagnosis easily. She suspected John had held off going to the doctor as long as he could, thereby minimizing treatment options. While Maddy dealt in death every day, she preferred to focus on life.

"I can see *you*. That's why I'm slightly different. I can't tell you when you'll die or any other hocus pocus stuff; however, I can see that your bones ache, your chest is compromised and you're having trouble breathing. Your body is suffering from major edema to the point you can't walk. There are energy blockages at several main intersections in your system that have been there for a long time."

Worry darkened his features. "What does all that mean?"

"It means getting here to my floor may not help you. I'm not sure there's anything I, or anyone, can do for you at this stage."

"But you're not sure?"

He latched onto the one straw she'd inadvertently offered. Maddy could understand the drowning man reaching for a life preserver. As much as she believed in the power of hope and positive thoughts, she also understood there had to be a level of acceptance, peace and belief. She didn't think he had much of those.

John looked to be rigid and grasping – not as if he were aware and accepting that he was close to the end of his life.

"No, I'm not a hundred percent sure."

John glared at her. "I've been to dozens of doctors. Each one says something different. No one can agree as to what's wrong with me because no one knows." He almost shouted the last words as his frustration rose to the boiling point. He coughed violently several times then collapsed back onto his bed, exhausted.

Using her most soothing voice, Maddy poured a glass of water for him from the carafe on his nightstand and said, "There are miracles in life. Still, you don't understand something here. This isn't just me working on your healing. You have to as well."

"How can I do anything? I'm sick. That's why I'm here. For you to work your magic."

He glared at her, using anger to hide the fear lurking in his eyes. Maddy stepped back ready to return to her office. "That's what I'm trying to say. This isn't a floor where you get to lie there and miracles happen. This is where people actively participate in their own healing. If you want to get better, you have to help make it happen."

She walked away, leaving him to think on that for a bit.

She wasn't trying to be cruel, but she needed to shake him out of the 'poor me' syndrome – to have him ask what he could do to help. Not that there was much in this case. He had weeks, maybe a few months, to live. The least she could do would be to make those as pain free and as enjoyable as possible.

On the other hand, she planned to roast Gerard alive – as soon as she found the damn weasel. He couldn't play with everyone's emotions like this. Damn that man. He shouldn't have let John in. Talk about setting up an important selection process, then failing to follow through.

Maddy walked past the nurses' station to the stairwell, pissed at Gerard, upset for John and disappointed in herself and her limited abilities. She needed to get away – even to another floor for a bit. To forget the machinations going on behind her back that threatened to sink her project, the bureaucratic bullshit that was all about money.

On the second floor, she walked through the wards, noting dinner had been delivered to most patients.

Dr. Susan Selsin, her carrot curls making her easily identifiable, stood talking with a colleague as Maddy approached. Her old friend's face lit up at the sight of Maddy. "Fancy that, Dr. Maddy's coming to visit."

Maddy grinned, feeling better already. "Hi, just thought I'd stop in and see how things are down here."

For the next hour, Maddy laughed and cheered everyone's progress. Susan concluded the tour when Maddy declared it was time to return to work.

It was time for her special energy work.

Sissy stretched and wiggled. She laughed at the odd sensation circulating through her body. It was as if she were adjusting to a new suit – a new birthday suit. She smirked at the other women in the ward. One glared at her, another shot her a disgusted look before turning away and reaching for her knitting.

"Don't know about you ladies, but I feel great." She giggled, like the fifteen-year-old she felt like inside.

"I need your drugs. Mine aren't doing anything for me," the old woman across the room said in disgust.

Murmurs and assenting groans answered.

Sissy's grin widened. Today, she felt great.

She looked over at the old woman beside her and couldn't prevent the pleased grin breaking out. That old biddy looked like she was one step away from death. Sad. Too bad for her.

Sissy knew that had been her future – once. Not now. She had a plan and it was finally working. Those damn doctors. You had to make it clear you weren't going to take their lack of care and progress lying down. If your doctor was no good, then get rid of him and get a new one. Like she'd done.

She didn't plan on living in bed 232 forever. Now she needed to work on the next stage of her healing. Everything was progressing, just like she'd planned.

She wiggled her toes. Perfect.

Back upstairs, the evening lights were on, dimming the fluorescent brightness to a mild soft light that was easier on everyone. Maddy let the nurses know where she was going before closing herself in her office. She turned off her phones, lowered the overhead lights and went to put on calming music. Standing in front of her music selection, she was hard pressed to decide between Zamfir and Yanni. Yanni won out. That man's piano skills were second to none.

Then she unbuttoned the top of her blouse, slipped off her jacket and kicked off her heels. Trying to relax, Maddy focused on her breathing and dropped into a deep meditative state. Having done this many times before, the routine was easy and comfortable. She sped through the process and expanded her consciousness out toward her patients. Moving easily, Maddy registered the energy levels on a grand scale. This was all about the big picture: looking for rents and tears in the fabric of the micro-ecosystem she was building. Like a giant pulsing bubble of warm, loving energy that worked to heal everyone on her floor – including the staff. Some of her nurses preferred nightshift because they experienced Maddy's work at its peak. Gerona had once suffered from terrible migraines, but no longer. Nancy used to suffer from ovarian cysts. They disappeared over a year ago.

Moving from the stairwell forward, she shifted the waves of energy, moving and adjusting as required to make a seamless blending of energy for the benefit of everyone there. It was slow work, and by the time Maddy made her way through the patient checks, she found herself tiring. Her forward movement stilled as she regrouped and assessed her progress.

Energy vibrated. How it vibrated said a lot about the type of energy, the health or strength of the energy and its purpose. It vibrated differently in an inanimate object, like the energy in a table, for example, versus the energy zipping around in a child.

It was the child, Felicia, she wanted to focus on.

Maddy planned to focus on the big picture for this trip, yet something about Felicia's aura disturbed her. Red swarmed her chest and lungs, not a pinkish red, but an angry blood red. Maddy frowned, drifting closer.

Felicia slept soundly.

Her body shimmered, active in sleep like that of everyone else. The red sat in the middle of her chest. It was pulsating, with mixed emotions, anger, love, pain – fear. Maddy pulled back slightly to look from a different angle. Yes, the energy was contained in Felicia's chest.

Just then, the bathroom door around the corner from Felicia's bed opened. It was Alexis, Felicia's mother, dressed all in black as if she already mourned the loss of her daughter. Only in her late thirties, her face had a reddish blush and her eyes were swollen. Her shoulders stooped in defeat though she put on a brave smile. Her emotions swarmed over Maddy. Maddy pulled back in an effort to distance herself from the pain, as the other woman's need and sorrow rushed at her.

Maddy struggled to detach from the mother's needy energy long enough to stay and complete her reading – except the woman's emotions were too strong. Maddy took one last look at Felicia. Now red energy filled the short distance between the mother and the daughter.

Disturbed, Maddy snapped back into her body and came out of the meditation. She grabbed her head with both hands as her temples resonated from the pounding energy shift that had created a massive headache. She rocked in place for several minutes until the pain eased. Gasping for breath, Maddy stretched out and groaned.

Alexis was hurting her daughter more than helping her. And she'd be horrified if she knew.

Somehow, Maddy had to help Alexis, before she killed her daughter – with fear and love.

Maddy walked quickly in the direction of Felicia's bed. This issue had to be dealt with now.

Felicia's mother sat in the same position as Maddy had seen her last, tears pouring down her face. Entering the small cheery area, Maddy quietly pulled up another visitor's chair and sat beside the grieving woman.

"Hello, Alexis."

The other woman gasped and spun around. "Oh my, I'm sorry. I never heard you."

Maddy placed one hand on the woman's arm. "You looked to be having a tough time right now. I hated to disturb you."

Alexis gave her a watery smile. "The feelings come and go. On the not so good days, they just live inside and leak all day."

"That's normal. Honor the feelings and honor the situation you're in. Let the tears pour when they need to and take time to do something nice for yourself." Maddy patted the painfully thin woman's hand. "You can't help her if you aren't doing so well yourself."

"I know that." She sniffled her tears back. "Honestly, I do. It's just so hard. She's all I have."

Sadness slipped into Maddy's heart. So much heartache for one person.

Felicia had a real opportunity here. Maddy had a good idea how she could help the child, except it was too early to tell the mother. It would be unethical to even mention a possibility of an improvement at this stage. Besides, the mother had to deal with the energy problems she was creating with her neediness. Loving energy was necessary, but it was destructive when delivered with the mother's negative emotions: anger, fear and sense of betrayal.

In this case, it became suffocating like the red energy Maddy had seen earlier.

Speaking slowly, gently feeling her way, Maddy made a couple suggestions. "One of the things that is the hardest to deal with is the lack of control, the helplessness. That feeling of being powerless to the whims of fate, which in this case seem less than benevolent."

"Isn't that the truth? I wish there was something I could do to help."

The perfect opening Maddy had been hoping for. "There is. It's called spirit talking."

Alexis turned to her, frowning, hope flickering in her eyes. "What's that? Will it help her?"

"It's easy, and it will help both of you. You do it while she's resting. She can be asleep or not; it doesn't matter. What matters is the tone of voice you use. It must be positive. Not teary, not negative – and definitely not needy. What you're going to do is talk to her. You're talking to the Felicia you have always known and loved. You want to tell her how much her presence in your life means to you. Be sure to tell her you love her. Not in a grasping way, like 'don't leave me,' but in a positive way, with gratitude. 'Felicia, you're a wonderful blessing in my life.'"

Maddy studied Alexis's face. "Do you understand what I mean?"

"I think so. Will she hear me?" Alexis wiped her eyes and straightened in her seat.

"Absolutely. That's the joy of this. You're speaking to her spirit, not to her body or mind. It's like the coma patients who know that someone is there loving them, coaxing them back into awareness."

Alexis gazed down at her daughter in a new way. "Oh, I've heard of things like that."

"The biggest things to watch for are your tone of voice and making sure your intentions come from the heart. Don't just say the words – make sure you mean them. Be there in your heart for her." Peering closer, Maddy tried to see if Alexis understood the subtle difference.

Optimism shining in Alexis's eyes told Maddy she got it. "Right. So it's like, don't lie to her. If I'm going to do this, be honest."

"If you can't be honest, don't do it. You'll cause more hurt than healing. I'm sure there is a lot of the loving mother inside of you waiting for a chance to do something useful here. Felicia needs to have a reason to live and to know that she's loved. So give her something to fight for."

Alexis stared down at her daughter, such naked love on her face, Maddy's heart ached for her. To lose a child had to be the hardest loss.

Maddy smiled, adding one more caution. "Remember to think about helping her. Not what you're going to do if her condition worsens or the multitude of other 'what ifs.' This isn't about you – it's about her. Remember that and you'll be fine." Maddy stood, happy with the session. Alexis had a direction and it was one that would benefit everyone.

Alexis got to her feet and threw her arms around Maddy in a quick hug. "You have no idea how you've helped me tonight. I really appreciate it."

Maddy returned the hug and stepped back. "No problem. Now might be a good time to try it out. I'll be down with my other patients. Call if you need me."

"Thank you," Alexis called to her retreating back.

He hadn't meant to listen in. He'd had no choice. Their voices carried in the silence. The echo from the largely unfinished empty room bounced conversations of the closest patients his way, like the conversation with John earlier. Maddy hadn't pulled her punches on that one. However, he had to admit that she'd handled it very well.

Adam Lenning hated the thought of that poor child dying beside him. It was yet another unique factor to Maddy's floor, mixing men and women and children in the same space. He'd had trouble with it when he found out. Now he understood. All the patients gelled into one big family. That understanding put everything in perspective. The strategy was quite smart, really.

Dr. Maddy was an enigma. He'd done her an injustice. Something he'd have to set right before his time came. He didn't know how yet. Maybe in a few weeks he'd work his way up to it. Apologies didn't come easy to him. They never had. It was hard to admit he'd been wrong – and in a big way. The more he saw of her active role here, the more he realized that Dr. Maddy had a gift. He didn't know much about the energy aspect of what she did, and because of his earlier criticism, chances were he wouldn't be included in the conversation for a while. They didn't trust him here. He didn't blame them.

One odd thing, though. As he learned more about her, understood her more and what she was trying to do, his sexual attraction had calmed. The fantasy relationship in his mind had changed to a more realistic goal, one of acceptance and friendship rather than romance.

Adam tucked himself deeper into his blankets. He'd yet to warm up from that lousy night and the obvious frailty of his body didn't help his mood. He knew he was dying. He didn't want to go quietly. He wanted to fight, kick and scream – rail at life's injustices. And he didn't have the energy to even start. His lips curled and damn him, he'd become a maudlin ass. How unforgivable.

"Dr. Lenning? How are you feeling today?"

Shit. Dr. Maddy.

Rolling over, he half-sat so he could see her. "Hello." He attempted a smile, unable to stop himself from drinking in the sight of her.

"The nurse said you didn't appear to be feeling well today."

The damn nurse hadn't said any such thing. Adam knew doctor speak as well as anyone. Better, in fact, because he had practiced it for over forty years. Being on the patient side, listening to it didn't feel very good, either. Still it was easier coming from her.

"I'm fine. A little tired maybe."

He followed Maddy's probing gaze as she checked him over. It was all he could do not to move restlessly under her perusal.

"You're still cold. I understand you didn't eat your breakfast this morning and only picked at your dinner last night."

Adam closed his eyes. Shit, he should be the one talking to the patients. Not her.

"Adam?"

Her soft voice was his undoing. Tears formed in the corners of his eyes. Christ, in a minute he was going to be bawling. Please, not in front of her. Never in front of her.

"I'm just having a tough day," he muttered under his breath. "Nothing to worry about."

"Maybe nothing to worry about but definitely something to talk about. Does your off day have to do with your pain level or your life level?"

His eyes open wider. "Life level? That's a new one for me."

"I use it to mean the stage of life you find yourself in. It wasn't too long ago you were in my shoes, handling a full roster of patients on your own. Now you find yourself on the other side. I can't imagine that being an easy shift to make."

He frowned, not expecting her warm, empathetic understanding. He didn't think he'd be so compassionate if their positions were reversed. "Maybe. I don't know. Can't say I like where I find myself today."

"Understandable. Still, for you, there are some treatment options. I'm sure you know them as well as I do. Plus, you have Dr. Cunningham on your side. That has to count for something."

"Not much. I've hardly seen him."

She laughed, her rich voice adding warmth and sparkle to the room. "He's not here tonight. He spends a lot of time in the hospital, as you know."

Not good. Dr. Maddy worked too hard. "He should be here, and you should be going home. You've been here since early this morning."

She stepped closer, smiling broadly. "And that's not unusual, either."

He smiled. True enough. Then he remembered what he'd planned to ask her. "Was someone in here recently?"

"In where?" She frowned at him. "We have visitors on the floor now, if that's what you mean."

"No. It felt like someone was looking in on me."

"Maybe someone did. They might have been lost or confused as to what bed their loved one was in."

"No. It was weirder than that. I thought I felt something similar a few nights ago. Tonight the sensation was much milder."

"Sensation?" she asked cautiously. He watched as she scanned his little corner of the world. He knew everything was in its place. He'd already checked.

"Before it was like a cold darkness washed over me. I know it sounds fanciful and undoctor-like, but I can't describe it any other way." He gave a helpless shrug. "It was different tonight – warmer, happier. It almost had a peacefulness to it."

She tilted her head, studying him. "Interesting. You felt this yet didn't see anything?"

"Right. Stupid, huh?" At least she didn't laugh.

"Not necessarily. I'll check with the nurses and see if anyone noticed anything out of the ordinary. Who knows, maybe a stranger wandered in here by accident."

He had to be content with that. He wanted to ask more. He had a million questions. There were things going on here, undercurrents he didn't understand, and he wanted to. Sure that revealed a bit of hypocrisy on his part. However, he dared anyone to do things differently if the tables were turned.

He had no proof that Dr. Maddy would be able to help him. He did know that he felt better here on this floor than he had anywhere else. He didn't understand it, and that aspect no longer mattered. He wanted to be included in whatever was going on here.

Now if only he had the courage to ask her for that favor.

Maddy left Adam's bedside, deep in thought. Was it possible he might have noticed her energy work from earlier? It wouldn't have been the first time a patient had felt her working, but she hadn't expected that level of sensitivity from him.

Maddy sighed in disgust at the judgmental thought. She wouldn't be able to help Adam if she didn't get rid of her own dislike for the man. If he shifted, warmed his energy – she glanced back at him – which he might be doing now, then the positive energy would move to encompass him on its own. That, in turn, would help to dissipate the remaining negativity he might be hanging onto.

Frowning, Maddy realized that having an old enemy in her bosom, so to speak, would have a profound effect on him. He might end up as a nice person.

And what about her? How would his presence here affect her? Maddy prided herself on being 'forward thinking' and 'in tune' with her own person. She didn't like to see herself as the one in the wrong. She needed to progress herself – in short, she needed to forgive him.

Yuck. Her stomach squeezed tight. He represented fear to her. Not so long ago, he had put her life's passion, her job, her beliefs and her reputation on the line. He'd raised her deepest, innermost fears, exposed them, forced her to see them. Maddy ran her fingers through her dark hair. She had a lot of work to do in that area of herself and not a whole lot of willingness to go there. Typical. Thankfully, energy work could be done in private.

For the sake of everyone on her floor, she needed to clear her own issues – regardless of how little she liked the idea.

TUESDAY

The next morning, Maddy yawned as she sat down at her office desk, staring at her espresso machine across from her. At this point, caffeine would need to be injected to do any good. She'd hardly slept.

"Dr. Maddy?"

Maddy glanced over to see one of the day nurses standing in her doorway. "What's the matter?"

"It's the new patient. He's unbelievable." Her cheeks bloomed with bright red flags of color.

New patient? "You mean John McNeil?"

"Yes. That guy's a madman."

Crap. Difficult patients were the norm for any hospital, but they couldn't stay that way here. Staff and patients alike either changed their attitude or were shipped downstairs. Not that it had happened before. Everyone was too grateful to be here to cause trouble. No one, including John, would be allowed to disturb the balance here.

"I'll go and speak with him."

Maddy marched toward John's bedside. She passed Felicia's mom, head bent over her daughter's hand, a soft smile on her face, and then by Adam's curled up body. Good, he slept.

Long before she made it to John's area, she heard John's voice, yelling at some hapless person.

"I said I don't want this. Get the hell away from me. Now!"

Maddy rounded the last curtain and stopped to observe the mess. Tina, one of the aides, had stripped his bed, trying to put on fresh sheets. A glance to the side showed the old ones had been soiled. Maddy checked John's energy and saw shame and anger radiating together. He'd had an accident, and because he needed help to fix the problem he was embarrassed. Anger was his weapon to hide his insecurities and the hatred he felt for his circumstances.

Maddy waited in silence for Tina to finish changing the bedding. She grinned at the woman, who rolled her eyes as she walked past, pushing the laundry cart.

John sat in a visitor's chair, oblivious to Maddy's presence. He dropped his head into his hands. Maddy gave him a minute longer. She approached him. "John. Bad night?"

He reared his head to glare at her. "A bad fucking life."

She had to cut through to the real problem. Patients had to come to terms with their situation before they could move forward. Their terminal conditions didn't give them the luxury of time to wallow. Sometimes she had to be hard in this business. "Only that's not quite true, is it? More like 'bad fucking end of life,' don't you think?"

He glared at her. "That's not funny."

"I wasn't trying to be funny. I deal in reality. The reality is you have a body that's in crisis. How that crisis is managed is up to you."

"I have no control over anything – not even my bowels, apparently." His growl held shame and embarrassment.

"Something that is to be expected, given your condition." She studied his face for a moment. "Or did you expect this not to happen after you achieved your transfer to The Haven?"

The pink on his face reddened. He stared down at the arm of his chair and refused to answer.

"If that's what your wish is, then you need to understand that such an improvement might happen, except healing is a process and tends to take time."

"I don't have any time."

"Hence the selection requirements to get on this floor."

He glared at her. "Gerard let me in, so I must have fit them."

"I'll discuss that with him soon. Why don't you take a nap? Rest will have a major impact on things, like making it to the bathroom on time. Let's get you back into bed."

"Sorry." He lumbered the few steps to the bed then clambered in. "I'm taking my temper out on you and I shouldn't be. I'm hoping with a little bit of time, you can help me."

Maddy walked forward and pulled the blankets up over his frail body. "And maybe I can. However, I need time. That means you need to give it to me. Avoid stress. Stop getting upset over the things you can't change and work on seeing something positive in your day. Find something to be grateful for every hour. Preferably every minute." She added the last bit as an afterthought.

"Why don't you ask me to do something easy, like pay off the national debt, or build a commune on the moon? I'm not much of a happy-vibe-type person," he grumped, pulling up his clean sheets.

Maddy laughed with real humor. Honest self-assessment was a great start. "Well, now is a good time to try. Your unhappy-vibe personality put you here, so what about trying something different to get you out of here?"

"Right. I'll let you know how that goes."

The wry look on his face made her laugh. "I'll see your progress, don't you worry. That's not exactly something you can hide."

"It doesn't appear that anything can be hidden from you anyway."

"True enough, so don't waste the energy. Just work on feeling better. Before you know it, you'll start thinking happier, healthier thoughts, and you'll manifest these in action."

"It's all gibberish, if you ask me."

For all his knocking of the process, John's eyes were brighter and he sat straighter.

"And if it works – who cares what you call it?" There was a hell of a lot more to it, but it gave John something concrete to focus on. Miracles did happen. She'd be the last one to shortchange his ability to create one.

He was the only one who could do that.

The morning light shone brightly into Stefan's studio. He picked up the paintbrush and hesitated as he held it above the pallet of colors. He was wading neck-deep in dark, unchartered waters – ones he wasn't sure how to navigate.

He'd done many weird psychic things over the past decade and his talents had always grown, sometimes in ways that had scared the crap out of him. This was no different. Except he needed information on Maddy's floor – and fast. He planned to use a technique like that used on his last painting. It had worked well then.

No time like the present to get started.

He dabbed his paintbrush into the black and started painting the newly renovated room at The Haven. Maddy's problem hadn't started there, but it was anchored there. Now he had to find a connection, something concrete so he could trace this energy to its source. She had emailed him several digital pictures of the room as a starting point.

The emailed pictures stood on the spare easel. He studied the details of the new wing then turned to his canvas.

Within minutes, he'd lost himself in the artistic process.

It took several hours for the image to take form. He switched colors several times as he layered in the details. When he came to adding the flooring around the finished bed, complete with patient, sheets and blankets, he switched to light browns. Placing the brush against the canvas, he tried to paint in the floor. The flooring laid down easily in the rest of the room, but the closer Stefan's brush went to the bed, the harder it was to force the brush to touch the canvas. Sweat filmed over his skin with the effort.

Breathing hard, he stopped to regroup. What the hell was going on? He tried to lift his arm again, but it suddenly felt as if it weighed two hundred pounds. He couldn't move it.

Stefan consciously relaxed his arm. Instantly the heavy sensation alleviated. Laying the brush on his palette, he shook his arm lightly. Next, he lifted his empty hand toward the painting.

That appeared to be fine.

The problem appeared to be in painting the floor around the bed, or rather, the color of the floor around the bed. Stefan quickly snatched up a fine brush and dabbed it in the white paint. He touched up the windowsill and accented the fold of a sheet. Then he moved to below the bed and tried to touch where the flooring should be.

His arm froze. It wouldn't allow his brush to connect with the canvas in that place.

Interesting.

Stefan stepped back and studied the picture. Only one color was going to be allowed there.

Stefan's inner senses strengthened as his 'knowing' kicked in: He was on the right path. He could feel the positive energy pulsing through his own veins. A sense of rightness. The recognition of another energy. An energy that wanted to be recognized.

And that would be this person's failing. Stefan knew the persona of this energy in some ways now. He 'couldn't recognize his signature yet, but he would. He had enough to search for him on the ethers. It might take a bit, but this painting would help.

With grim determination, Stefan picked up the black paint and finished the image, painting the blackness in where the brown hadn't been allowed to go.

This would be his starting point.

***

Gerard tried to write the report explaining why he'd allowed John onto Maddy's floor…without making it sound like he'd sold the bed to the highest bidder. That John was already in place helped, only not enough, as Maddy had reminded him. Gerard still had to justify his actions to the Board.

Shit.

Sandra walked in without warning. "That nice detective is on line one." She sauntered back out. "I told him you'd speak with him."

Picking up the phone, he used his most his professional sales voice. "Drew? What can I do for you?"

"Sorry to bother you, but I'm looking for a diary that went missing in the ER while a patient was being worked on. He and several nurses swear it was there at the time. However, it didn't move with him and his personal effects when he was transferred to a room for the night."

Gerard frowned. Issues like this wouldn't normally make it to his desk, unless a patient threatened to file a lawsuit for loss of personal property. Insurance usually dealt with it. Was Drew asking about it personally or professionally?

"There is a lost and found department. Have you checked with them?"

"Several times. This diary relates to a cold case. I'm sure you can see that I need to follow up all leads to help me retrieve it."

"Hmmm." A cold case, so it was professional. Good luck with that. Time wasn't kind to evidence. "The only thing would be to ask everyone who was on shift that night—"

"Which I've done." Drew sighed, frustration and impatience obvious in his voice. "I don't know if it's stupidity, negligence or a criminal element at play here."

"I can ask the staff myself, see if that helps, but I can't imagine I'll get a different answer than you have."

"No, probably not. If you hear anything about it or if it turns up, please let me know. This is a police matter."

"I'll send out a staff-wide email and explain the importance of locating the diary. Maybe someone thought it was pretty and didn't realize its importance."

"Yes. That might be enough impetus to make someone do the right thing. Thanks."

After Drew hung up, Gerard shook his head. CEO of a major company and he was sending out emails about a missing diary. Who'd have thought? Shrugging at the comedy of his life, he brought up his email and starting writing.

Doris stared out the window. Embittered and diseased was not what she'd hoped for in this stage of her life. She hated her life. She felt out of control, on a train taking her somewhere she didn't want to go. Depression, they called it. She didn't care what name was given to it, it felt weird. Surely something was wrong.

She'd had enough to deal with over the last several decades. She didn't want to deal with anything else in this lifetime. Just the thought of reincarnation and repeating this process scared the crap out of her. Karma, yuck. She'd not been exactly a good girl this time around, and didn't have enough time to fix that, even if she had the inclination to do so.

No, she'd hang on as long as she could before going, kicking and screaming, through the final door. All that other New Age stuff fascinated her – as long as she was allowed to pick and choose what she wanted to believe.

Damn her brother, anyway. She wished her mind would shut up about it. Except the angry thoughts recycled endlessly.

The asshole was gloating. Well, maybe his move to Dr. Maddy's floor would come too late to save him. Damn if Doris wasn't going to have a party when his time came. A big one too, with everything he liked so he couldn't have any of it. And she'd use his damn money. Money that should have been hers. They'd been a family after all...at least some of the time. John had hated her mental instability, almost as much as he hated her constant boyfriends and her lifestyle. She shrugged. Too damn bad.

She groaned as she shifted on her bed. Everything hurt these days and nothing they gave her helped. Trapped inside a rotting body was not an experience for the lighthearted. She hoped her brother was suffering, too.

If he'd shared his wealth, she might have felt differently, particularly in light of their history. But he hadn't and now his actions had a direct negative impact on her life. He'd gotten in and she hadn't. She refused to let that be the end. Her pride wanted her to heal so badly. She wanted to parade in front of him before walking out the front doors of The Haven forever – preferably leaving him behind and suffering mightily.

She hadn't even heard about her transfer request yet. Surely, it had to be complete by now. It had been months. Damn it, she deserved Dr. Maddy's floor, not him.

Maddy wanted to go home. Her working day had once again extended well into the evening. She needed fresh air and a decent night's sleep. After shutting down and locking up her office, she pulled on her jacket and walked toward the stairwell. With a good-bye wave to the other nurses, she said, "I'm off."

The fresh air revived her somewhat. She stopped outside the hospital door and took several bracing gulps, appreciating the fresh air. Sometime during the day, it had rained, giving the air the feeling of renewal. Though she'd been eager to get some rest, walking toward her apartment, she realized she wasn't quite ready to go home and be cooped up inside again. That intimate little coffee bistro around the corner would be perfect. A bite to eat wouldn't hurt, either.

At the bistro, she chose a spot on the outdoor patio where the evening lanterns swayed in the warm breeze. Truly, it was a peaceful setting. The waitress brought her a latte with a beautiful heart design in the cream. With a happy sigh, Maddy settled back and sipped her coffee. Perfect. Too bad she was alone. A particular male would be a great addition to her evening.

"Excuse me, Dr. Maddy." A shadow fell across her table. "May I join you?"

Maddy looked up, startled, as her imagination manifested him beside her. "Detective? I didn't expect to see you here." Her heart bounced with joy.

"Please, call me Drew. And actually, I followed you in," he added with a sheepish grin.

She blinked. Did he have more questions or was there a more personal reason? Flustered, she said inanely, "Oh." Heat climbed her cheeks. "Please, sit down." Maddy's eyes widened as he folded his long frame onto the small bistro chair.

"It's okay. I won't break it." He laughed at her.

Her cheeks burned. "Sorry. It's always a concern, being tall myself. So much of the world appears a little fragile from up here."

"You wear your height well."

The heat on her cheeks deepened. "Thanks," she muttered, unsure what to say next. "So, why did you follow me in?"

Drew grimaced. "I wanted to double check on my uncle's condition after the transfer, I know it really isn't fair to ask, as you're off duty." His coffee arrived. He thanked the waitress. Maddy watched his interactions. Friendly, but not flirty. Nice. From the wattage on the waitress's face, she obviously thought so, too.

When he faced her, curiosity lit up his features. "What's that smile for?"

"I was thinking the waitress likes you."

"Who?" He turned around to see who she was talking about, then shrugged. "Really? I didn't notice."

"I know, that's why the smile. It's kind of nice."

His gaze narrowed and he took another hot sip of the brew. "Nice? Oh." He gulped, shrugging uncomfortably. "Uhm. So, is Uncle John settling in?"

"Yes, he is." Maddy studied the wrought iron table before looking straight into his eyes. "You know he's seriously ill."

Drew leaned forward. "Yes. He won't talk about it."

"No, he wouldn't. I have to admit, I'm troubled by his transfer." At Drew's frown, she explained, "His application shouldn't have been approved. He doesn't fit the strict protocols for the project."

"I wondered about that earlier when you explained the rules for your floor." Drew frowned. "I spoke to Gerard about it. He brushed me off with something like not everyone has to follow the same rules."

She didn't want to hear that. Stirrings of frustrated anger whipped through her. The viability of her research and the well-being of patients on her floor depended on everyone following the same strict entrance requirements. Damn Gerard. Everyone *had* to follow the same rules, or the medical community would dismiss the project. She eyed him curiously. "Do you know anything about how Gerard and John know each other?"

"Only that they've been acquainted for years."

"Well, I'm going to have a talk with Gerard in the morning. As for your uncle, his prognosis isn't good. You'll have to speak with his physician for the details."

"I have. Not that it's done much good. No one seems to be able to pinpoint the root of the problem."

"There's not always an answer or a single cause. Several of your uncle's systems are crashing. Talk to Dr. Cunningham about him if you're concerned about his treatment."

Drew frowned. "I will. Did we put him at risk, moving him at this stage?" He paused and reconsidered. "I guess moving him couldn't do much more damage. He was adamant about getting onto your floor."

This time it was Maddy who winced. "That's because he seems to think I can work miracles. He wants me to heal him or seriously slow down the progression of his condition."

Drew blew out his breath and sat back to study her. "That doesn't sound like him. He's usually pretty grounded."

Maddy studied the caring in his face. That was kind of nice, too.

"We often find that people will grasp at any solution when facing imminent death." Hiding behind her own mug, Maddy studied him. His high cheekbones and squared off chin gave him a Nordic appearance. The dark hair with the slight curl to it added a youthfulness he probably wouldn't appreciate. There was dark stubble on his chin, an indication the detective had a long, hard day.

But then so had she.

They both had difficult jobs where they were in service to others. Another thing she liked about him.

He stretched out his legs, his shoulders relaxing. "You know, I have to say you're easy to be around."

Surprised, she answered lightly, "So are you."

Sipping her latte, she watched the surprised gleam in his eyes and chuckled. "I gather most people don't feel that way, do they?"

He shook his head and grinned. "The exact opposite, actually. Most women say I don't talk enough and that I'm too devoted to my job."

"Now, I've heard that one a time or two." Her candid answer drew a startled laugh from him, bringing out an endearing dimple in his cheek.

He leaned forward to study her face closer. "Do you think two workaholics might find time to go out for dinner together?"

"We do have to eat sometime." She pushed her coffee cup ahead of her on the table. "And if it means eating Chinese, absolutely, although I might consider something else as well. I've got an awful hankering for Almond Gai Ding."

"Tomorrow night? Would that work for you?"
Maddy grinned. "Tomorrow sounds great."

WEDNESDAY

A deep sense of unease woke Stefan from his restless sleep. *Now what?* He groaned and rolled over. What a horrible night. He hadn't slept more than a couple hours.

Lying flat on his back, he stared up at the ceiling, wondering about the dread pulsating through his veins. Something was stirring in the world. Something at The Haven. Again, he recognized it as something *evil.* He hated that term.

So many people gave it a religious connotation. He didn't. He defined the term as those who had no remorse, no conscious, no caring for the numerous people they hurt, tortured and killed. Evil wasn't a force from some horrible underworld. It was the force inside people that allowed them to act in horrible ways. He turned to his latest painting hanging on the wall opposite and talked to it.

"The Haven is the center of it all – why?" The painting and the empty room offered no answer, but it didn't stop him from thinking out loud.

"How can such negativity exist in such a warm, positive environment? The answer: It can't. Maddy's Floor should be a deterrent for this type of energy." Sitting, he pursed his lips. By the very laws of nature, that negativity would have to change and become more positive. Therefore, the negative energy isn't in the bubble – yet – but it's attracted to it, like a moth to a flame. The lovely healing energy Maddy is working hard to maintain for her patients is also a lure for this other energy.

Only how would anyone know unless they practiced energy work? Then they'd know, as the very energy would call to them.

However, The Haven had stringent admission requirements for Maddy's floor. It had to. Anything less would destroy the delicate balance.

Then again, he surmised this energy wasn't on the floor itself – or at least not inside the bubble.

He froze. The colors in the painting shifted ever so slightly.

Something here held a glimmer of truth. What if someone made it onto Maddy's floor, someone who shouldn't have? What difference would that make? Would it shift the delicate balance between health and disease? Good and bad? Would it be enough to open a tear in the energy field? Or would it widen the rent that already existed?

He needed to talk to Maddy.

Throwing back the blankets, he swung his legs over the side and sat up.

And froze.

A vision snaked through his mind. Black curtains dropped before his eyes, taking him out of his reality into the world in-between. Then the curtain ripped back, showing him his new surroundings.

He blinked several times at the cheerfully bright, yet soothing walls staring back at him. The Haven. Blinking again, he found himself on Maddy's floor. The vision showed him nothing unusual. Here, the energy had lightness, and a warmth he recognized as Maddy's signature.

He circled the floor, wondering what the vision was attempting to show him. The new wing sat outside the main bubble. There the energy was slightly less warm, less healing and definitely less energized. He frowned. There were several beds out there, only the people in them weren't included in the same healing bubble as the rest of the floor. The bubble wall between the two areas held strong and pulsated with a joyous blue radiance.

One bed touched the inside of the healing bubble. That would need to be fixed. It was a child. Stefan went there first.

Maddy's heart would break if she weren't able to help the little one. The child's meridian pathways throbbed with power, and although thinner than he'd like to see, there was a determination that reassured him. She might be one of the lucky ones – brought to Maddy just in time.

Studying the energy layers, Stefan found two black spots sitting low on the first chakra. Both blended in together, easy to miss and big enough to cause problems. Maddy needed to start working on them right away.

He turned his attention to the two males in the new wing. Distracted by a sudden movement out of the corner of his eye, he noticed a small black thread under one of the beds. The strand, so black, so shiny, so full of life, its very presence throbbed. *What the hell?*

Stefan tried to move closer and couldn't. The vision froze him in place. The thread snaked out from under the bed, sliding maybe six inches before retreating until it completely disappeared. Stefan knew it sat underneath, waiting.

This is why he had been drawn here.

Just like his paintings, the black wispiness hid under the bed.

The thread slipped out again to wind around the metal leg of the bed.

It stopped. Then in a snake-like motion, it raised its head and appeared to stare in his direction.

Stefan shook his head. No. Not possible. No way could it see him. There's no way anyone had the strength, the skill to actually do that. God, he hoped not.

The snake's head never wavered.

Then it lunged.

Shocked, Stefan reared back and snapped through multiple dimensions, before finally slamming back into his body and his bedroom. The world wavered, distorted, and then finally sucked back into place with a loud pop. The last image he'd seen was the black snake-like thing heading toward the child's bed.

Stunned, Stefan barely moved. He focused on trying to catch a breath. His chest was so constricted he could barely gulp air. Everything in his room appeared the same, except for the goose bumps taking over his skin, and the chills racing down his spine.

Shaking, he reached for his cell phone.

✳✳✳

Maddy's panicked arrival at The Haven was less than stellar. Still shaken from the convoluted information Stefan had delivered over the phone – way too early for her brain to grasp – she took the elevator to the top floor. The place was deserted. It wasn't even six in the morning. Stefan had woken her from a deep sleep with his confusing message, sending her racing back to work.

Something about a black thread that had been as aware of Stefan's out of body journey as Stefan had been aware of it. Somehow, it connected to one of the two new arrivals in the renovated space. She hadn't had a chance to rebuild the energy on the floor to the levels that existed before Jansen's death. Felicia's arrival would have aggravated the balance as well. Extending the bubble to the new area wasn't something she'd complete overnight. At least not alone.

Maybe Stefan would help her widen the boundaries of the protected space, or create a secondary space. She didn't know the right way to move forward.

The current bubble had taken months to establish. The new area needed to vibrate at the same frequency as the older established area before both could be joined into one all-encompassing system. The process needed either more energy workers or more time.

Better yet, both.

The elevator crawled to a stop. She stepped onto her floor and stopped, assessing the energetic atmosphere and balance of the floor. Jansen's death had caused a ripple effect, though most others wouldn't recognize it. And it was to be expected. It wasn't like this was their first death on the floor.

Yet underneath all this energy, was a faint suggestion of something else. She leaned against the wall and closed her eyes. Something was wrong. How else could she describe the odd sensation? Stefan would help her, but only if he knew what they were dealing with. He'd told her to find out as much as possible this morning.

He'd ordered her to move Felicia's bed further into the protected area, and away from the bubble edge, no matter what.

"Dr. Maddy, are you all right?"

She opened her eyes. "I guess. At least I hope so." Walking toward the nurses' station, she delivered a reassuring smile to the two women watching her.

Gerona walked closer. "Bad night?"

Maddy shrugged off her jacket, hooking it over her shoulder. "Bad morning, actually."

"Well, for once, we had a good night. All the patients appear to have recovered their equilibrium and most everyone slept well."

Unlocking her office door, Maddy threw her a big cheery smile. "Now that's a good start to my day. No bad turns in the night? No calls for medics, nothing?"

"Nope. All calm."

"Great." Maddy strode over to the blinds, moved them aside and opened the windows, letting the fresh air filter through the small room. Then she made a quick dash to Felicia's room. Stopping at the entranceway, she saw Felicia, sound asleep on her left. Maddy shifted her vision. Carefully, going from side to side, she searched for any anomaly in the area.

Spinning around, she considered the position of Felicia's bed. It was in the protected healing bubble, only damn close to the edge. Too close. Maddy would take care of that as soon as possible, as Stefan suggested.

Everything seemed clear. Then she stepped into the new wing.

The air had an odd flatness to it. As if something weird had played out on the ethers. There was no discernible odor, not that she'd been expecting one. Still...something was off. She quietly checked on both sleeping patients. Their energy was clear, calm.

Striding back toward the nurses' center, she ordered the shifting of Felicia's bed and said, "I need to head down to security and check out that the new camera feeds are working. Hold my calls for a bit, will you?"

Once at the main office, she stepped into the security room, with its wall of monitors and counter of computers. She wanted to speak with Jean Paul, the man who headed the security department. He preferred the morning shift, but he rarely left on time. Most long-term care facilities had minimal security, but with the hospital attached and Maddy's project, it had been beefed up several years ago.

"Good morning, Dr. Maddy. Figures that you'd be in so early. I suppose you'd like to see how the new cameras are working upstairs, huh?" Jean Paul was small in stature with the charm of ten men. She liked him and his wife for the genuine people they were. That Jean Paul worked hard to keep The Haven secure and running smoothly was an added bonus.

"Yes, please. I presume they're functioning properly?"

"Of course. I always run a check on new equipment." He shrugged. "And as they were, I haven't checked since."

"I'd like to run through last night, if you don't mind."

"Sure enough." He motioned to a monitor on the wall. "I'll set up the digital feed here." He fiddled with a series of knobs and dials, punched in the date she wanted, then stopped and looked at her. "Is there one camera you'd like to see over another?"

"The one in the newly renovated section."

"Good." He made several adjustments before asking, "Any time frame in particular?"

Maddy pondered for a quick second. "If I don't have to watch in real time, then I'd like to go through the entire night." She turned to look at him. "But if it's like eight hours of sitting and watching, then no. I really would like to see around four to five am this morning."

"You can go as fast as you like." He reached forward and pointed out the controls for her. "Here is fast forward. You can slowly move forward or speed up until you reach a specific hour by watching this clock here. Then you can slow it back down or stop it altogether."

"That's perfect, thank you." Maddy pulled up an empty chair, waited until the digital feed started, then she sped it up slightly, watching as nurses went through their normal shifts. Maddy watched herself as she crossed in front of the camera lens on the way to speak with Felicia's mother, then Adam Lenning and John McNeil.

So far, all appeared normal.

She continued to watch, recognizing the hour when she'd gone home and left The Haven in the capable hands of the night shift. Hours passed by in a continuous, rarely disturbed mode. Adam got up and used the bathroom around three. She noticed how stiffly he moved. He made it back to bed without incident.

John shifted restlessly in his bed, for no apparent reason that she could see. He might not have taken a sleeping pill and that might account for his tossing and turning. She'd check when she went back upstairs. The video didn't allow much energy reading. In fact, she wasn't sure she'd be able to see much at all. The wee hours of the morning disappeared in a flash. Maddy thought she might have been wasting her time but then something odd flashed on screen.

She hit the stop button, backed up the feed and then went forward at a snail's pace. The area up by the ceiling showed a snowy fleck that hadn't been there before. She wondered if it represented Stefan's astral body. It wasn't obvious what it was. Most people wouldn't even recognize it was there unless it was pointed out. She'd been looking for it. Freezing the frame, she turned to ask Jean Paul about it, only to find he'd left the room.

She started the feed again. The snowy projection moved slightly, shifting, almost rippling as though floating on a breeze wafting through the room. Then it appeared to stop, freeze in place.

The camera didn't give a close-up of the snowy image or of the end of the bed in its view. There. She rewound the feed and bent close to the monitor. The picture was clear, except she couldn't make another item out.

What was at the foot of the bed? Something black popped up then slid back under. To Jean Paul, it would likely appear as a fault in the film or a dirt smudge, but to Maddy, it was something else entirely. That's what Stefan had seen in his vision.

She sat back. This black thread was under John McNeil's bed.

The snow flecks disappeared from one frame to the next, however, the black smudge stayed, inching out in the direction of Felicia's bed. Maddy stared in horror until it shrank back in itself, as if unable to go out further.

She rewound it once again and stared at the foot of the bed as the feed replayed the same few minutes. Checking the time, she realized this had taken place at 5:14 am this morning. Stefan had called her around half past five. She scanned the rest of the film but there wasn't much more to see. The camera couldn't capture the space under John's bed or the other side of the bed.

John was dying, from unknown causes. And his health was declining faster than expected. Now she just might know why.

Yet, he'd just arrived. So this black energy couldn't have come with him. She'd seen it or something similar hanging over Jansen's bed days ago. Jansen's bed *had* been partially out of the bubble due to the renovations. That's when he'd been attacked. Therefore the energy had been here first, had a connection to Jensen and theoretically, as it went after John, the person doing this knew him as well.

What were the odds of that?

Too much conjecture. It was giving her a headache.

All she knew for sure right now was that the black energy had anchored itself to John. He may have harbored this thread-connection a long time. In fact, it would feel like his energy after all this time. Not that John would have noticed. Few people did. That this energy didn't have a happy, healthy feel to it didn't mean it was evil or bad. Everyone wanted something and this energy was no different.

Now if only she knew what it was and what it wanted.

Sissy sat up slowly, testing her bones and her muscles. She felt like Sissy today, not an invalid. The pain had diminished slightly, but not enough to notice and not enough to count on. She frowned. Surely, her new health program should have had a stronger or at least a longer-acting effect. As much as she was delighted with her obvious progress, it also pissed her off that she wasn't getting to the end of this road faster.

Every time she seemed to make a step forward, she slipped back several steps. She had to change that, and fast. Her patience was running out. Everyone else here was dying. It might be contagious.

She giggled. Her deathbed humor brightened her spirits.

"My, aren't we in a good mood today." The nurse bustled around, wrapped the blood pressure cuff on Sissy's arm and checked her temperature at the same time. Those tasks done, the nurse patted her arm and walked to the next bed.

Twenty minutes later, breakfast was served.

Sissy played with the food. Only ate because she needed the energy. She hadn't even finished before an aide, an older woman who looked like she should have retired years ago, showed up and began laying out clothes and makeup.

She sat and complied through the woman's hurried ministrations. Sissy wondered how the aides managed to keep up this pace all day. The staff was overworked and underpaid, the cliché of today's lifestyle. Everyone raced as if the world would end before nightfall. She didn't understand it.

Still, she was in a race too – a race against death.

***

Maddy strode toward Gerard's office, her long gray tunic swishing from side to side. Endless questions streamed through her mind. The security tapes had added more of them. She had to do something. Her mind was ready to explode. Gerard was the target she'd chosen to vent some of her frustration. John was an issue – and he shouldn't be.

"He's on the phone, Dr. Maddy," Sandra said to her as she stormed to Gerard's door. "I don't think he wants to be disturbed."

She came to a dead stop and spun on her heels. Narrowing her gaze, she stared at Sandra. "Any idea how long he's going to be?"

"Not too long. He's arguing with someone again."

Maddy wrinkled her nose. Great, if he were already arguing, he'd be primed for a fight. She thought about that for a brief moment, only to realize she relished the idea. She'd been brooding over this since reading John's charts. Someone had bent the rules to get him onto her floor and in so doing, had jeopardized the project's integrity.

She smiled, showing her teeth. "No problem. I'll wait."

"Ohh. You want a piece of him too, huh? He's not having a good day." She perked up as a light on her phone console went out. "He's off. You can go in."

"Thanks." Maddy opened the door.

"I'm busy."

Maddy ignored his blustery yell.

"Too bad. I think you can find the time to see me." Maddy strode across the spacious office and took a seat in the chair facing Gerard's desk. She glared at him. "I've left several messages, so you should have expected me."

Gerard took one look at her and groaned. "Now what?"

"What kind of blackmail did John pull to make it onto my floor?" At the word blackmail, all the color disappeared from Gerard's face, making his pallor an almost perfect match to his white dress shirt. Maddy raised an eyebrow in surprise. Her off-the-cuff words had an effect that she hadn't expected. Interesting. As much as she'd said underhanded methods had been used, she hadn't really given serious thought to specifics.

"Sorry. What?" Gerard's gaze touched her face briefly before dropping down to his desk.

"I'm asking how and why John McNeil made it onto my floor?"

He glared at her, bravado written all over his face. "Maddy, you don't have ultimate control over who comes and who goes through The Haven."

She stared at him...hard. He dropped his gaze again, his fingers turning a pen over and over.

"What did you just say?" she asked softly, not sure what he was implying. The process was in place for many reasons. To say she didn't have ultimate control was true. Yet, if she didn't have the power to say who she could help and who she couldn't, why was she doing this project at all?

"Now, Maddy. Don't get upset. I didn't mean to imply that your vote isn't important. But sometimes there are extenuating circumstances..."

"Really." She crossed her legs and stared at him in disbelief. "That would make sense if we're talking about The Haven as a whole, but not for my floor. There were requirements for me starting this project, if you care to remember." Her voice rose as her anger flared. "John is more than welcome on any other floor.

However, he does not fit on mine. He doesn't fit the health criteria in any way, and I'd like to know exactly why you decided to let him in."

His chin jutted out, his eyes narrowing in defiance "And I'm not going to tell you. I have to run this place based on many different factors, not just your criteria."

"Is that so?" Maddy stood up. "I guess we'll see about that. The success of this project, the extra money pouring into The Haven, is based on the results that I can produce. There are many reasons for the exacting criteria to get into the third-floor project, as you well know. I set the standards to make the program not only a success, but so it can be sustainable. And if you're not going to honor that..." She let the threat hang in the air.

Gerard bolted upright, alarm spreading across his face. He held his hands out as if he could stop her by that very motion. "Whoa, there's no need to become hostile here, Maddy. You don't want to do anything that might affect the long-term success of The Haven."

"Like you did? You've put my entire project – a project that paid for this new wing expansion, entirely by donations of these generous people, I might add – at risk. Do you know how many offers I've had to leave here and set up elsewhere? The inducements?" She gave him a hard look. "I refused the last one because I care about what I've built here. I care about my patients here. I care about what I can do here. However, if you are going to sell beds to the highest bidders and completely ignore what I can sustain – thereby destroying everything we've created – I'll go somewhere else where I can help patients without interference."

Gerard tugged at his shirt collar before finally loosening his tie and unbuttoning the top button of his shirt. "Dr. Chandler, by any chance?"

Watching Gerard sweat made her feel much better. About time. After what he'd done, he needed a reality check. "Dr. Chandler is very persuasive. I don't want to have to start all over again, but if you keep undermining my system, I will. If my energy is spread too thin to help my patients, the program is ruined."

Gerard gulped, then leaned forward earnestly. "Then leave John out of the project. Think of him as an isolated incident. He's on the same floor, only not on *your* floor," he wheedled. "And I'm sorry. It won't happen again."

She didn't believe it. How typical. Threaten the money and he crumbled. "It's not that easy. I can't exclude him. Energy is malleable to a certain extent so he'll benefit from being close."

"There's nothing wrong with it benefiting him, is there? The man's dying. If he gets a few extra weeks by being there, surely that's a good thing."

"A few extra weeks – the man's death will still be around the corner. Putting him into the program skews the result because he doesn't fit the criteria. Not to mention the effect his death will have on the other patients. You know that." She was frustrated and wanted him to know. "You did this on purpose, and I want to know why."

Goaded, Gerard snapped. "I didn't have any choice." He glared at her. "Our budgetary requirements are unbelievable right now. John offered to pay – and in a big way, I might add – for some necessary equipment. My hands were tied and we needed his money to help other patients. Okay?"

Maddy shifted back down into her chair. Gerard's face had blown into a cherry red color and the lines of his face had deepened with anger. She'd been right. John had bought his way in, an easy trick to play on the moneyman.

Maddy wasn't sure how she felt about everything now. That he'd sacrifice her trials was unacceptable. To lose necessary equipment due to a lack of funding? That didn't make sense either.

She stared at Gerard, who shifted like a truant child waiting for his punishment. What were the options? Could she keep John out of the project? He was in the renovated area with Adam

Lenning. For the moment, that *was* outside the research floor's boundary.

And Felicia had been included in the trial. That was a good thing, as she had the potential for remarkable improvement – in fact, she'd shown wonderful stabilization, as of this morning. Maddy had high hopes she's make a complete recovery.

Mentally, Maddy sorted the possibilities before she gave in. She didn't know what would be more debilitating to the other patients, to have John removed right now or to have him die within weeks of arriving. They wouldn't have much contact with each other. He wasn't in the same area, and not mobile enough to make use of the common areas.

Patients who died after being there for a while had a much bigger impact on the others. They might just think John's illness had advanced too far when he arrived. Hell, that's exactly what she'd thought herself.

Now she wasn't so sure. The black energy hanging around him could be interfering with his health and recovery.

What the hell, she might as well include him in the energy. Besides, it would take a meaner doctor than she was to kick him out. Especially as she'd seen the possibility of a way to help him.

However, she also owed the people that had put their trust in her. She couldn't let the investors or her patients down. Her project was valuable and to lose the investors was to sideline the project. And that would slow the number of people she could help.

Maddy gave in and stood up. "I'll see what I can do. Don't do it again. This isn't what our investors want and I won't turn a blind eye again. I can understand the temptation to let patients buy their way in, but no more. They can damn well buy their way onto another floor."

She glared at him, not liking the gleam of hope in his eyes. If she let him get away with this, there'd be no end to his meddling in her affairs. "Do you understand? Don't get smug. That offer I refused won't go away for a long time."

Gerard bounded to his feet, relief washing over his face. He walked around the desk, his arm outstretched. "I promise, this one time only. Thank you." He clasped her hand with both of his, shaking it with fervent enthusiasm. "Thanks, Maddy. I really appreciate this."

"I mean what I said," she snapped, afraid he hadn't understood the severity of his actions. "No more going behind my back."

He grinned, the perfect salesman persona back in place. "I know, I know. I promise."

Pulling her hand free, she jabbed her finger at him, wanting him to understand how wrong he'd been and the severity of his actions. "And see that you don't forget it."

Maddy walked back out. Sandra smiled at her. "I see you know how to handle him, too."

"We'll see if my 'handling,' as you call it, is successful." She motioned to the closed door behind her. "He's definitely a wild card."

"Only if you give him rein. Hold tight and he's not bad. Give him too much rope and that boy will get into trouble every time..." Sandra's tone was light and airy, but with serious undercurrents.

Maddy's mood plummeted. Damn Gerard and his conniving ways. That he should put her project at risk for a bit of money was untenable. It had been unbelievably difficult to get this off the ground in the first place. To jeopardize it now... She tried to shrug off her mood.

Balance, peace and everything nice are what she needed as her focus. It was impossible to keep any type of healing energy flowing if there were a disturbance in her own mind – especially as she needed to do energy work right now.

Back in her office, she switched off her lights, switched on her music and took up a comfortable position on the floor.

Her mantra. Peace. Happiness. Joy.

Surprisingly, it only took a few minutes to go into a meditative state, where she consciously dropped the accumulated tension from her spine, unspoken words from her mind and the less-than-ideal emotions from her heart. She slowly deepened her state. Drifting down lower, she went even deeper until she slid out from this reality. Focusing on the people in her care, Maddy detached from her physical reality and moved out in her astral form. This was a common form of travel, usually done by people during their dream state. While in this state, and though generally involuntary, people often visited people and places they loved…and hated.

To do this consciously wasn't something one learned overnight.

For the first few seconds, she stretched, enjoying the sense of freedom. This reality left every opportunity open, the imagination unbelievable in its scope, the possibilities limitless. She knew from experience that she'd lose hours here, wallowing in this other existence. She also knew she wouldn't be able to stay here alone in her office without being disturbed for too long.

It was time to get to work.

***

John didn't feel too good. No. It was more like he didn't expect to ever feel good again. He'd achieved something he'd plotted, agonized over and had been striving for since he'd first fallen ill. For what? He'd bought his way in and had managed to piss off Dr. Maddy. Worse, she might not be able to help him. After all he'd done, defeat left a bitter taste in his mouth.

A specter of death hung over him. Sure, he might not die today or tomorrow, yet within a few months he'd be gone. His stomach almost heaved at the thought.

Darkness seemed to cover his world and his soul. He snorted, the sound so light as to be irrelevant if anyone else heard. That's how he felt these days, insignificant and unimportant, as if he had nothing left to offer.

A hot tear welled at the corner of his eye. John rolled his face into the pillow. He hated feeling so weak and helpless. He wasn't a goddamn wuss. He wasn't. And he wouldn't be. He refused.

Good, John. Don't give in. Don't give up.

John bolted upright, wincing at the pain as he did so. "Who's there? Who said that?"

His corner of the floor was empty except for that other doctor working on Adam over by the far wall. John sank back down. "Great, now I'm hearing things."

A light, tingling laughter filled the air. John's eyes narrowed. "Dr. Maddy?"

No answer.

Neither did she materialize around the corner. John searched around again. He didn't know what the hell was happening. The air warmed and lightened around him. A soothing heat slipped into his toes and worked its way slowly, inch by worn-out inch, up his legs. His knees throbbed when the heat reached them, making them feel good. Stronger. Something they hadn't felt like in years. He lay there, enjoying the healing power or whatever was going on. This had to be the secret of Dr. Maddy's floor.

Whatever it was, it felt real. It felt good.

The warmth reached his spine. He moaned in relief as the constant chaffing and brittleness in his bones eased. He didn't know what was happening, why or by whom but he was so damn grateful he didn't care. Prone and at peace, John lay in awe. So great was his joy, tears of wonder streamed down his cheeks. His poor body thrummed with healing effervescence.

As the heat slipped higher and higher, his heart calmed, his blood pulsed stronger, yet with serenity. The healing energy shifted, finally encompassing his face and head. His eyes closed. He rejoiced in the warmth bathing them from the inside. As the heat hit the top of his head, it seeped ever upward, as if squeezing through the very pores at the top of his head. He wanted the sensation to stay, the heat to turn around and slide down again, yet somehow he knew it wouldn't.

I will come again.

Tears streaked down the side of his face, only instead of feeling sad, John felt only grace and thankfulness.

Remember, find joy and acceptance in life and appreciate all that you have.

"Thank you," he whispered softly, afraid to dispel the magic of the moment.

Soft beautiful laughter tickled the air.

He felt a deep connection with the voice. Nothing lustful or lover-like. Instead, it was spiritual – something he never would have expected. He hadn't given the New Age crap any airtime in his world, and now all he could do was lie in his bed in amazement, wondering at the most beautiful experience of his life. He floated on that wave of wellness, until a sigh climbed his spine and escaped, taking with it years of toxic emotions, stress and negativity. He sank deeper and deeper into the feeling.

His last thought before succumbing to sleep was of Dr. Maddy.

What a class act.

WEDNESDAY EVENING

A hard knock sounded on the office door.

"Dr. Maddy? Are you in there? It's been over an hour."

Silence.

"Dr. Maddy?" The knock became a pounding. The doorknob twisted uselessly. The door was locked. "Maddy!" This time, the door rattled as the person on the other side tried to get in.

Maddy heard the noise, she understood the concern, but she hadn't returned to a functional enough state to answer Nancy.

"I'm here," she croaked out in a whisper, barely audible over the music still streaming throughout her room in soft muted tunes. She uncurled slowly from the yoga position she'd been twisted into for the last hour or so. Blood rushed through the veins in her legs and up her spine. She stretched, waited another quick moment, and tried her voice again.

"Nancy, I'm back. Everything's fine."

"Jesus, Maddy, don't do that to me. You promised you'd never lock this door again." She heard the sound of a heavy sigh, followed by a thunk as if Nancy dropped her forehead against the door. Or maybe it was her fist.

Maddy finished stretching and opened her eyes. After drawing a deep breath, she walked to the door and unlocked it.

As she opened the door, Nancy slumped against the doorjamb, staring at her grimly. "Jesus, you scared the crap out of me."

Smiling, Maddy tried to reassure her. "Sorry. This ended up being a pretty intense session."

Nancy huffed. "That's it. If you won't keep this room unlocked during your sessions, then I want a set of keys."

That was probably a good idea. Maddy's smile slipped. "I'll get you a set. I'm still feeling the effects of this session."

"Coffee. Your blood has peace, quiet and oxygen flowing through. It can't comprehend the lack of caffeine." Nancy eyed the counter area with its coffee maker. "I'll make you a fresh pot."

"You only want a cup for yourself." Maddy let Nancy propel her out to the small balcony. She took several deep breaths, feeling her blood pulse with life as it always did after a strong healing session. Basking in the sun, she waited another long moment to allow her awareness to fully return. When Nancy brought the coffee, she took a seat beside her in the shade to enjoy it.

"What happened this time that you went so deep?"

Maddy closed her eyes for a moment, letting the residual power flow through her body. "Nothing odd, just incredibly powerful. I haven't had a session like that for a while."

"Who were you working on this time?"

Opening her eyes, Maddy glanced at Nancy. "Several people. Felicia and John, the new patients, then some maintenance and tweaks on most of the others. I didn't make it through half of the patients though. I'll do another session this afternoon or tomorrow morning and see if I can touch the rest."

"Don't overdo it. You know how much this takes from you. Too bad management doesn't understand that."

"Hah, you wish." Maddy refused to rise to the bait. The two of them had been close friends for years. They often shared dinner, had coffee or rode bikes together on days off. Nancy was permanently watching her weight and Maddy was always eating – and getting skinnier – a contrast that drove Nancy nuts.

During the years of their friendship, Nancy had married and divorced and Maddy had gone through a couple of boyfriends. Through it all, they'd shared most things, especially their laughter and their tears.

"That's because they don't understand what goes on here." Maddy explained about the idea of blackmail. "John's arrival being the end result."

Nancy screwed up her face in exasperation, the words bursting out. "Unbelievable. If you don't get the results, then the donations dry up and not even the brass will have jobs. Yet, they let in the wrong people." Nancy sipped her coffee. "Good for John, I suppose, *if* you can help him. However, this shouldn't become healthcare available only to the rich and generous."

The coffee had cooled enough to drink. Maddy thought for a moment before answering. She took a long sip, reveling in the dark roasted flavor. "Gerard means well. But he likes the shine of gold." She refused to let the reminder of how John had arrived mar the peace and contentment coursing through her. "Anything going on while I was busy?"

"No, all's well." Nancy looked at Maddy over her cup. "That cute detective popped in, asking about you."

Startled, she almost spilled her coffee. "Drew?"

Nancy turned her full attention to Maddy's face. "Drew, is it? Interesting."

Heat rose on Maddy's cheeks. She hadn't meant to say Drew's name in quite that tone of voice. "We had coffee last night." And they were heading out for dinner tonight, only she didn't want to share that tidbit yet. "Did he leave a message?" she asked casually, shifting her legs. Perhaps a little too casually. She hoped Nancy wouldn't notice.

"Are you expecting one? Is there something going on here?" Nancy's grin widened. Her knowing gaze gave her a mischievous look.

Maddy didn't want to share her plans. She held the dinner date private, close to her heart. She couldn't imagine the relationship going anywhere, but there was nothing like the bloom of attraction in its initial stages.

"What was that look for?"

Maddy turned wide eyes to Nancy. "What?"

Nancy shifted so she could stare into Maddy's eyes. "Oh, wow." Nancy positively bounced. "You're really fascinated by the detective, aren't you?"

Maddy tried to appear interested in the garden. The sunlight danced on the bright white roses until they dominated the garden below. An unusual effect. She glanced at her friend. "I might be a little attracted. I mean, the guy's taller than me. You know how I feel about that."

"Yeah. For you, they're hot. For me, they're impossibly tall." Nancy stared down at her stubby legs. "You two can't get together. Your babies would be giraffes."

"Hah. Better than you and him. You'd have to use a stepladder to kiss him."

"Nah, I'd knock his knees out from under him. He's a good-looking hunk."

"Go find your own. He's mine."

"I knew it."

"Shit," Maddy groaned, caught by her own quick mouth. "Fine, okay. I'm interested." Maddy sipped her coffee, barely holding back her smirk.

"Yup, I thought so. So where are you going for dinner and are you taking him home afterwards?"

"Chinese. And I don't know." Maddy rolled her head back to study the sky. "Crap. Me and my big mouth."

Nancy howled. "You never were any good at keeping anything back."

Just then, the emergency alarms crashed through their peaceful idyll.

Cardiac arrest.

Both women raced down the hallway.

The nurses shouted out the bed number as they raced past. Number 364. Maddy's mind raced. Bed 364 was Adam Lenning. The code team converged ahead of Maddy, with two of her nurses already doing two-person CPR. Even as she joined them, the crash board went under him as the team efficiently went into action. Once monitors and IV were hooked up, Adam was bagged, and the first of the drugs administered. Maddy coordinated the resuscitation efforts, grateful that Gerard had followed through on her demands a couple years ago to updating the nurses' training – particularly on the AED units. For several frantic moments, they all worked on Adam.

Everyone watched for a heart rate. The irregular pulse was sweet. Now with any luck, they'd shock it into a regular beat. The defibrillator nurse stepped up. One shock. Nothing.

"Again."

A strong rhythmic pattern moved across the monitor. A sigh of relief swept the group.

"Okay, he's back." Maddy stepped back, surveying the organized chaos that always accompanied a code blue. Her document nurse was furiously writing everything up. She would need to contact Adam's family and let them know that he would be transferred to the hospital side for further tests. A warmed blanket was placed over his chilled flesh.

"I wonder what brought that on." Nancy stepped back over to Maddy's side. "How was he this morning?"

"He's one of the ones I didn't get to." And damned if she didn't feel guilty about that. There's no guarantee that she might have been able to hold off this attack even if she had reached him earlier. But that didn't stop her from her wondering.

"He doesn't have any history of heart problems."

Maddy looked up from the chart in her hand. "He does now." Glancing back, she examined Adam's energy level thoroughly. The orderlies had arrived and the cardiologist, who would order a battery of tests, had been notified. Adam was stabilized – for now.

Maddy wanted to know what had brought on the attack, and whether that black energy had anything to do with it.

It wasn't unusual for energy to build up to a critical point where the balance tipped in favor of mass development. There'd been no indication Maddy's floor had reached that point. In fact, with the renovations disturbing everyone, the energy humming throughout the floor had actually thinned. But was it thin enough to allow someone through? She'd kept the energy wall thick and strong so the healing energy could resonate, but the expansion of the new wing had changed that and the new patients had also affected it. Heart attacks were an all too possible result. She'd have to do a session on Dr. Lenning tonight or tomorrow. Who knew what she might find.

Her energy work was going deeper now, faster, and even more smoothly. She'd been surprised at the sheer enjoyment John had felt during his session. Often, patients had no awareness while she was working on them – especially new ones. His awareness had increased her enjoyment, which had thereby increased the power of the session. It had been a pleasure this morning.

Another oddity slipped back into her mind.

What she hadn't felt was evidence of any debilitating disease racing throughout his body. She frowned. Every person reacted differently to illnesses and in John's case, there'd certainly been a lot going on. She'd expected that, except his pain level had hit her hard and she'd gone straight into healing mode to help him feel better instead of analyzing the problems – like she had with Felicia. But she needed to find out what his health issues were, or she'd never be able to sort out the best ways to help him. She had to go back in as soon as possible. And she needed to check for that black thread.

The news filtered downstairs. Gerard was speaking with the nutritionist when one of the staff approached them with the news. Adam had worked at The Haven for years. Staff and patients knew him, although not everyone liked him.

Shock socked him in the gut. *Shit.*

"He's pulled through, apparently. Dr. Maddy was on the spot."

"Good. He's a good man."

The nurse stared at him, one eyebrow raised. "I'm not one to speak ill of the dead and in his case, the almost dead; however, Dr. Lenning...a good man? That is debatable. He's damn lucky Dr. Maddy tried as hard as she did to revive him. Many in her position, with their history, wouldn't have."

And that's how the gossip would go. There'd be the critics that wondered why she'd brought him back after he'd been such a thorn in her side. Then there'd be others who knew that Maddy would do nothing but her best. And her best was pretty damn spectacular.

"Unless there's a no revive order, you know we have to try."

"And she did and it worked. I wonder how happy Adam will be when he wakes up."

Gerard listened quietly as various staff members discussed Adam Lenning's medical condition. Adam wasn't an easy person to begin with.

He excused himself from the now-raging discussion on life and death issues. In a place like The Haven, there was never an end to these discussions. They stormed one way, then the next, as fickle as the wind and the individuals that came and went.

Two hours later, he found Dr. Maddy at Adam's bedside. He appeared to be sleeping comfortably.

"Is he going to be okay?"

She nodded. "The cardiologist is running tests."

Just then, Adam's eyes opened, unfocused and with widened pupils. He stilled, and then searched for something that obviously disturbed him.

Maddy approached him, her hand on his shoulder. "Take it easy, Dr. Lenning. You've had a heart attack. Please stay calm."

His eyes locked on hers. "Where is it?" His voice trembled with the effort to speak. "I don't want it to get me."

Gerard exchanged glances with Maddy.

"What's after you, Adam?" Gerard stepped to the other side of the bed. "Did you see it? Can you describe it to me?"

"Yes." His voice dropped to a mere whisper. "It was a snake."

Dread filtered through Maddy. A snake. The black energy or a hallucination? Some drugs might cause hallucinations as side effect. She didn't see anything listed here that would do that. There'd been no change in his medication. Her frown deepened.

"When did you see the snake?"

Gerard frowned at her. "We don't have snakes loose in The Haven."

Maddy ignored him. "Adam, talk to me. Where and when did you see this snake?"

Calming down, as if realizing the snake must have been long gone or was no threat when they were there, Adam's eyes became less wild looking and more focused. He took a deep breath. "Gerard said it, didn't he? There are no snakes here."

"Still, I'd like to know what you saw." Maddy kept her voice gentle but firm.

He took another deep breath. "I thought I saw a black snake twisting around the end of my bed. It was thin and had no discernible markings. All I can say is I *seriously* thought it was there."

Gerard frowned, yet stayed quiet at Maddy's warning hand signal.

"How did the snake make you feel?" She ignored the questioning glance he sent her way. The answer was more important than either of them knew.

Adam's response was instantaneous. "Cold. Icy. Empty. As if it were the end. That snake represented death, I know it. I just never expected the grim reaper to be so small."

***

Maddy raced inside her front door, locked it behind her and started tugging her clothes off as fast as she could. Turning on her shower, she slipped off her underclothes and stepped into the hot spray. Her shoulders dropped three inches as the water washed away the tension and pressure she'd felt as she tried to get out of the office. She wanted to melt under this heat for hours.

Except she had less than an hour, probably half that now, before Drew arrived. She shut off the water and toweled dry. Clutching the towel to her chest, she scanned the walk-in closet for the perfect outfit.

Five minutes later, she stood on one foot, chewing her bottom lip, no further along in her decision process. In a fit of frustration, she snatched up black skin-tight slacks with a tiny path of butterflies flying up the outside of one leg. Dropping her towel, she slid into red lace bottoms and matching bra that had butterflies racing across the swell of her breast. Pulling on the pants, she topped it with a long red-hot sweater that hung to mid-thigh. After adding a black belt around her waist and black and red earrings for accessories, she stepped to the mirror to check her reflection. Yes, she was ready for anything – but her sopping hair wasn't.

Checking her watch, she grabbed the blow dryer and attacked her hair. With only minutes to spare, she slid her feet into four-inch red heels with tiny straps at the toes. She stood straight up and grinned. Now she felt more like herself.

The doorbell rang.

Opening the door, she watched Drew's face as he took in her outfit.

"Wow." He stopped in his tracks, blatant male appreciation obvious in his gaze.

Tingles rippled up and down her spine. Excited, nervous, she found herself attacked by shyness. To help cover up, she asked, "Is this appropriate? I didn't want to dress up too much."

He was wearing a suit. She didn't know whether it was an evening suit or he'd just come from work.

"You look great. Are you ready?"

She nodded. "Let me grab my purse." Leaving the door open, she walked into the living room where she'd tossed it in her mad dash to the shower earlier. "Okay, I'm ready."

She turned to find Drew wandering the room, stopping to look at the artifacts of her life. He studied a huge, complex oil painting on her wall, then stepped back a couple of feet and frowned. His head tilted.

Maddy suppressed a smirk. "Like it?"

He took another step back and shook his head. Finally, he turned to her, his brow furrowed. "What is it?"

Motioning with her hand, she said, "Step over here."

Drew frowned. "The view's different from there?" Backing up toward her, he studied the painting again. Maddy studied him. Would he see the different faces when viewed from this side?

It took about ten seconds. Then lightning struck. He glanced at her, wonder in his eye. "What the hell? Is this for real?" Puzzled delight lit his features as he walked around her living room, keeping an eye on the picture. "Who created this?"

"Stefan Kronos."

"Never heard of him." He walked to the other side, his gaze never leaving the painting. Stunned comprehension washed over his face.

"Most people haven't." Maddy smiled in delight at his reaction. She loved how Stefan, using copious amounts of paint in a three-dimensional way, had made different faces shine through, depending on where you stood to view the painting.

"That is the most striking piece of art I've ever seen."

"Stefan's a dear friend. I thought that perhaps you had heard of him because he's quite famous in the law enforcement world. As a psychic."

"As a *what*?" He slid her a sideways glance. "Did you say psychic?" He glanced back at the painting. "I don't know how good his psychic skills are, but he's one hell of a painter."

"I think his psychic skills are second to none. He works with law enforcement agencies across the country." She walked toward the front door. "Are we ready to go?"

"What?" Drew had turned back to the painting. "Yes, yes. Let's head out."

He led the way to his truck parked out front. "We're heading to a new classy Asian restaurant downtown." Turning on the engine, he pulled the truck out into the traffic. The evening light was bright with an almost-full moon riding high. Recognizing a capable driver, Maddy crossed her legs at the ankles and relaxed back into the seat.

She was game. All Chinese was good to her. "Have you been to this restaurant before?"

"Not for a few months." He glanced at her in the dim interior. "You did want Chinese food?"

"Thank you. I'm looking forward to it."

"There's fresh seafood on the buffet."

"Oh yummm." Maddy rested her head back and closed her eyes. She so needed this tonight, just to have a break from all the problems – to not have to think about anything for a while. Then Nancy's question about taking Drew home with her tonight flitted into her mind.

She shouldn't. Short-term affairs weren't her thing. They didn't know each other very well either...

None of that really mattered. She wanted him. The single question floating through her mind – what did she want him as – a friend or a lover?

"Tough day?"

"Hmmm."

"Not to worry. Tonight you'll forget all about it."

At the smug tone of voice, she rolled her head toward him. "Yeah? How's that?"

"We're going dancing afterwards."

Maddy sat up. "Really?"

At his grin, her stomach started to bounce. She didn't remember the last time she'd really let loose on the dance floor. Her toes wiggled. They were so going to get a work out tonight.

John rolled over for the umpteenth time. Another bad evening. What the hell was wrong now? Today, he'd had one of the best days in a long time, and if he could get some sleep for once, he might actually heal.

He pulled up the blankets, shivering in the night. The lights never went out here. There were night-lights along the hallways, and street lights giving a glow outside. Tonight, the moon aggravated the problem. He should ask for a sleeping pill.

"Or not," he muttered to himself.

Why did the sound of his voice not give him the same comforting feeling it usually did?

He hunkered deeper and sighed. He couldn't sleep. He was too freakin' scared.

Scared of dying. Afraid of death itself. Terrified of what came after – if anything.

Not that acknowledging his feelings would change them. Death was waiting for him.

One of the lights in the hallway flickered, throwing eerie shadows on the walls in his room, crawling on the ceiling, dancing through the emptiness. His back stiffened. His breathing rasped unevenly.

This was stupid. He was a grown man – a cop, for God's sake. Too old and experienced in the ways of the world to let flickering lights scare him. Yet, nothing would stop the pit in his stomach from sinking. Something was out there.

John stared in the direction of the light, nervous, his stomach clenching. Closing his eyes, he gasped for breath, desperate to control his anxiety level before it controlled him. A second light flickered. He whimpered as the darkness encroached, coming ever closer to his bed. He squeezed his eyes tightly closed. His heart pounded against his chest, screaming warnings at him. Please, not tonight. He didn't want to die tonight.

The blackness approached.

THURSDAY EARLY MORNING

Maddy ate her way through the phenomenal buffet, then danced the night away at The Pandosy. Drew moved with the best of them, and she loved the chance to toss her stress away. They danced and laughed their way into the wee hours of the morning.

They closed the club and Maddy still felt like rocking. However, by the time Drew pulled up outside her condo complex, her adrenaline had seeped out through her toes. Her feet were killing her and although her heart sang with happiness, her body's song slid toward slumber.

"I had a phenomenal night. Thank you so much for the dancing. I had forgotten what fun it was." She'd danced his socks off.

Drew switched off the ignition, leaning his head back against the headrest. "Come on, I'll walk you to the front door.

Maddy smiled and unlocked her door. "Not required." She motioned toward her building. "It's right there. You can watch me walk the twenty feet. You're tired, too. Go home to bed. I'll be fine."

She watched the argument rise on his face, but he bit his lip and stayed quiet. *Good on him.* He was a protector and that was nice.

His long fingers grasped her chin. "Thank you for spending the evening," he said, glancing at the clock on the dashboard, "or maybe I should say – the night – with me." He grinned.

She smirked back at him. "You wish."

"I do," he whispered. "Are you sure?"

She leaned across and gave him a kiss on the cheek. At the last moment, Drew turned his head and her lips stroked across his. He held the kiss a brief moment, letting her taste him, get a feel for him. His lips teased yet didn't force, tantalized yet didn't take over.

She knew she had to leave before he tempted her more. And he did tempt her. The man was dynamite, on and off the dance floor. "I'm sure." She smiled wickedly. "Then again, I'm not against a second date tomorrow?"

A light fired in his eyes. "Tomorrow," he promised. "One kiss to hold me until then." A tiny smile crinkled the corner of his eyes and he lowered his head again. This was no gentle good-bye. No longer was he enticing or teasing. A small part of her brain dimly wondered if he was giving her a taste of what she'd be missing. Then her brain shut down.

He took her mouth in a possessive full-on promise, ravaging her lips with his heat. Their tongues danced and plunged, tasted then retreated. He gently stroked her swollen lips, his tongue soothing but promising more heat to come…and then he left Maddy gasping.

The man was magic.

Trembling, she barely managed to open her eyes to stare at him in wonder when he set her away from him. A tic pulsed at the side of his stern mouth. Deep blue velvet pulsed deep in his gaze. Good, she wasn't the only one affected.

"Get inside. I can't promise to be good any longer." He reached up to caress her bottom lip with his thumb, while his gaze hungrily devoured her. "You belong under lock and key."

Maddy was charmed.

A noise jarred her from the spell. "My phone. Someone's calling me. At this hour?"

"Then you'd better answer it," he whispered against her ear.

Maddy cleared her throat once, then again. "Hello."

"Dr Maddy? This is Amber on night shift. I wasn't sure if I should call you or not, as technically he's Dr. Cunningham's patient, but we can't reach him."

"What's the matter?"

"It's John. He's awake and incoherent."

"Meaning he can't speak clearly, his speech is slurring or he can't talk, period?"

"All of them."

"I'm coming in. Keep trying Dr. Cunningham as well. Did you call Emergency?"

"Yes, someone's on the way."

"They should be there by now. Emergency is in the same building, for heaven's sake. Who's on tonight?"

"I don't know. I put in two calls, except the hospital is crazy busy with some multiple car pileup on the freeway."

"Right. That's where Dr. Cunningham will be. Check with the hospital. I'll be there in ten. Stay on John. Make sure his breathing doesn't become impaired and hook him up to the heart machine. It sounds like he's heading for a stroke. And call Emergency again." Maddy slammed the phone closed and snatched up her handbag.

"Problems?"

Maddy stared at him, surprised by the question. She shook her head to clear it. "Your uncle has taken a turn for the worse. I need to go."

Eyebrows raised, he never said a word. He put the truck in drive, checked the traffic and pulled out onto the main road.

Maddy sighed with relief. "Thank you."

"He's my family."

"Let's hope he's okay. I can't do anything over a phone."

He shot her a sideways glance. "Can you do anything at all at this point?"

She glanced at him, unsure of what to say. "Maybe. I don't know." God, now she was babbling. Making a sudden decision, she said, "I'll try."

"Try what?" Confusion colored Drew's voice. "I don't understand what you do."

"And you won't understand this, either." She shifted into a more comfortable position. "Don't touch me. Tell me when you have parked so I can come back out."

With that, Maddy's consciousness jumped out of her body.

"Back out? Out of what?"

She recognized the shock and worry clouding Drew's face as he glanced from her to the road and back again. She didn't have time to soothe his nerves. John needed her help. Right now.

As fast as she thought his name, Maddy zipped to John's bedside in her astral form. Gerona was there, checking his vitals. Dr. Cunningham, his normal gray hair tousled, appeared to have just shown up. With a concerned frown on his face and tablet in hand he checked something on the minicomputer. She glanced at the machinery that registered John's heart rate. His color had faded, showing there had been some trauma to his system.

John's energy shuffled in a sluggish movement among the sheets. Below the bed, however, snug against the floor, were faint remnants of a black, darker energy. And not much of it, either. Gazing at the matrix of different energy fields mixing and blending, Maddy deciphered several other energies besides Gerona's and Dr. Cunningham's that she assumed belonged to other nurses, aides and visitors. Taking her time, she followed each energy pathway as they entered and left the area.

The black energy never left.

Even as she watched, it faded, starting to disperse slightly. Moving closer, she saw the broken hazy energy beneath John's bed had an aged appearance, as if it had been there for a while. Could this be the same snake-like blur Stefan had seen earlier and that she'd noticed on the film? If so, there was nothing snake-like about it now. This energy had shattered into globules versus normal dark energy that resembled a black heavy cloud. Sometimes, she identified dark lines within the clouds, woven through the fog like a spider web, which showed her the level of damage in the body she was scanning.

Here though, instead of spider webs, the blackness wobbled, like shiny gobs of Jell-O. She approached them, wondering about the shimmer deep inside each piece. They were almost pretty. Except looking at them made her stomach heave at their alien sense of wrongness.

She wanted to touch them, yet wasn't sure how they would react. She wished she understood what they were and where they'd come from – not to mention their relationship to John.

Surrounding John with white light, she poured healing energy into stabilizing his heart rate. Seconds later, the machines beside John showed he'd stabilized.

Relief flooded her.

"What the hell?" Dr. Cunningham stood at the machine, hands on his hips. "That's bizarre. What's the chance he was only having a bad dream?"

"He wasn't talking properly." Gerona picked up the chart and wrote down the current vitals. "Maybe we should wake him up and check again."

"We tried waking him and it didn't work," Dr. Cunningham snapped.

John moaned and snuffled, shifting his thin legs in bed.

"John, wake up. Talk to me." Gerona prodded his shoulder gently.

Maddy watched as John opened his eyes and frowned.

"What's everyone doing here? Am I dying?"

Dr. Cunningham snorted. "Not today. The nurses overreacted, as usual."

Gerona's face thinned at the criticism. She stayed silent. Maddy frowned. Dr. Cunningham had never been anything other than respectful in her presence. Then again, he probably wasn't himself because he'd been swamped at the ER because of the accident. He also hated being bothered with trivial things.

However, Gerona was an experienced nurse. If she said there was something off, then Maddy would believe her. Amber had been the one who'd called her, but on Gerona's urging.

Maddy took another long assessing glance at John. The white energy would hold for a few hours, maybe a day or two. Somehow, they had to deal with this dark energy, fast and permanently. In the distance, she could hear Drew calling to her. She disconnected from John.

"Maddy? Maddy, we're here at the hospital. Come back, please."

After a heavy pause while she struggled to shift through realities, she sensed him lean over her. Maddy opened her eyes.

***

Drew reared back in surprise. "Jesus." He closed his eyes in relief before reaching over and kissing her hard. "I don't know what you did. Just don't do it again *ever*, please. That's bloody scary." The cop in him had wanted to call 911; he'd been unsure enough to wait it out. Thank heavens she'd woken up when she had, if waking up was the right term for this.

She sat up slowly, and then closed her eyes as color washed over her face before quickly receding. "I'm fine," she whispered. "Thanks."

"Good," he retorted. "I'm not. How's my uncle?"

"Dying."

"What? Now?" *Jesus.* He looked up at the imposing structure outside the car window.

"No." She chuckled lightly. "That's not what I meant. There's something weird going on with him that I can't figure out."

"Will he make it through the night?" Drew studied her face closely, as if the answers to the universe rested there.

Maybe they did. He knew his own beliefs in life and death, evidence and cold facts, were slowly eroding. Maddy had him questioning everything he thought he knew. He didn't know what the result would be – he hoped Maddy would be there at the end.

"As far as I can tell, yes. However, there are no guarantees here, remember that."

He tugged her into his arms. "Got it. You're not God. You're one of His angels."

Her snort was muffled by his shirt. She nestled in closer. Drew squeezed her gently, enjoying the rare comfort of holding her tight. Chances were good she didn't let this happen very often. He'd like nothing more than to take her home and hold her close for the rest of the night. "Do we need to go inside still?"

"No." She yawned and lifted her head. "I think he's fine now. Besides, his doctor is there with him, so I'm no longer needed."

He stroked a large hand over her face, smoothing the tousled locks back behind her ears. "And what do you need?" Leaning closer, he peered into her eyes. "This has obviously taken a toll on you."

"It has. It doesn't always, though. Tonight, I have to admit, I am tired."

"Let's get you home."

Tucking her up against his side, Drew started his truck. Maddy mumbled a slight protest as he removed his arm from around her shoulders. "It's all right. I'm not going anywhere. However you, my dear, are going to bed."

Maddy smiled up at him. "Sounds good to me," she whispered sleepily.

Sounded good to him too, only she was beyond anything more than crashing. True to his word, Drew had her back to her apartment within minutes. This time though, there was no suggestion of letting her walk up on her own. Drew came around and opened the passenger door and helped her to her feet.

Attempting to get out of the vehicle and walk up the sidewalk, Maddy stumbled. Drew held her close, clasped her around the waist with one arm and guided her through the front door to the elevator. At her apartment, she fumbled for her keys. Pulling them out, she handed them over to Drew.

Once inside, he shut the door behind them and gave her a gentle push toward her bedroom. "Bedtime."

"I'm going. I'm going," she muttered, stumbling through the doorway. "Good night."

"I'm not going anywhere. I want to make sure you're all right."

Holding onto the doorframe, she twisted around enough to face him. Surprise lit her features. "I'm fine, honest. I did do some energy work tonight, but it wasn't bad. The long night has just caught up with me."

"If you say so." Like hell. He'd seen how she'd looked in his car. A day-old corpse had more life.

"Honest. It's safe to leave me. I'll be in bed in like five minutes."

"Good, get going. I'm not leaving."

Exasperated, she turned around and kicked off her heels. "Then you might as well sleep in the spare room for the night. It's so late now, you're not going to get any sleep otherwise."

Not a bad idea. Drew swallowed hard as Maddy stripped off the red sweater as she went into her bedroom, leaving him with a stunning view of her slim back, ribs encased in a black and red bra, gentle curves heading down to the top of black pants.

So close and yet so far.

Resolutely, he walked toward the spare room and considered. Should he stay or go home? Home wasn't that far away, except leaving her might take more energy than he had. This way, he'd see her in the morning, even if only for an hour.

It would also give him a chance to take the relationship one step further.

Anything was worth that opportunity. He'd made a few discreet inquiries and everyone said the same thing. Maddy was known to be very selective when it came to male friends. Not a prude from what he'd learned – just careful.

He liked that. He didn't consider himself in the tomcat category, and it was nice to see she felt the same. Now if only he had some idea how she felt about him.

***

Gerard walked into the office very early, worn out from yet another sleepless night. For the first time since he'd been a young boy, he'd been plagued with nightmares. Endless hours remembering stuff he'd spent most of his lifetime forgetting. Just a horrible night.

These last few days had been hard. He hadn't realized how hard or how badly the stress had affected him. Jesus. What was he going to do down the road? But that wasn't fair. He was coming out of a long year of tight budget constraints, nonexistent wiggle room and staff shortages. Then there was John and that mess.

He wanted this stage of his life to be over and to move on to smoother times. He frowned. Since when had he ever had smoother times?

That brought him back to last night and his childhood nightmare. Demons had chased him. Blackness took over his mind and body. It controlled his hospital and the people in it. Sweat formed on his brow, even thinking about it.

Why were all those childhood memories he'd fought so long and so hard to forget coming back now? He'd walked away from his mother years ago. Begged to be taken away actually, and family services had honored his request. He'd had little contact in the intervening years. Good thing, too. The woman was nuts.

Gerard's secret fear was that it was genetic – that he'd end up as crazy as his mother.

He looked around. Sandra wasn't at her desk. Good. He didn't think he was up to speaking with her this morning. He shut and locked his door, hard pressed to not look around the darkened room. He hit the light switch, heaving a sigh of relief as the light washed away the darkness.

Maybe he needed to take a break. Take a holiday, if he still remembered what that was.

THURSDAY MORNING

It was morning. And that had to be wrong. There was no reason in the world that Maddy could think of to explain why she was awake. After last night's dancing, followed by the panicked visit to The Haven, she should be sound asleep. Only she wasn't and that sucked.

Her cell phone rang as she slipped on her Egyptian cotton dress with the beautiful flowers winding down the left side and back.

It was Stefan. "Maddy, update on The Haven, please."

"John had an attack of some kind last night." Maddy walked out to the living room to slump down on the couch. "His symptoms mimicked a stroke. He's stable, and will need to be closely monitored." She sighed heavily. "I haven't contacted The Haven so I don't have an update yet." She went on to explain what she'd found.

Silence.

Maddy rubbed her temples. "These are psychic attacks, right?" This would be her first experience with something like this – but not for Stefan or other energy workers she knew. "I can't think of what else they could be. I know people are people. They always want something they don't have. And many are prepared to do some pretty horrible things to get it."

Stefan hesitated. "We have to assume this dangerous energy is anchored to John." His voice deepened. "It might have started with Jansen. We don't know enough at this point."

"True enough. From what I've seen, the energy slid around the base of the bed, moving and shifting. It always stayed close.

Contained. Anchored." Closing her eyes, Maddy winced at the question even before she'd managed to ask it. "Stefan, is there any chance that John is doing this himself?"

"Unlikely, although with the little we know, we can't discount that."

"There has to be something more going on than what's related to John. The attack on Jansen happened prior to John's arrival." This was all so bizarre. "John's very pragmatic. He has no patience with any of this stuff. It's hard to imagine he has a hand in it."

Maddy didn't see it. She walked into her kitchen and pulled out the coffee grinder. She chose the setting she wanted before filling it with dark Costa Rican beans. She turned on the grinder, stepping away from the noise to continue talking. "We've both seen black energy causing problems in a person's energy system. It's the basis for all health problems, only the bigger blockages can cause personality changes, mental problems, diseases and, eventually...death."

"True, however, all we have to go on for the moment is the attack on John, regardless of whether he brought it or the energy latched onto him for some reason when he arrived."

"Right. I did a full session on him yesterday. I put the markers in place and ran some healing energy up and down his spine." The coffee grinder shut down. She walked back, filled the coffee carafe for two cups and poured the water into the back of the coffee maker.

"Did you notice anything wrong?"

She paused before placing the carafe on the maker. "Not at the time. This session went deeper and longer than I'd ever gone before. One of the nurses actually brought me out." Maddy measured the coffee and hit the start button. "It hit me afterwards that he didn't feel the same as my sick patients usually do. There wasn't the same sense of disease eating away at him or even the same sense of finality I get from terminal patients."

"This is new territory here. We don't know what might happen."

"Great." Maddy leaned against the counter, waiting for enough coffee to drip for her to steal a cup. "We've done so much work already in the main part that it could take months for the energy in the new section to match the level of the rest of the floor."

"Search for someone connected to him. In order to do this when they are not physically in the same room, they would have to be incredibly skilled and strong. Or desperate."

She said, "It has to be someone he knows and trusts. A lover, best friend or family member, most likely."

"Remember, this person might have been in John's life decades ago. Few people understand how much energy we get on a day-to-day basis from other people, much less how long we carry it once we do." Stefan paused, then added, "They could have placed hooks into his system years ago, an insignificant amount, initially, and then slowly increased it over time. And it's quite possible they didn't realize what they were doing."

"Then they've learned quickly," she retorted. "I've seen cords stretching from person to person, but these black clusters are new on me." And Maddy'd be fine if she never saw them again.

"Energy work is one of the greatest unknowns in our lifetime." Stefan sighed, as if the weight of the world rested on his shoulders. "Keep an eye on it. Anchor a field of your own to keep watch. Set it to trigger with any movement."

"How do we protect the other patients?"

"Set a stronger border. Strengthen the healing energy inside. You might want to set up a Kirlian camera too."

Maddy frowned. Kirlian photography took pictures of a person's energy. It would be interesting to see the images captured on her floor at night, but the cost would be horrific. "That's expensive. How can we minimize the cost?"

"Get a digital one?" He suggested. "I can lend you mine, only it's an older film model."

"Hmmm." The film would be used up an hour. It would have to be changed often and that cost would be prohibitive. "Digital would be better." She sighed. "There's no budget money for toys like this." Another thought occurred. "What if John dies? Would this clump of dark energy be able to transfer to a new host?"

"Anything's possible. We don't know enough. Make sure it doesn't shift to you. If you suddenly have a new person in your life, someone who's on your mind all the time, I'd be leery.

"Take a hard close look at them. The person tied to this black energy would need a way to get in somehow, but once he's there, this person appears to be able to do all kinds of things."

Maddy's mind sorted through Stefan's words. She leaned back against the counter and nearly dropped the phone.

"Oh my God!"

A very sleepy Drew raised an eyebrow at her. Dressed only in pants, Drew stood there, pinup perfect. Maddy gulped. How was it possible she'd forgotten him? He must think she'd lost it completely.

"Maddy!" Stefan's voice reverberated through the phone. "What's wrong?" A thick pause filled the phone. "Oh. That's what."

Heat rushed through her cheeks. Trust Stefan. He read her mind every time.

"I wouldn't if you didn't constantly advertise what you were thinking." There was a second heavy pause. "He's involved in a murder case, an old case and a new one." Stefan's voice took on an odd note, distant with an odd echo. Maddy sat back to listen as Stefan shifted into a different reality. She listened but kept her gaze locked on the virile male dominating her kitchen and her senses.

Drew reached into the open cupboard beside her, snagged two cups and poured coffee from the freshly made pot. He held one out for her.

Maddy nodded, struggling to stay focused on Stefan. A little hard to do with a half-naked man in her kitchen.

"He's got trouble. Dead kids, dead man. And that's not the end…this is just the beginning." Stefan spoke clearly but quietly.

"Can you help?" Maddy kept her voice calm and even. She needed Stefan's vision to continue and anything jarring or loud had the potential to snap him out of it.

Stefan's voice dropped, slurred. "Same energy."

Maddy leaned forward. "What? Stefan? Same energy as what?"

"The Haven. *Maddy's floor.* Same energy."

Maddy ran her fingers through her hair. "Stefan," she whispered. "Talk to me, please. What about Maddy's floor? Stefan, what does this killer have to do with my floor?"

"Wait…" His voice died. "Not…quite the same. Same, yet different." Stefan's voice had deteriorated to a deep slur. His words faded with his effort to maintain conscious awareness in both spheres.

"Can you see the person?"

"No. Energy."

"Can you trace it to the person?"

"Death. Drew is in danger."

"Drew?"

"Weird energy. Can't hold…" His voice warbled before draining away.

There was only blankness on the phone. A tinny sound gave her the sense he was still there, but not speaking. "Stefan." No answer. "Stefan, answer me."

Click.

***

Drew sipped the coffee, enjoying the unusual sensation of being with someone first thing in the morning. He'd woken suddenly, reaching for a ringing phone. But it wasn't his, so he lay back and listened to the sound of Maddy's voice drifting to him from the kitchen.

He watched Maddy as she studied him. Then again, he was standing shirtless in her kitchen. Hopefully not a sight she was accustomed to seeing too often. And one she liked.

With one ear tuned to the conversation, he studied her face. Sleep had helped to restore the bloom of pink across her cheeks, and in that long cotton dress, she glowed. That woman wore her height well. She wasn't shy or self-conscious about it. That made all the difference in the world. Confidence was sexy.

He sighed. What an idiot. He was acting like a lovesick teenager.

***

Maddy whipped up breakfast while Drew got dressed. Even without much practice entertaining males early in the morning, making breakfast didn't take long. With her mind full of Stefan's disturbing words, she finished the job quickly and set two full plates of pancakes on the table. "Let's eat, then we'll talk."

Finishing first, Maddy sat back with a second cup of coffee and watched Drew polish off his plateful. Every bite went down with gusto. This man loved his food. He looked up.

"So what did you want to talk about?"

"Remember the painting you saw in the other room last night?" She raised her eyebrow in question. "That was the artist, Stefan, calling." Unsure how to continue, she sipped her coffee.

"What did he have to say?"

It wasn't that easy. If Drew didn't have working experience with psychics or knowledge of energy work, he wouldn't understand the gist of her answer. Even more complicated, he wouldn't understand the bits and pieces, the incompleteness of the information. "He's worked alongside the police for years and probably has names to give you as references."

He sipped his coffee and stared at her quizzically. "Why would I care?"

"Because he's a powerful psychic and while talking to him, he slipped in and out of a vision. Your name came up. He said that you were busy with murder, an old case and a new one."

Drew's mouth opened, then closed before opening again. "He said *what?*"

She quickly went over the little bit that Stefan had picked up. When she mentioned dead kids, his cheeks sucked in and his eyes chilled. Black reached deep into his eyes. "I need to talk to him." Curt, sharp and no arguments allowed. She wasn't planning to argue, but knew Stefan usually avoided people.

"I'll have to call him."

"Do that." He took out his cell phone and tossed it at her.

She grimaced. "Now?"

"Now. Remember those dead kids? If he has any information that might help with that case, I need to know. The father of one of those children was attacked on Sunday, and with that bruise on Jansen's back that might link the old and new cases, well…"

Maddy sobered as she grasped the connection to his cold case. "I understand."

"Good. Thank you." Drew took a sip of coffee and motioned toward his cell.

Maddy slipped her own cell phone out instead. "He won't answer if he doesn't know who's calling. Even then, he doesn't always answer."

Stefan didn't answer her call. Reaching out mentally, she frowned. She couldn't sense him. A curl of unease unfurled deep in her stomach. "I think maybe we should go to his place. The phone went dead when I was talking to him earlier. I didn't worry at the time because I sensed he'd dropped into a deep sleep." She tilted her head. "Now I'm not getting a reading at all."

The decision made, she stood up abruptly. "I'm going."

Drew stared at his half-finished coffee. "Going? Now?"

"Now." Maddy snatched up her purse. "Sorry, but I mean *now*."

She hurried for the front door, not caring whether Drew was behind her or not.

When she arrived at the parking lot, she glanced back to see him rushing to catch up, shirt open and billowing behind him, his jacket hanging off two fingers over his shoulder. She paused. He looked like he'd enjoyed a hell of a wild night. Damn. She felt cheated.

"My truck or your car?" he asked.

"Your truck. And fast."

John huddled under his covers. He'd barely closed his eyes all night. He'd been too scared. How many people were actually ready to meet their maker when the time came? He'd been sure he wouldn't see the dawn today. In his life, he'd done things he wasn't exactly proud of – getting onto Dr. Maddy's floor was just one more.

He hadn't done anywhere near enough for friends or family over the years. Drew would lose all respect for him if he knew. He'd do a lot to keep that from happening. He'd been hell on wheels throughout his years on the police force and he was proud of that, yet he'd not been easy on his family. He'd never married because he hadn't seen himself committing to one woman. But he could have helped his stepsister out when her son was so sick. The boy damn near died.

His stepsister hadn't done as well. Whether it was the scare of her son's close brush with death, her loose lifestyle or just an encroaching mental weakness, she'd slipped mentally. When Doris's mental state was first called into question, the boy had struggled – a lot, yet instead of stepping up and helping out, John had stayed in the background, not wanting to get involved.

He hadn't treated Drew much better, except he was his younger brother's boy and that made all the difference. Blood counted. He hadn't wanted kids and had regarded his nephew as his own. Drew would get everything when John was gone. He could help Doris now, if he wanted to. But some habits were too hard to break.

Tugging the blankets higher, John sank deeper into the mire he'd made for himself.

God, he'd never planned on *this* as his end.

What irony. What hell.

Stefan, for the first time, wondered at the sensibility of his actions. He thought he was lost, and in the etheric plane, no less. It wasn't the first time, but damn it, he hadn't expected it now. During the call with Maddy, he'd thought about following the trace energy back to the source. Once the thought went out, the action had followed. He'd zipped out of his body to travel the energy field in search of who was doing this.

It was nice in theory but difficult in practice – at least like this. He'd wandered Maddy's floor and probably scared the crap out of John, who couldn't see him. Instinctively John had still known something wasn't quite right.

Stefan found Maddy's dark faded *blob*, as she'd called it.

He'd tried several tricks. He'd tried to smother it, then to join with it, anything to get a handle on where it was coming from.

Nothing had worked. He didn't understand how or why, only it seemed the black globs were attached to, or maybe even originated from John. For the past ten minutes, he'd been trying to see through the dense material to see what and how and where it was attached. Was it to John or his bed?

Stefan hadn't been able to figure it out. That had pissed him off, and made him try harder.

And in the process, Stefan had burned up too much energy. He cast a cautious glance at the throbbing blackness that instinct said had helped drain his reserves faster than he'd expected. There was always enough energy available, but in he still required a certain level of power to access it. It was an easy mistake to make if you were inexperienced. He wasn't. Shit. He hadn't made a mistake like this in years, decades even.

He didn't have enough reserves to get back home.

Maddy's sense of urgency refused to abate on the trip to Stefan's. Her anxiousness even prevented her from reading his energy clearly. When she finally connected with him, it was faint at best. Maddy knew she was capable of connecting and scanning the energy of people around the world, but only when her emotional state was calm and balanced. If it were, then the physical distance *could* be crossed as fast as the thought was understood.

If her own energy were chaotic with worry, nothing would allow her to bridge even the shortest of distances.

The trip took close to twenty minutes, with Drew at the wheel. He drove up the long, winding gravel driveway and stopped outside Stefan's cedar house. As soon as the vehicle rolled to a stop Maddy hopped out.

She paid little attention to the oversized plants lining the driveway, noting only that Stefan's truck and car were both parked in front. She pounded on his door.

No answer.

She tested the knob and it turned easily under her hand. She pushed the door open and tossed a quick backward glance to make sure Drew was behind her, then stepped inside.

"Stefan, are you here?" She walked down the hallway. "It's Maddy. Stefan?"

"Any idea where he'd be?"

"Anywhere. He's very unconventional. He'll paint in a tuxedo if he feels like it, and as his days and nights are his, he abuses traditional constraints of time, does as he pleases."

The living room was empty. Maddy crossed the gleaming hardwood floor into the glass-enclosed sunroom that faced the wooded backyard. Stefan's special place. She walked in and almost missed him. He sat cross-legged in an oversized wicker chair.

"Stefan?" Maddy bent down to his level. His face was gray and lax. Switching her view, she searched his aura, finding it thin and discolored – dangerously so.

Drew crouched beside her. "He doesn't look so good." He flipped his cell phone open and dialed for emergency help.

Maddy slid a sideways glance his way, reached over and closed his phone.

Startled, he glanced at her. "What? I'm not supposed to call for an ambulance?"

Keeping her voice low, she murmured, "No medical professional can help with this."

Ignoring him, she studied Stefan's energy. Scanning him from his head to his toes, she saw no obvious cause for the energy drain. She knew he often took trips. Astral travel was one of his specialties. His silver cord appeared almost nonexistent, even fainter than his energy. She frowned. Crap, she was so worried about him she wasn't thinking straight.

Glancing at Drew, she found him staring at Stefan with a puzzled frown on his face.

"What?" Maddy struggled to understand his expression.

"If a doctor can't help him, and you're a doctor, how are you planning to do what others can't?"

"Well put." She grimaced. What should she tell him and how? He had very little understanding of energy work. He didn't even believe in psychics. She decided to take a chance. "I've told you about being a medical intuitive, and you've seen some weird stuff, like in the car this morning. This is just a little more. I do energy work that's similar to what Stefan does."

"So you've said before. I don't know what that means."

"It means a lot of things. I don't have time to explain now." She motioned toward the comatose Stefan. "Not if I'm going to save him."

"Right. Later you are going to have a long talk." He stared at Stefan. "How do we help him?" Drew stood and studied the tasteful but minimalist style of the room. "Should we lay him down somewhere?"

"No, he can't be touched right now. Even the slightest disturbance of his energy can kill him."

"Shit. Are you serious?"

"Yes. His energy has dissipated. It's too fragile for much right now."

He shook his head. "Then what can you do?"

"Everything and nothing." She stepped back slightly and chose a spot directly beside Stefan.

"Can I help?"

"Pick a spot, sit down and don't talk." She waited until he sat. "I'm going in after him and bring him back. While I'm out, you can't touch either of us." She narrowed her eyes at him. "Do you understand? You can't touch me or him."

He grabbed her arm. "Whoa. And what am I to do if you end up looking like him?"

She frowned. "Then it's too late for both of us, but it won't happen. I'm not going to do the same thing he's doing. I'm not going to leave my body."

"What?" Drew turned his attention back to study Stefan. "What the hell does that mean? And is that what you did this morning?"

"It means he's walking around the planet consciously, in spirit form – without his body. He's very good at it. Many people are doing the same, you know. They just don't know they are doing it. And yes, that's similar to what I did…only not quite."

"Really," he murmured, disbelief caging his voice.

"Really."

"And you're not going to do that? So you won't end up looking dead like he does, right?"

"Right. Don't panic. I'll be back."

She closed her eyes and dropped her head forward. It took several precious minutes to calm her breathing and open her chakras to build the energy she needed for this. She was good, but Stefan was better. She could infuse his chakras with energy, both in physical form and etheric, but this was faster, safer.

Maddy sensed the lightness within her mind. She stretched toward it. She wasn't going to astral travel, she would astral project – follow his silver cord in her mind. Find him and figure out what was happening to him because he should have been able to get home by thought alone.

Lightness entered her heart, her spirit, her very soul. Maddy tilted her face skyward and smiled as her very blood sang with joy. Only by becoming one with the energy, to the emotion attached, could she free her mind to travel the etheric plane.

A heavy sigh worked up from deep inside. She slipped out on the warm breath and opened her eyes. The sensation gave everything a muted appearance, making the experience easier on her senses than if she'd truly left her body. This was like a foggy day in England. A bit eerie, a bit slower, but she could still get to where she needed to go.

Picking up Stefan's silver cord in a white haze was a little difficult. It wasn't possible to change the color of his cord, but she could change the color of the fog. All thoughts manifested immediately here. The hazy fog instantly changed to a lavender overtone, showing the silver cord as a glowing streak across the room. Maddy followed it out onto the etheric plane. The path twisted and turned, dipped and swerved, and through it all Maddy kept the silvery cord in sight.

Her focus stayed on Stefan, calling to him, sending him loving energy and a message that she was coming – to hold on until she arrived. The cord strengthened slightly. It brightened and pulsed. He had to be close.

She rounded several more corners and fell, literally, into a vast chamber of space. Stefan's cord lay crumpled, as did his astral body. Maddy saw her surroundings clearly, although they appeared as if on the other side of thick glass. She blinked once, and then blinked again as she recognized the location. Stefan had traveled here to her floor at The Haven – and here he'd fallen.

Moving around his prone astral body, Maddy studied his position. He was exhausted. With luck, that was the only problem. Maddy moved closer. His cord pulsed. The thinness and fragile look of it, said he'd just gone too far, done too much. That was typical of him. Still, he shouldn't have run his system down to this level so fast.

She frowned.

He was lying within ten yards of John's bed.

Giving John a quick study, Maddy saw his silver cord, not as strong as she'd like to see it, but pulsing happily along. He appeared to be much better off than Stefan at the moment. Beneath the bed, the faded black patch now consisted of even smaller gobs of energy, as she'd come to think of them. They were softer looking, swollen, and they pulsed in an obscene gloating manner.

They gave her the creeps.

And she knew instinctively they were very dangerous – for everyone that came into contact with them.

Like Stefan had.

Glancing down, Maddy realized she needed to help him – now.

She leaned over Stefan. Being only energy, she stretched over him completely. Slowly, ever so slowly, soft as a feather, she let herself sink into him.

"Maddy?" Stefan's voice was as frail as that of someone over a hundred and twenty years old.

"Yes," she whispered into his mind. *"Stay calm. You need to absorb enough of my energy to get yourself back home where you belong."*

"Knew you'd come. Love you, kiddo."

Maddy smiled, her warmth and joy spreading deep into his astral body, blending and morphing into something else. She felt he'd revived sufficiently. *"Let's go."*

Instantly, they were flung back into their bodies like arrows from a bow.

Stefan's body jerked, collapsing him backward. For Maddy, who had only been energy on the outside, the homecoming wasn't so harsh. Still, she groaned as she fell backwards onto the hardwood floor and opened her eyes. Stefan's stained glass window stared down at her. Beautiful mermaids flaunted their bodies on the sunny rocks, as rain poured in a torrential downpour from above, making the window a more realistic portrait than she'd have thought possible.

"Maddy?"

Stefan's faint whisper galvanized her into action. She sat up and shuffled closer. "Stefan, how do you feel?"

"Like butter spread too thin on a slice of day-old bread."

Maddy related to his imagery. How many times had she felt the same way? "I still think you look good enough to eat."

The color slowly seeped into Stefan's face, chasing out the gray pallor. He smirked, bringing a rosy blush of color to his cheeks. "You're biased. You love me."

"True." Maddy reached out a gentle hand and pushed a fallen lock of hair back across his forehead. "What the hell happened?"

"That's something I'd sure as hell like to know, too."

Maddy spun around, surprised at the harshness of Drew's voice. Given the weird events he'd been thrown into, his reaction shouldn't have been unexpected.

He reached out and squeezed her shoulder. "You scared the crap out of me, you know that?"

Tossing him an intimate smile that eased the lines on his forehead, she nodded. For anyone who didn't know how this stuff worked, it would have been incredibly difficult to sit still and wait, not knowing if there'd be two gray bodies or none. "Thank you – for keeping your head and not panicking."

"And that was damn close, I'm telling you." Drew got up and paced the small room as Stefan and Maddy watched. "Don't ever leave me to watch over you two like that again."

After a couple of moments, Stefan pushed up from the chair to stand. He stretched and wiggled slightly, as if adjusting his body suit. Maddy grinned. He was the only person she knew who did that. Drew raised his eyebrow and shook his head in disbelief.

Stefan held out his hand. "I'm Stefan, by the way. Sorry for the initial introduction. It's not my usual style. You're Maddy's cop, I presume. Drew McNeil?"

Drew stepped forward and held out his hand. "Maddy's cop. I kinda like that. Yes, I'm Drew. She was worried after you disappeared during your phone conversation this morning. Although, if you two can do all of this..." He wafted his hand toward the papasan chair. "Then I don't understand why you'd bother with a phone. Can someone please explain what the hell just happened? And what's this you said earlier, about my murder cases?"

Maddy studied Drew's face, pale and drawn as he struggled to understand. He'd obviously had a difficult time when she'd left him alone, but he was handling it well. Secretly, she admitted liking Stefan's name for him, too. She wanted to see if Drew and her had a chance at a relationship. A real one, not a hot-affair-and-be-done-with-it sort of thing.

She'd done those; not anymore. They left a bad taste in her mouth. Although she wasn't exactly looking, she wasn't opposed to accepting what was before her. There was no denying the attraction between them. More than the heat they generated whenever their eyes met, was the energy that melded when they were together. Drew wouldn't be aware of it, yet his energy slid close to hers and snuggled at every opportune moment. She had to admit, she really liked that. She knew hers reached out and touched his energy often too.

They'd burn the sheets to hell and back when they finally got there.

And she, for one, couldn't wait.

***

Stefan watched the two people now seated comfortably in his solarium. So this was the new man he'd seen in her life. Interesting. Close, yet not touching, their bodies had yet to match their minds. Their energies were way ahead of both. Snuggled up tight as they were, their auras blended naturally. He smiled. It wouldn't take them much longer. Danger and drama had a way of pushing people together and making them get over their differences faster. He was happy for them.

The best sound in the world had been Maddy's words when he'd been caught in no man's land.

"Stefan, are you all right?"

Startled, Stefan realized he'd been staring off for several minutes. "That black energy under John's bed did something to me, drained my energy faster than I've ever experienced before."

"I wondered about that when I found you. I've been watching those energy strands and clumps for a couple of days now. Today they were different."

"Different how?" Those fuller globules scared the hell out of him.

"Swollen, as if they'd just eaten."

"Nice." Stefan winced. "Thanks for that imagery, seeing as how I was probably the last meal."

"Today the globs were softer, almost happy, content. I don't know how to explain it."

"You're doing fine, and I think you're right. That energy is feeding on other, healthier, energy."

"For what purpose though?" Maddy stood up and wandered over to the front window. "Healing?"

Stefan studied Drew's face. He hadn't added much to the conversation, but he seemed to be trying to take everything in. "Has to be."

Drew interrupted. "Are you saying someone is stealing another person's energy from the new wing on Maddy's floor?"

The disbelief in his voice reminded Stefan how odd this business would be to an onlooker. In Drew's case, he'd seen more than most. "Potentially, yes."

"And why are they still doing this? Wouldn't they have taken what they needed and stopped by now?" Drew stared hard at Stefan.

Stefan shook his head. "They can only access sick energy so they need so much more of it to be viable. That may be why this black energy is located where it is. I can't say for sure that it originated there. However, it's currently sitting under the bed of one of the patients on Maddy's floor."

"There's only one patient in there now – John McNeil." Drew glanced over at Maddy.

Stefan could only guess at the discomfort sliding across her face.

Nodding slowly, she said, "That's correct."

"So, you're saying this is his energy. That's he's the one doing this?"

Stefan said, "It's possible, although that's the least likely scenario. It's more likely to be someone close to him, like a family member." A fine tremor slipped over Stefan's body. He needed recovery time. He glanced over, catching Maddy's grimace. He turned his attention to Drew, watching as his brows came together and his gaze narrowed on Maddy's face.

Drew asked, "A family member, like a stepsister? Or better yet, a blood relative, like a nephew?"

Stefan shrugged. "If they were close."

"Well, he has a nephew and they are close, but it's sure as hell is not him doing this."

"How do you know?"

"Because I'm that nephew."

THURSDAY AFTERNOON

Drew's announcement that he was John's nephew raised Stefan's eyebrows. Maddy had forgotten to mention that fact to Stefan. Not that it had mattered. Drew wasn't the one causing the black energy. She'd seen his energy and knew he wasn't the one causing the trouble.

Besides, explanations would have to wait. Stefan desperately needed rest and Maddy needed to get back to work.

The trip back had been silent and uncomfortable. During the drive, Maddy made several important phone calls. The first was to request that the newly installed security cameras be checked to make sure they were working properly and that there was no unusual activity. Too bad there was no way to track visitors to Maddy's floor, or The Haven in general. Maddy didn't know of one extended care home that had such a system in place. It would be helpful right now though.

In between these calls, a pulsating silence filled the car. She knew Drew didn't understand what he'd seen today and that he had questions. Not knowing how or what to say, she hoped he'd give her a chance to sort it out before demanding an explanation.

In the back of her mind, she remembered the warning about Drew being in danger. She still hadn't figured that out either. And she needed to.

Maddy asked Drew to drop her off at The Haven. After the tense return journey, he pulled in front of The Haven and parked. She hopped out of his truck, gave him a hurried good-bye and practically ran to the front entrance.

"Maddy?" Drew asked.

Maddy turned around to face him. He'd hopped out but stood beside his truck.

"Where are you running to and why?"

She sighed. "To your uncle. Something's going on and I want to see if I can figure it out. I need to know who else is in your uncle's life. People he knew really well in the past. And now. That includes those that he currently loves, who might love him, and those he may have loved at one time and definitely doesn't now."

"Do you have any idea how many people that could be?"

"People are getting sick, possibly dying, and you're a detective who's close to the victim," she said, exasperated. "Help us figure this out before someone else gets hurt."

He studied her, his eyes narrowed and assessing. "Say I do find these people, the ones who are still alive anyway, what can you do?"

"I'm not sure yet." She stared past him, considering. "It might narrow down the options. If I see these people, see their energies, I might be able to tell if they have anything to do with this. I can't guarantee it, of course. Energy is unique, like a fingerprint." She gazed at him. "Remember, Stefan thinks it's the same person who may have been involved with the deaths of all those kids. Cross reference the people from today with them and…"

"Right, I get it." He held up a hand. "Please keep me in the loop. When will it be safe to call Stefan to ask more questions?"

Maddy checked her watch. "Give him an hour, at least, if not twice that. He should have recovered enough by then."

"Good enough. Is my uncle safe?"

"I'm hoping so, at least for a little bit longer. We believe that whoever is doing this set their hooks into him a long time ago. And are acting on them now. I'm pretty sure that's the reason for his rapid physical decline recently. I don't know what they might do next."

"Can I put a guard on him? Move him to a safer place? What?"

Maddy's laugh was sad. "With energy work, they wouldn't need to be physically close to do this. Alibis are useless. I've scanned people in Egypt from my apartment. He's not safe anywhere. Consider The Haven one of the safest places for him to be right now because it's one of the few places where someone can see what's happening." She was adamant on that point.

Poor Drew, he was grappling with this new idea but he was getting it. The horrified understanding on his face said it all.

"Right. If someone wants to and has the skill to, they can cause the death of anyone, anywhere in the world," she said. "It wouldn't be easy and it would depend on the other person's health and mental state, but it's possible from any distance."

She kept talking as she reached for the front door. Drew followed. "I am suspicious this person had something to do with two other patients at the hospital, Dr. Lenning and Jansen Svaar – possibly for many more attacks and deaths over the years. Find a connection. Find your killer." She didn't want to bring up Eric Colgan as another potential victim at this point.

She'd follow up on him if this trail panned out. Pulling open the door, she glanced back over her shoulder. "And fast. Chances are this person will kill again, and soon."

Drew stared after her as she raced inside.

Could she and Stefan be right? If death were as simple as disconnecting someone's cord then, as impossible as it sounded, it would explain how those kids long ago had literally dropped dead on the spot. Like unplugging a lamp from a socket, they'd been unplugged from their cords.

Why those kids? Why no one else in the last twenty years? Were there other deaths that had gone unnoticed by law enforcement? Not that he'd blame them, with so little evidence and such a far-out cause of death – well, he was sure no one would have considered such a possibility. He wasn't sure he believed it himself. Getting other law enforcement to agree would be impossible. Obtaining a conviction based on conjecture – never.

Ice settled in his stomach. Perhaps it was something unrelated to his uncle – like the Internet had given this killer access to millions of potential victims?

No. Maddy said they had to have a personal connection. She also said with a connection, they didn't need to be close in order to do something like this. He couldn't imagine a world where killers chose victims by their ability to connect with the person, regardless of where they lived in the world. Civilization could degenerate into chaos.

In a smaller way, this could be happening right here and now, and might have been going on for decades. Uncle John wasn't doing this to himself – there was no way. Therefore, someone was doing it to him, and had been affecting his health for who knows how long. But who? He walked back to his truck. How many up-close-and-personal friends, lovers and enemies had his uncle collected over the years? Hundreds, if not thousands.

Drew pulled his car out of the lot and drove toward the office.

Wilson was working on his computer when Drew walked in. The man glanced up with a big smirk on his face. "About time you showed up. Figured I'd be working alone today. Hot date?"

Working with Wilson had to be one of the biggest blessings of the new job. Easy to work with, and open to ideas, he was like a gentle family dog – agreeable all the time.

Tossing him a glowering look, Drew booted up his computer and replied, "Yeah, hot date, followed by a panicked visit to hospital, then crashing in hot date's spare room, followed by a second panic visit to a different hot date's friend's home."

"Nice. What are you planning for a second date?" Wilson sat at his desk, leaning back comfortably. "Did the emergencies turn out to be okay?"

Drew plunked down in his chair, suddenly more tired than he cared to admit. He'd grabbed a few hours of sleep at Maddy's place but not enough. "They will be. A little scary for a while. My uncle took a turn for the worse, but he's expected to pull through, and the friend...well, I guess you might say he was unconscious for a while."

"Not quite the outing you'd planned, I presume?"

"No, not quite." Drew played with a pencil on the top of his desk, switching it end over end while he considered mentioning Stefan.

"Something wrong?"

"How do you feel about psychics?"

Wilson shrugged.

Encouraged, Drew continued. "Does the name Stefan Kronos mean anything to you?" He studied his partner's face carefully, looking for any scoffing.

Wilson's face registered surprise, not shock. "Ah." Wilson sat forward. "That must have been a hell of a date."

"You've heard of him?" Maddy had said he'd done work for the police. He hadn't expected Wilson to know him.

"Absolutely. He's one of the best in the business. A bit freaky, though. And the man is a genius artist, producing some of the most incredible paintings imaginable. It's a little too raw for the common folk. He's had phenomenal success working with law enforcement in this country and others. Scary dude for the stuff he knows. It's like he can look right through you – and apparently he can."

"So I've heard. So in your opinion, he's for real?"

"Solid gold."

"He's the one who had trouble this morning."

Wilson jumped to his feet. "What? How do you know him? He won't work with just anyone."

"Dr. Maddy is a good friend of his."

"Dr. Maddy? From The Haven? Wow, don't you move in high circles." Wilson reached the stack of folders on his desk. "I see transferring your uncle to The Haven moved you up in life, too."

"She was my hot date last night."

A long whistle of appreciation circled the room. "Wow. Wait..." Wilson paused, then a grin cracked his face.

Drew watched him put two and two together.

"So you spent last night in Dr. Maddy's spare room?" His smirk widened until he burst out laughing. "Talk about being so close…"

"And yet so far." Drew finished for him. "Right. You got it. So back to Stefan. Does his work stand up in court?"

"He hates courts. He tries to show you where to look so you can find the evidence to put these assholes away without him. It's his way of avoiding courts."

"Good enough." Drew refreshed the screen on his computer and while it did he reached for his notepad. Standing up, he walked to the wallboard holding the photos of the six dead kids. He tapped it gently with the notepad. "We may have caught a break on this case."

***

John sank deeper into his bedclothes, hating the chill that ran through his veins. Would he ever feel warm again? He shivered and pulled the covers up. He wanted to move to another area of the floor. One not so cold, empty and lonely. He had liked having Adam close by, only Adam was still in ICU. None of the medical team had been able to tell him when he would return. There was an eerie feeling, lying in a room full of gleaming empty beds. Definitely weird.

Then, his whole life was that way lately.

Maybe they'd changed his drugs. The doctor had gone over a bunch of stuff, but John hadn't paid too much attention. He didn't want to focus on the constant pain or the debilitating mess his body had become. Still, new medications would explain the hallucinations, the paranoid feelings, even the weird nightmares he'd been experiencing.

Feeling better with that realization, he shuffled his butt slightly until he was half-sitting.

This wasn't so bad. He smoothed the bedcovers down and reached for his remote. It lay at the end of his bed. Getting there was a little harder. Pulling his wasted legs over the edge of the bed, he shifted to a sitting position and reached again. He picked it up and wiggled back toward the head of his bed. As he swung his arm around to use the metal side for support, he dropped the television remote. It slid from the blankets against the metal frame and down to the floor.

"Shit."

He slid his feet to the floor. "Well, I had to go to the bathroom anyway." He tottered slowly in that direction, careful because of his unsteady gait. After washing his hands, he made his way back, painfully aware of every step. At the side of his bed, he bent slowly, hanging on to the metal frame for support. As his fingers reached for the remote, he twisted his head to look under the bed...and frowned.

What the hell was that?

He moved down the end of the bed and searched for something to poke underneath. An empty IV stand stood beside his bed.

Knowing he probably shouldn't try this and determined to give it a go, regardless, he bent down, lowering himself onto his knees and then he reached under the bed. He felt around. A weird tingling sensation started at his fingertips and slid up toward his elbow. John pulled his hand out and turned it this way and that, wondering what had changed.

The tingling slid up to his shoulder and across his chest.

Something was wrong, really wrong. Kneeling on the floor, he struggled to his feet only to collapse from the effort. He wasn't going to make it to his call button. Damn it.

The numbness carried down his chest, back, and deeper into his spine. The room spun. His vision blurred. He pitched head first to the floor.

***

Maddy was delayed on the main floor of The Haven. Two doctors had questions for her about their patients and her project. She couldn't exactly brush them off; neither could she get rid of the sense of wrongness building inside the place. It took a good fifteen minutes before the three of them reached the point of setting up a meeting.

By the time she managed to excuse herself, the feeling of being too late had her racing to the stairs.

Entering the stairwell, urgency slammed into her. Not understanding, but incapable of ignoring the energetic vibes, Maddy sprinted up the stairwell, her heels clacking with each step. The urgency built higher and grew stronger the closer she got to her floor. Her heart pounded as her stress levels topped out and a film of sweat covered her face. "Oh, God." She wrenched open the door and bolted down the corridor.

"Dr. Maddy?"

"What's wrong?"

The voices called out as she fled past the nurses' station. In the background, Maddy heard footsteps rushing in her wake.

She entered the new wing. John's bed was empty. Skidding to a stop, she spied his foot on the far side. Dropping to her knees beside him, she checked his vital signs while simultaneously shifting her vision to her inner eye. The black energy blob pulsed under the bed. It surrounded John's silver cord several feet away from his body, almost suffocating him. It was climbing ever so slowly up the length of the silvery lifeline. The energy of his arm closest to the silver cord had a gray tinge to it as the life force had weakened under the power of the draining blackness.

Two nurses dropped to their knees beside her.

Nancy asked. "What happened?"

"Don't know yet. Get him stabilized. Call for help, just don't move him yet."

Amelia raced off. Maddy glanced at Nancy. "I have to go under."

Nancy stared back, one eyebrow raised. "Can you do that here?"

She answered instinctively. "I have to. I don't have time to go to my office."

She lay down on the floor, took a deep breath and jumped free of her body.

Opening her astral eyes, Maddy studied the black threatening ooze surrounding John's cord. Releasing the tension in her chakras, she reached out to the region of John's cord the energy would envelope next. Mentally, she projected blue and lavender healing waves to that one spot. As if hit by a shock wave, the black energy rippled.

Like a war between titans, Maddy sized up the resistance immediately. There was a person attached to this mess. She sensed the intelligence, their surprise and their frustration. Force was no answer in working to change energy. It engaged the senses and fired up the mind and emotions. Energy, to work effectively, was all about stepping out of the way, sinking into the sensation while detaching from the ego. Maddy had learned to become one with the source of her being, the source of who she was inside, blanking out the issues of her life and awaking fresh from the experience – one with the world.

To work energy positively, she had to be full of grace and joy, content with herself – anything less and it would be too easy to leave a shadow, a tiny piece of herself, behind.

Maddy focused on the area of John's chest. She studied the shadowy energy carefully, needing to see how it reacted. Would it pull back in retreat? Or would it spread so thin as to disappear?

This energy tried to blend into John's energy.

Keeping her wall of healing energy in place, Maddy gently moved the blackness backwards. It thinned out, slinking tightly against John's aura. Her energy block held, maintained the pressure, forcing the apex of the slender layer of blackness to retreat. She sensed a building fury, the absolute blinding tension as the energy was thwarted. It vibrated in place for another moment, before receding down his arm.

Instantly, Maddy moved her energy forward, keeping a firm edge against the receding darkness. Keeping the block in place, she watched it detach from John's arm. The last final bit, infinitesimal in size, fell off, to sit on the floor quivering. She stretched out a finger, her hand full of warm lavender energy. And almost touched it. If the energy were a puppy, she'd be holding out her hand for it to sniff.

The blob wiggled.

Maddy frowned, pulling her hand back slightly. The blob followed. She stopped her retreat and waited to see what it would do. It came closer and closer. Her brows pulled together as realization struck. It was attracted to her energy, her healing energy. Only it wasn't strong enough to attach itself to her.

It wanted to be, though.

Stefan was right. It wasn't necessarily trying to kill anyone. It wanted the energy for itself.

It wanted energy it could use to heal. Healing, loving energy, like hers, would be at the top of the list. Old, sick energy had to be all this person had access to, meaning they were likely to be in the same physical health as those it victimized...feeding on those weaker than itself. A healthy person could repulse a weak attack without even being aware it was happening – unless the attacker had learned the art of killing instantly.

Who was doing this?

"Dr. Maddy?"

She blinked. Nancy was staring at her, or rather, at her body. Maddy gave the blob one last glance, settled two anchors in place for future use then realigned her energy to her physical body.

She closed her eyes for a long moment and when she reopened them, she was viewing the world with her physical eyes. Turning her head toward Nancy, her voice still slow and slurred, she said, "I'm here."

"Good." With a relieved voice, Nancy continued briskly, "John seems to be coming around. His color has improved and his vitals are picking up."

Moving slowly, Maddy sat up and studied John's face. His skin had taken on a more natural appearance, losing the dry, paper-thin look. Hearing footsteps approach, she stood slowly, using the bed for support. Nancy handed her the tablet.

She stepped out of the way as two brawny orderlies arrived and lifted John gently onto his bed. Nancy wrapped a warm blanket around his cool body and settled him in before checking his vitals. Maddy checked his file on her computer and perused his medications. She wrote a couple of quick notes and made a mental one to contact Dr. Cunningham.

John needed to have someone keep a close eye on him. The Kirlian cameras were a moot point. Maddy absolutely knew what was wrong on this floor now. She just didn't know how to stop it.

Most sick people wouldn't be able to save themselves. The attacks, as in John's case, would appear to be a natural decline in health. If energy were drained slowly but regularly, the process would also become familiar. Anything that becomes familiar then becomes harder to recognize or identify as wrong and therefore it would be almost impossible for someone to fight against its damaging effects. It would be viewed as chronic decline.

How would she combat something she couldn't see or recognize?

Walking back to her office, she massaged the back of her neck. Tension had collected there in a tightening pool of aches. She rotated her neck to loosen it.

"Is John okay?" Amelia raced to her side and walked beside her down the hall.

Maddy nodded. "Who attended him last?"

"I'll check. I haven't personally seen him since ten this morning. Candy should have seen him after lunch for his medications, and of course the staff served him lunch and picked up the dishes."

Maddy glanced at Nancy. "Find out names and when they were here, please."

Nancy nodded, but instead of leaving, she touched Maddy's arm. "Is something wrong? Some weird stuff's been going on lately."

"Yes. I don't have all the details. But I will." She refused to let anyone do this type of damage, to her patients or her project.

Maddy's floor was for healing. It was hers to guard and to protect.

Occupant of Bed 232 stretched out on her bed and pouted. She felt like a bedridden failure and therefore the nurses could damn well call her by her bed name today. Damn it, she hated to fail. She'd almost had it all. She'd wanted more, she'd needed more. She shouldn't have tried a second time today. Only this morning's session had been so brilliant, so wonderfully stimulating that like a crack addict, she had to try it again.

Damn that interfering upstart from the second session – whoever the hell they were. And she'd find out. Nudging up against her anger, fear threatened to settle in. She needed that energy. Without her daily healing injection, she wouldn't be able to function.

Her options were limited. John was the only one she had access to up there now, and his energy had sweetened. Had to be the influence of Dr. Maddy's floor. What the hell was that damn shield anyway? She'd sensed the power of it, she'd seen the loving energies inside of it, and she hadn't been able to enter – she'd tried, though.

She sighed. If she managed to figure out how to get to those people in that bubble, she wouldn't have to go after so many other people. And that child's energy, wow. Was she improving or what? Jealously twisted inside her. Just one smidgen of the child's energy and she would be free from pain for days, not to mention that would kick-start her healing and raise it to new levels.

It wasn't because she hadn't tried, because she had – many times. Somehow, Dr. Maddy had managed to create that bubble to block energy drainers like her. Wasn't that a sneaky thing to do? She stared at the ceiling tiles for a moment. She'd never been able to access Dr. Maddy's energy.

She'd have to consider that though. She needed to know more and do more. Damn doctors. Her skills would have blown this hospital apart if she'd been able to develop them as she should have.

Sinking deeper under the covers, she tugged fretfully at the bedding. She'd have to do without for now. But she had to find another source soon or the drought would send her physical condition spiraling downward. Best if her next donor were to carry Dr. Maddy's sweet, pure energy.

She'd have healed ten times over with that wonderful, positive energy. It was worth fifty of these dying old farts. Their life force was already dried out and decaying. Their energy helped sustain her, kept the worst of the pain away, but theirs would never heal her. She needed to access those patients under Dr. Maddy's care. Better yet, she needed to be under Dr. Maddy's care herself. Then she'd grab all the energy she needed.

Jansen. Now that had been a mistake. She'd gotten greedy. She'd been siphoning little bits off him for a long time, when all of a sudden she hadn't been able to access his energy. That damn bubble had kept her out and away from him, until his bed had been shifted. When she had access again, after so long, she'd lost control and gorged – had taken everything he had. She never experienced a healing quite like that before. It had felt so good she hadn't been able to stop. She might even have killed him. He'd certainly been dead the next day.

That had saddened her. They'd had good times years ago. Then he'd gotten back with his wife and had broken off the relationship. She hadn't meant to kill him.

But, oh Lord, it had felt good.

***

What a day. Gerard dropped his head into his hands. The Board had called with more bad news, and he was on the firing line himself. He'd managed to duck – today. There was no doubt that his ass was being watched and his fingers had been slapped.

Gerard didn't like who he'd become. How had it happened? How had he become a person who sold beds to the highest bidder? Someone who held Maddy's floor up as an enticement to desperate, dying people? Sure, Maddy was good, but as Jansen's death had proven, she wasn't perfect.

Although that blame might need to be placed at his feet, too. He'd forced her to take Adam on, snuck John in, and already had several fat checks in his hands for the next beds. Dr. Maddy had warned him that breaking away from protocols would change the project, and it had.

His pride had placed him in this position. When the budgets had gotten so bad, he'd wanted to show the others he could handle it. Prove that he could successfully run The Haven, despite the problems and the economy. God, what a fool he'd been then. His ego had won over his sense of right and wrong.

Dispirited, he crossed his arms on his desk and laid his head down.

***

Maddy closed her phone and placed it on her desk, confused and slightly disoriented. She stared down at it as if it might explain what had just happened. Gerard had actually apologized for the way he'd been bringing patients on board and disregarding the system specifically designed to maximize the healing abilities of The Haven. He'd agreed that there needed to be a solid rethink of their current policies and procedures, and was setting up a special meeting. Today he sounded more his old self, the strong-in-charge man who'd recruited her years earlier. His voice had surged with power, brimmed with resolution. What the hell had happened to him?

Her cell phone rang. This time it was Drew.

"How long has Nancy Colfax worked for you?"

Maddy started, her mind struggling to switch subjects so fast. "What? Nancy? Uhmmm, I don't know. Four, five years maybe? Why?"

"Did you know her mother had an affair with Uncle John? About six or seven years ago?"

Maddy glanced toward her closed office door. "No, although I can't say I'm surprised. I've heard John was quite a womanizer, and at his age, there might be any number of women connected in one way or other to my circle."

"So you didn't know?"

"No. I did not know." Maddy sighed, slumping back in her chair. "Then again, Nancy probably didn't, either."

"Oh?"

"She hasn't been close to her mother in a couple decades. They exchange the odd phone call. That's the extent of it. Why, are you checking up on her?"

"Not only her. I've extended the parameters to include everyone on the floor with a connection to John, no matter how tenuous. Another avenue to explore would be his caregivers."

Maddy rubbed the bridge of her nose. That would be a long list. "Talk to John. Let him know what's going on and see if he can narrow the list down. By the way, I went over the information Nancy compiled for me, but nothing pops."

"Right. I'll run a few more names, then come over."

She would get to see him again. She smiled "I think I know what caused the bruising," she said abruptly. "At least I might know. I had to think about whether this was possible or not." With a grimace, Maddy forged ahead. "I believe the bruises represent energy entering or exiting the body with extreme force. Normal energy movement wouldn't cause any damage."

A long silence filled the phone line. His voice, harsh and curt stepped in. "What kind of training does someone need to do this?"

"There's no formal training. However, several spiritual groups work with this energy. Some people can stumble on their own power without realizing it. There are people who hop out of their body on a daily basis and never realize it's an unusual skill."

"Can *you* access this energy?"

"Yes, but I wouldn't without the person's permission."

"Okay, I'll keep that in mind. I've got to go."

Her voice dropped to an intimate whisper. "See you later then."

After closing her phone, Maddy got to her feet. She grabbed her tablet and the large stack of paperwork on the side of her desk, strode down to the nurses' station and gratefully dumped the paperwork on the counter.

She greeted the two nurses who were busy working and continued down the hall to check on her patients. Belle slept, something she did most of the day now. Maddy gave her energy a cursory glance, checking for anything out of the ordinary. Everything appeared fine.

Feeling reassured, Maddy moved on from one to another, stopping to talk with those awake and to smile at those sleeping peacefully. With every patient, she searched their energy for any abnormalities, noting changes in blockages of their meridians and updating their files on her tablet.

As she moved toward Felicia, she was aware the energy of the space had changed – was becoming edgy, irritated.

Maddy frowned and picked up the pace.

A shriek split the air.

Maddy ran to Felicia's side.

Alexis sat on the other side of her daughter's bed. "Felicia, take it easy. It was just a nightmare. It's over now."

Felicia opened her eyes and gasped several times. A heavy sweat drenched her skin and sheets as she shuddered. "That wasn't much fun."

Maddy patted her hand as she noted the rapid vibration of the child's energy. Something had scared her badly. "Bad dreams can be like that."

Alexis thanked her. "I'm sure it was bad, baby. But it's all over. You're awake and the dream can't hurt you."

Felicia groaned. "I know, but I'm still scared."

Maddy checked her pulse, noting her heightened color and rapid breathing. Normal signs after a bad shock. "Do you want to tell me about it? The dream?"

Like a frightened rabbit, Felicia retreated deeper into the bedding, shaking her head rapidly. "No, I really don't."

Alexis patted her hand. "It's okay, sweetheart. You don't have to share if you don't want to."

"I don't want to," she whispered, wiping her eyes and face with the sheet.

Maddy settled on the edge of the bedside. Felicia might not want to tell her, yet it would help her a lot if she did. It would also give Maddy a good idea whether she had been affected by the aberrant energy, or something else.

From the box of tissues on the small side table, Alexis handed one to her daughter. "Use this, honey. Dry your tears then get some rest."

"I don't want to go back to sleep." Felicia struggled to shift herself upwards.

Maddy leaned over and gently helped the child sit up against the headboard. She gave a comical groan. "I'm not going to be able to do this much longer, you've gotten so big." She sat back down again. "You know, I think you've gained weight in the short time you've been here." And that was big news.

The two adults glanced at each other in pleased surprise. The fight, as always, was to stop the rapid weight decline. Weight gain was a dream rarely achieved with terminal patients.

Felicia grinned, hope a bright beacon shining on her face.

"Wow. What a smile, young lady." Maddy beamed back at her.

The blankets rippled as Felicia wiggled. "Thanks, I'm feeling lots better."

"That's what I want to hear. Now if we could only do something about those nightmares, huh?"

The smile slipped away from Felicia's face. She twisted the sheets around her fingers.

Reaching over, Maddy held Felicia's hand gently. "I know it's tough, but it would help me to stop them if I knew what they were about. Have you had these often?" Maddy watched the emotions cross her young charge's face. She loved working with children for that reason. They were so open so innocent so trusting. That's why they healed so beautifully.

Felicia shook her head. "No, I'm sleeping really well. It's just today when I had a nap. That's when it happened."

"What happened?"

"I don't know. I went to sleep while Mom read *Harry Potter* to me. The dream started fine, then it turned nasty."

That's the part Maddy needed to hear. Keeping her voice soft and gentle, she asked, "Nasty, how?"

When Felicia didn't answer and wouldn't raise her head, Maddy squeezed her hand gently, comforting her. "It's going to be okay, Felicia. Sometimes the medication we give people can make the mind do funny things."

In a faltering voice, Felicia tried to explain about the meadow and the black cloud that had started like rain and ended up chasing her. She'd fallen down and that's when the blackness tried to smother her. She'd sat up screaming, only to realize she was inside a bubble with the blackness clawing at the outside trying to get in.

Nice. Maddy gave her a bright smile. "Then it was a good dream, Felicia. You were protected inside this bubble. The darkness wasn't able to get you."

Felicia frowned, thinking hard, then her face cleared and she a huge grin split her face. "That's right. I was screaming because I was afraid it would get me, but it didn't. It couldn't because I was safe inside."

"And now you don't have to be scared anymore." Maddy's heart warmed. Felicia's spirit understood she was safe here. Not only safe, she was thriving. Since moving to The Haven, Felicia had shown steady improvement, and it was early. She slept better, mostly, and her arms and legs had strengthened a lot, giving her better mobility. Then there was her appetite. Maddy didn't have her prior record to go by, except the nurses had reported that Felicia was eating often and well. The food was probably better here, too. Maddy would strengthen the bubble around her even more. Felicia would stay safe. Now if only she could figure out how to keep John and Adam safe.

Grinning, Felicia reached her arms up. Maddy gave the child a big hug while her mother watched, tears in her eyes. Walking away, Maddy increased her pace as she moved toward John. Acid bubbled in her stomach. Worry chewed on her consciousness. Maddy needed to find the person doing this and fast. She skidded to a stop at the sound of voices.

Drew's.

"Maddy?"

Startled, Maddy found Drew standing beside his uncle's bed, eye to eye – concern all over his face.

She flushed. "Sorry. Lost in thought." She turned toward John, who lay on the bed. She noted a healthier tone to his skin. Odd to think that he might actually experience a miracle cure and walk out of here – if they could stop the person who was trying to kill him. Grinning at the two men, she said, "So what are you doing, shooting the breeze like two old women?"

John grunted. "Old women? Speak for yourself, young lady. You'll get old yourself one day."

The disgruntled look on his face matched the disgruntled tone of his voice. Maddy chuckled.

"You're perfect the way you are." Drew leaned forward and dropped a kiss on her cheek.

John whistled.

Maddy walked over to John, doing her best to ignore the heat washing over her cheeks and the even stronger heat pooling inside. John smiled at her.

"You dating my nephew?"

"Why?" Maddy kept her tone professional, her smile polite. Her doctor face.

John blustered. "What do you mean, why? Drew's family. What's his business is my business."

Maddy grinned. "Oh, good. So of course, you've given him a full list of all your lovers, haters and wannabes. Because what's your business is his business."

Drew laughed. "She's got you there, Uncle John."

John grumped. "That's private."

"Not anymore." Maddy kept her voice cheerful. She walked over and picked up John's wrist, automatically checking his pulse rate. She frowned. His rate was up.

John jerked his hand free. "I gave him the names already, damn it."

"Good." Maddy made a notation on the screen of her tablet. "This has to stop, Drew. I need to know my patients are safe."

"I'm working on it."

Maddy tapped her foot impatiently. "Not good enough."

John rose to Drew's defense. "Leave the detecting to him and focus on treating people. God knows I'm not cured yet."

Maddy gave him a hard gaze, her hands on her hips. He was right but still… "That's fine. I can transfer you back to your old ward, or Drew can help you to find another place you'd like more."

"Now wait." John struggled to sit up, his thin frame almost quivering with shock. "I'm sorry. I'm not wanting to get transferred."

"Well, maybe I'm wanting to transfer you. Especially after finding out you bribed your way in here."

John blustered, "So what if I did? Gerard needed some equipment and I needed a bed. It's called a trade." His face turned an indignant red.

Maddy glared at him.

John glared back. "You don't understand. They said I was dying and no one could give any answers as to why. I knew you were my only chance. Hell, I've been to every other damn doctor. Nothing. Being here has worked. I feel much better today. I don't know what you did, but it felt wonderful." Hope crossed his face. "I don't suppose I can get that every day?"

"Nope. So any method is fine as long as it works?" Maddy raised one eyebrow as she studied him. "And this from our old chief of police?"

He had the grace to look ashamed. His glance going one to the other and back again. "I admit to using underhanded methods to jump the list. I was desperate."

"Yeah, I got that. But what methods?"

"It's not pertinent." Spit formed at the corner of John's mouth. His gaze circled the room, avoiding hers.

Only it could be pertinent. Maddy's neck tingled. Whatever John was hiding had to come out. "Tell me. No more lies."

Drew held up a hand, except it had no effect.

"All right!" he yelled. "I did blackmail him into it. Okay?"

Maddy sniffed. "I figured that much out already. I want to know over what."

Drew walked over and placed a calming hand on her shoulder. "I understand that you're pissed about this." He turned to his uncle. "Now what did you blackmail Gerard about?"

"It's complicated." John glared at Drew. "And private."

"Too bad. Most things in life are. Give." Drew refused to back down.

"These are family secrets. Ours, too."

Drew reared back. "Ours? What are you talking about?"

"Gerard's sister."

Maddy scrunched up her face, confused. "What about her? I don't think I knew Gerard had a sister. He never mentions her." She shrugged. Her relationship with Gerard hadn't extended to personal conversations. She presumed he had a family like everyone else in the world.

"Well, he does, sort of... At least he's kept up the façade that she's his sister. Only she's not. She's his mother and she's on the second floor of The Haven. Has been for a while. She wants to transfer to your floor, but Gerard won't let her. She scared the hell out of him years ago." John grumped at her, distaste in his voice.

John glared at the two of them, before his shoulders sagged. The wrinkles on his face deepened with pain. "There's decades of family secrets here and I'm not going to tell you all of them. So don't ask. That's Gerard's personal hell – not for public knowledge. But his mother and I were close for a time, way back then. For all I know, Gerard is my son. And that relationship with his mother is not something I'm proud of and I'd just as soon not make it public knowledge."

He groaned and flopped backwards. "And just in case you didn't put two and two together, Gerard's mother is my stepsister, your Aunt Doris."

"You're talking about Aunt Doris?" Shock sharpened Drew's voice.

"That means you're saying Gerard is my cousin? Why didn't I know?" He straightened and stared at Maddy. She raised one eyebrow and stared back. They both turned to frown at John.

He frowned back. "Yes, Doris. Damn it, don't look so shocked. It wasn't incest; she's not really your aunt and never was. There's no blood between us. I've told you that before. Why do you think her transfer to Maddy's floor was never approved? Mental stability is one of the criteria to get here." His face puffed with outrage, the color darkening even more. "When things fell apart for him, Gerard and I worked to keep their relationship hidden."

Maddy stared at John. "And you blackmailed him with his own paternity?" Did nothing make any sense here?

Drew stared at him. "Blackmail? Really? Why would he care if anyone found out?"

John's face flushed a deeper red. He growled, "I didn't really blackmail him. I kinda threatened to. She's not all there, mentally. Been sliding in and out for years. He never wanted people to know about his parentage. It all goes back to a bad time when Gerard was about nine and he almost died in a car accident. He pulled through, obviously. Only his mother started to deteriorate around then and she hasn't been the same since.

"She knew a bunch of kids that died around the same time. Their deaths affected her weird like. The whole thing broke her up." John sat straighter, terrible memories clouding his expression. "She can't handle anyone even talking about it."

Maddy's antennae went up. She met Drew's gaze. *Dead kids.* "How long ago?"

The bluster was long gone from John's face. Weariness and shadows filled his eyes. "Almost thirty years ago. I tried to help her back then, only it was tough and I'm not much of a communicator. She wasn't easy to talk to. She'd spend hours at Gerard's bedside in marathon visits that exhausted her. She'd go home and sleep, then go back to the hospital again.

He gazed off in the distance. "Somewhere around the same time, these kids turned up dead. I remember the case well, because so many of us were undecided as to whether there'd been foul play involved or not. However, for her...hoping and praying so hard for Gerard to live, when all around kids were dying around the community...well, she was so afraid that Gerard would be next. Needless to say, the stress damn near broke her."

"Had she known the kids? I mean the ones that died?" Drew asked.

"Several of them, if not all of them. It was a small, tightly knit community back then. I think we all knew them in one capacity or other. She'd done daycare for years and had gone on to teach piano, choir, and singing lessons." He shifted uncomfortably on the bed.

"That must have been hard for her." Twisting, Maddy tried to see how Drew was handling this. Confusion clouded his features.

"Well, it certainly did something to her. It seemed that the longer Gerard was in hospital, the more unstable she became."

"Has her mental state improved over the years?" Maddy frowned.

"She was really bad after Gerard recovered. It was a surprise because I thought she'd be fine then. Instead, she became worse. Kept talking about the dead kids as if they were still alive, as if through talking about them, she could make it so. Especially the first one that died, Sissy. She'd known her better than the others. Bad enough as it was, she was into that weird New Age stuff." His jaw clenched.

"Gerard asked to go into foster care, and he eventually changed his name. He said he didn't feel safe with her. I should have helped him then." He glared at both of them. "But I didn't and now he's still hiding the fact that she's his mother. Not sure she even recognizes him. Must be pretty hard... and I never helped."

His anger and guilt had caused him more than a few sleepless nights, Maddy could see. An inkling of an idea, a possibility grew in the back of her mind. She needed more information to see if it fit.

With a heavy sigh and a dark glare toward the window, John said, "Her doctor kept trying new medicine, hoping for improvements, and she did improve but had multiple setbacks as well. She was institutionalized at one time. Then after that doctor passed away, she got a new one and he seemed to be more knowledgeable. With this new medication, she's shown remarkable improvement. She's like a split personality. One day is good and the next she's a different person – even names herself differently at times." John shook his head. "I don't know. I used to visit every once in a while, then I got ill...and well, I haven't been able to. I call her often though."

Maddy stared at Drew. There it was. Her possibility grew into full-grown probability as her mind raced through the events with lightning speed. Could Gerard's sister, aka his mother, have something to do with the energy attacks going on here? Even worse, could she have done something to those kids thirty years ago? There was no motive more powerful than the love of a mother for her dying child, and if this woman felt she was losing Gerard, chances are she'd have done anything to save him.

Desperate people did desperate things, including killing other people's kids to save their own. Maddy had no idea if Doris's actions had saved Gerard. If she'd succeeded in killing these kids, and hadn't cleansed the children's energies from her own aura, then bits and pieces would have stayed with her – slowly poisoning her, and quite possibly manifesting as mental illness. The development of a personality disorder would be a given, and split personality disorder, a distinct possibility. A fascinating case.

Her medical training wanted to delve deeper. The medical intuitive side of her was stunned.

Drew stared at her. "Maddy? Is it possible she could be the person we're looking for?" he asked, his voice hard.

Doris was only one floor below, close enough to keep tabs on Maddy's floor. Close enough to hear gossip about who was arriving and who was dying. Close enough for her weak, sick mind and body to access other sick people. Close enough to allow a small portion of her energy to float free and live attached to her lover, stepbrother and possibly…to the father of her child – the child being Gerard. That would explain John's ill health these last few years and the recent aggressive attacks on him since his arrival at the Haven.

What about Jansen though – had she known him? How many other deaths could she be responsible for on the floors below? Maybe Jansen – if there were a connection between them.

Yes, definitely possible.

"Yes," she whispered. "It might be." Maddy was stunned by the enormity of what this woman might have done, and what she would continue to do if she weren't stopped. "But you're never going to prove it. And if she's not in her right mind, she may not realize what she's been doing, either."

THURSDAY EVENING

Stefan glared at the phone. He glanced down at the paint on his hands, his smock, the floor. Damn it, even the phone had yellow on it. And it was Maddy calling. He pushed the speaker button.

"I'm fine. You don't need to keep checking up on me." He rolled his eyes at Maddy's musical laugh. God he loved that woman. She could switch his moods on a dime.

"Glad to hear it. And I'm still going to check up on you, the same as you'd do for me."

He grinned. "Fair enough." Pausing, he shifted energies. Something had changed. He heard it in her tone of voice. "What's wrong?"

Whatever it was involved The Haven. He scanned the markers Maddy had placed. All was normal.

"We think we finally understand some of what's going on, but we don't know how to proceed." Maddy explained how Doris played into the scenario, her relationship with the individuals and her mental state.

We? Oh, Drew was with her. Stefan frowned. "Her mental state makes sense if she's not protecting herself during her 'healing' sessions. We all know many people in psych wards are actually strong psychics that never learned control. What do you want me to do?"

"Drew doesn't have any way to prove what's happening. He's going to talk to his captain in the morning. Doris will have to undergo mental assessment. They will require legal advice as to how to proceed. The protective markers are still intact in

John's aura. He appears fine. I've also placed markers on the edges of the bubble and Felicia's bed," she confessed.

She would. Stefan smiled. "That's unnecessary but understandable."

The smile in her voice made his widen. "I know, but she's a child." Her voice became brisk. "What do you think about Doris?"

Stefan finally spoke, slowly, carefully, as if working through a problem. "We know people accidentally bring away pieces of another person's energy with them for many reasons. Over time, Doris would have started disassociating with her reality and splintering off and connecting with these other people – even if they were dead. But…"

"But? Where are you going with all of this?"

Stefan rubbed his temple, only to stare at the smeared splotch of yellow on his fingers. Shit. Shaking his head, he returned to the conversation. "I'm not sure I'm convinced that in her condition she's strong enough to do everything that's been going on there."

"Energy work doesn't require physical strength…" she reminded him.

"No, but it does require some mental strength."

"True. And if she's shown this level of deterioration, then she might not be capable of such focus?" So how could she be stripping these people of their life force now? The answer was she shouldn't be able to. So if she wasn't, then who was?

"Unless one of her realities is strong enough to dominate – then we're dealing with a different person altogether, and that individual might be very capable."

"Exactly." With a heavy sigh, Maddy said, "I'm not sure what to do overnight. We need to keep her locked down, maybe sedated so she can't hurt anyone. Tomorrow, decisions can be made." Her voice thinned. "I really don't want to alert her. We won't know what to do until we know what our options are."

Stefan frowned. He could help. This painting wasn't going anywhere tonight. An emotional mess of bright oranges and yellows sat on the large square canvas. He'd come back to it. Besides, he wouldn't mind looking at this Doris person. See if she'd been the one who'd drained him so quickly. Or connect to another someone who did. "I'll keep an eye on them. I'm doing energy work myself this evening. I'll put in markers and check for any movement, while you *sleep*." Stefan chuckled at Maddy's gasp on the other end.

"Thanks," she said, her voice calm and steady. "Do the same for John, please, just in case. I need to know she's not going to be able to do any more damage tonight."

Snatching up a rag, Stefan tossed his paintbrush and cleaned his hands. "I'll keep an eye on her. If it's Doris, I might know when I check out her energy."

Hesitation tinged her voice. "You won't do anything foolish?"

Stefan groaned. "No. I won't. Everything will be fine. Go home, relax and for once – get some rest."

"Thanks," she said dryly.

His voice dropped the teasing tone, becoming distant and cool. "This isn't over, Maddy. All hell is going to break loose soon."

"What? Stefan, what did you say?"

Silence.

"Stefan?" she added sharply. "Are you there?"

Blinking hard, Stefan realized he'd drifted off somewhere. He cleared his throat. "I'm here. Sorry about that."

"Damn it Stefan…you did it again. You warned that things are going to get worse but gave no details."

He chuckled. "You know I have no control over that. If I get more information, I'll pass it on. In the meantime, say hello to Drew and tell him if he hurts you, he'll have me to deal with."

She laughed lightly. "I'm so not going to tell him that."

"Actually, I heard just fine," Drew spoke into the phone. "Hurting Maddy is not in my plans, Stefan. No worries there."

"Forewarned and all that." Stefan hung up, leaving Maddy gasping. Stefan shut off his phone and headed to his living room. He couldn't wait to see this woman.

Ten minutes later, he settled comfortably in his chair, and slipped free of his body. Stretching at the wonderful sense of freedom, he thought himself to The Haven. According to Maddy, this woman was a floor below hers, in bed 232. He found himself at her bedside instantly.

And stopped. Pink scalp showing through thinning hair, her skin translucent with age, she slept, the covers pulled tightly up to her chin.

This is the person who'd caused such havoc upstairs? He frowned. Surely not. Searching for her cord, he found her spirit inside her body, also resting. Not walking the ethers as he'd expected. Nothing about this scenario made sense. Still, asleep was good for him. He set a protective marker that would alert him if she left her space. There was no way she'd get out without him knowing.

Casting a final glance back at the old, frail-looking woman in the bed, he shook his head and left.

Surely not.

* * *

Maddy protested the highhandedness of the males in her life, but accepted Drew's lead as he placed his hands on her shoulders and nudged her forward to the stairwell.

She stumbled in the hallway. "Okay, maybe I am tired."

"You need food and rest. Believe me, stress is more exhausting than anything else."

The stairwell was deserted as always. Maddy yawned. "Sounds good. Even better, a pepperoni pizza dripping with double cheese…but in a minute. I'm not going to rest until I check on your aunt's state myself."

Surprise lit his face. He followed willingly enough though, keeping a warm supportive hand on her back as they walked. She loved that protectiveness in him. The caring. That innate strength.

At the door to the landing he stepped forward and held it open. "Are you sure you're up for this?"

Striding through, her back straighter than it had been coming down the stairs, she nodded. "I won't sleep if I don't. Stefan will keep an eye on her, but if I can see her energy, scan her system, it will ease my mind."

By focusing on her destination, Maddy hoped to keep the fatigue at bay long enough to reach Doris's bedside. Drew called out, "Aunt Doris." He strolled closer. Doris was curled up in a ball, sleeping soundly.

Maddy stood at the end of the bed. It was so hard to see this tiny aged woman as a killer. That she was close enough in appearance to the woman she recalled seeing in the hallway outside Eric's ward only confirmed her suspicions and underlined her dismay.

Drew stood beside her.

There was no sign of the killer in her energy that lay close to her body, shimmering as in a deep sleep. Her cord was snuggled up peacefully inside her aura. She wasn't walking the ethers. She slept like a normal person.

Wrapping an arm around Maddy's shoulders, Drew tugged her closer. "Well?"

Maddy closed her eyes briefly. "She's calm, quiet. And she so doesn't look like a killer. Nor does her energy."

He squeezed her shoulders in a quick hug. "You're telling me." He dropped a lingering kiss on her temple, before dropping his arm to turn her toward him. He searched her eyes. "Is it safe to leave? Are you ready to leave this here and go home to get some rest?"

She rubbed her eyes then glanced up at him with a quick smile. Warmth lit her gaze. "With the bubble strengthened, and Stefan looking after John and Doris, yes, it's safe. It's time to go home to that pizza." Her gaze deepened. "I have to admit to being very hungry."

Drew raised one brow at her. A hint of heat warming his gaze. "No problem," he whispered softly. "Shall I order it now, so it's there for us when we get to your place?"

"What, you have a pizza place on speed dial?" Maddy led the way to the elevators, their hands entwined.

Drew lifted her hand to press a kiss to the back of her wrist. "Of course. I'm a single male and a cop to boot. Pizza is a major food group."

She giggled. "Right, except don't forget, I'm a doctor, and I know what's good for you."

There was a pregnant pause.

Maddy caught his hesitation as she entered the elevator. She turned to face him, instantly caught by the possessive look in his eye. The air becoming still and hot. Her gaze caught. Her pulse raced. Her mind stalled at the look in his eyes.

Electricity flashed.

"I'm counting on that, Doctor... That you really do know what's good for me," he murmured, his voice deep and dark, "because I have high hopes of getting it."

Maddy gazed into Drew's eyes – they'd gone dark with emotion. Heat pooled in her lower belly, her breasts tingling in response. Her breath caught in her throat as heat arced between them.

Drew's jaw firmed and his cheeks hollowed out. "I suggest we go straight home."

Swallowing hard, Maddy didn't dare try for words. She just nodded.

The elevator dinged at the correct floor, opening its cage doors.

Maddy pulled herself together, threw off her lethargy and forced her gaze away from the promise in his. She didn't know how long it would take to get home, only that it would be too long. She shuddered and headed for the exit.

"My truck's over here."

Mutely, she fell into step beside him. Her entire being pulsed with tension. Christ, she couldn't believe how badly she wanted him. Here. Now.

Looking around the interior of his truck, she reached for control. She so didn't want to have their first time together as a mad grapple in the front seat like sex-starved teenagers.

The drive seemed interminable, yet probably lasted less than five minutes. Drew threw the vehicle into park and unlocked the doors. Maddy, still silent, gripped by a fever she'd never experienced before, exited the truck and ran to her front door.

Drew stayed close behind.

"Christ," she whispered as she pounded on the button to call the elevator.

"Here. Let's take this one," Drew said beside her. The doors opened and both bolted inside, careful not to touch.

Maddy shuddered. Drew held out a hand. She took a step back. "No, don't," she whispered. "Not here."

His jaw clenched and he closed his eyes briefly, his outstretched hand dropping to his side, closing into a tight fist.

If he touched her, she'd be lost. Here in an elevator, with her apartment only seconds away. This wasn't the time for that kind of sex. She wanted to make it home. She needed this heat – scorching, driving flames to spread throughout her body, setting fire to her nerve endings.

The elevator was taking too long.

She whimpered.

Drew sucked in his breath, tension radiating from his body. He whispered, like a prayer, "Almost there."

The elevator dinged and opened its doors.

They exploded from the interior and sped past the two doors to her apartment. Maddy fumbled for her keys, swearing under her breath as the lock refused to cooperate. Finally, she pushed the door open.

Drew gave her a gentle shove inside, following her in and slamming the door behind them. Locked it.

They both stopped to look at the other.

Drew opened his arms.

Maddy raced into them.

Their mouths met in a ravenous kiss that provided as much relief as promise. She snuggled up tight and close, molding herself to the hard ridge between them. Maddy moaned again.

"Shhh." Drew took a deep breath and pulled back slightly, dropping his forehead against hers. "Take it easy. We have all night."

A broken laugh escaped, despite her best efforts. "Doesn't feel like it," she whispered. "It feels like it has to be now or I'm going to die."

A groan wrenched from deep in his chest, his gaze a gentle caress. "Me, too. Let's go to your bedroom."

Maddy blinked, and then glanced around, realizing they were jammed against the front closet. "Oh my God." Desperately trying to collect her thoughts, she said, "I can't believe this. I'm never like this."

"Oh?" The light in his eyes deepened and he bent his head once more.

Maddy evaded his touch. "Beat you there," she called behind her, leaving Drew standing startled in the hallway...but not for long. She'd barely reached her doorway when strong arms slid around her from behind, scooping her into his arms and moving forward in the same motion.

She shrieked and laughed as he tossed her onto her huge bed with such force the mound of comforter poofed up around her. He dropped on top of her.

Her laughter died as flames ignited inside. She kicked off her high heels, wrapped her silk-stockinged legs around his hips and levered tight against him.

Perfect.

His rigid penis rested against her pelvis.

She moaned.

He groaned.

She rocked her hips experimentally.

"Witch," he gasped against her lips as shudders wracked the long length of him. Frantic, he reared back and grabbed her shirt, tugging it up and over her head. Her arms were pulled up and back with the clothing when he stopped.

"What? What's wrong," she gasped, finally popping her head free.

Drew stared down at her, lust in every line of his face, his eyes filled with desire.

Maddy followed his gaze and smiled.

She arched her back, and winked at him. "Like that, do you?"

He flicked his gaze up to hers in disbelief before dropping back down again. "Christ, you are something else, you know that? There's got to be a law against that."

She giggled. "I guess that means you don't like it."

"I love it," he said reverently, "but what is it?"

"A bustier." And one of her favorites, with its black fishnet lacings across the front red lace panels that barely covered her ample breasts.

"Christ."

"I can take it off if you'd prefer," she whispered.

He reared back. "No! Never take it off. Good God." As if unable to contain himself, he bent over and traced the skin between the laces, tasting, teasing and touching.

Maddy cried out as pleasure screamed across her skin. Her nipples pressed hard against the fabric, almost popping free as she arched her back higher, begging and pleading for more. Drew slid his tongue across the lace edge of the bra and shuddered when he found the hardened points peeking out. Using his chin to drag the material lower, he took her left nipple into his mouth and sucked hard.

"Drew," she cried, her pelvis grinding up against him as tiny explosions began deep inside.

"Yes, let go. Fly, I'll be here when you come down."

Shudders rippled across her skin. She closed her eyes, arching higher.

"Let go," he whispered again, taking the right nipple deep inside his mouth and sucking hard.

Maddy cried out as the orgasm slammed through her.

Everything ceased to exist but this moment, this man and, oh God, that mouth. Only he didn't let her rest. He moved up to ravage her mouth, his own need rising to a frenzy.

"Yes," she whispered against his lips. "Oh, yes." Her fingers worked on his shirt buttons, popping the last one as she ripped it open, sliding the material partway down his arms. Taut muscles flexed and rippled under her questing hands as she found his belt buckle, loosening it before attacking the button on his pants.

"Shit." Drew shrugged out of his shirt. With an extraordinary effort, he rolled to the side. He brushed her hands away and stripped off his pants and underwear, even snagged his socks in the process. Within seconds, he peeled her skirt down and came to another sudden halt.

"Christ, woman, you're going to kill me."

He stroked her leg from one slim foot to the top of her thigh where the stockings ended. Her underwear? Only a tiny thong nestled at the top with thin ribbons rising high on her hips. He shuddered, dropped his head, and kissed her in the center of the thong.

Maddy cried out as her need for him once again picked up, threatening to consume her. She reached to slide her thong off, but he stopped her.

"I want you with me this time," she pleaded.

"Oh, I will be." He dropped one more kiss to the heart on the surface of the material and slid a finger under the edge, to stroke the plump moist skin underneath.

She moaned, twisting against him, crying when he removed his hand to slide the material off. Maddy surged up. She couldn't wait. She needed him now. She grabbed his head and tugged his mouth to hers, devouring his lips, nibbling at them, and then kissing them better.

Lowering himself until he rested over her, he held his weight on his forearms, his erection gently nudging against her. Maddy wrapped her legs around him, rubbing against him.

Drew plunged downward until he'd seated himself deep in her center. He dropped his head against her temple and swore.

She smoothed her hands down his back to the hollow at the base of his spine and teased the indent at the top of his muscled cheeks. Tremors rippled down her body. God, she needed this. She needed him.

He lifted his head, locked his gaze with hers and started to move. His hips thrust deeper and deeper. He slowed once, to reach under her backside to open her more, then plunged repeatedly. Increasing the tempo to a frenzied pace, Drew drove them back to the breaking point. Taking her mouth in a ravishing kiss, he withdrew almost all the way.

She cried out in protest.

Drew plunged deep, crushing his hips against hers.

Once again, Maddy's cries soared free as Drew sent her flying off the chasm. With a loud groan, he followed. Collapsing, he shifted his weight to his forearms again and rested his forehead against hers until his breath calmed. Shifting gently, he fell to the side and pulled her close.

Still trembling, Maddy curled into his arms and closed her eyes. With the rapid beat of his heart pounding under her ear, she smiled. Exhausted and exultant, she let the night take her under and she slept.

FRIDAY

When Maddy opened her eyes the next morning, early rays of sunshine were already peeking through her curtains. She lay there for a long moment, enjoying the sensation of being held as if she were the most precious thing in the world.

"I wondered when you'd wake up." Tucked behind her, Drew's warm breath bathed the side of her face. "I wasn't sure what time you needed to go to work."

From the circle of his arms, she saw the clock register seven in the morning. "This is fine." She murmured. "This is better than fine. This is wonderful."

He cuddled her closer. Maddy snuggled in, loving the full naked-body embrace. She closed her eyes for a brief second.

"Maddy?" Her shoulders were being gently shaken.

She moaned, and tried to burrow deeper into the blankets.

"Come on, sweetheart. We fell back asleep. It's 8:30 am. Time to get moving."

Her eyes blinked open and she sat upright in shock. "What?" She stared at the clock. "Okay, now I'm late."

She threw back the covers and stood, wincing at the unaccustomed achiness. She'd been well loved last night. After making love for the first time, they'd followed with a second, gentler session that had ended up with the rest of her clothing taken off. After that, they decided other hungers needed to be appeased and they'd ordered pizza. That and a bottle of wine had led to yet another session of wild lovemaking lasting well into the night. No wonder they'd slept in.

Ten minutes later, showered and wrapped in a towel, she stood in front of her bedroom closet.

Drew, bare-chested with his shirt in his hand, walked over to her. He dropped a kiss on her temple. "Are you okay?" Warm, loving concern followed his gaze from her to the tossed room.

She smiled. "Yes. I'm more than okay, but I do have to get moving." Bending down, she collected the lingerie and one stocking on the floor at her feet, and dropped them in the hamper.

"I hope I didn't destroy those last night."

She turned with a silk stocking draped across her arm. "What, these?" She added the stocking to the rest of the items. "They are hardy. Besides," she said with a wicked grin, "I have more."

"Be still my beating heart."

She smirked. She placed one hand on either side of his face and kissed him, long, lovingly and with enough heat to send her pulse skyrocketing. Pulling back, she stared at his flushed skin and the glazed look in his eyes. "Now it's a good morning."

He shuddered and closed his eyes. "That was not fair."

Her laughter filled the room as she dressed quickly, heat still pulsing through her veins. "Tonight, I'll make it up to you."

"Oh, God."

Slipping into navy slacks, she asked, "Did you make coffee?"

"Couldn't find any to make," he replied. He shrugged into his shirt and started to do up the buttons, pausing to study the spot where the last one should have been.

"Do you have time to stop and pick up something on the way?" he said, tucking his shirt in.

She checked the clock and made a face. "No, I'll go straight in and make coffee at my office."

"Great, that gets you coffee. What about breakfast?"

With a cheeky grin, she ran to the kitchen, where she grabbed her purse and keys. She opened the breadbox. "Good thing I remembered these blueberry muffins from Nancy. You take two and I'll take two." She bagged them quickly and handed him his.

"I'm going to see my uncle, so I'll drive you there."

"Perfect, thanks."

At The Haven, he parked in 'visitor parking' and walked in together. While they waited for the elevator, Drew cocked an eyebrow at her. "No sign of the wild woman running up the stairs today?"

She laughed, stepping into the elevator in front of him. Thankfully, they were alone. She punched the buttons for her floor. "No. Wild woman was in full swing last night. She's going to rest up today." A smile played at the corner of her lips.

He eyed her intently. "Rest up for what?"

Just as the doors were about to open, she reached over, kissed him on the corner of the lips and whispered into his ear, "For tonight!"

And walked out of the elevator and into her world.

***

Dr. Lenning shifted slowly into a sitting position in his bed and looked around. He'd been in more than his fair share of hospitals, but he didn't recognize this room. Where was he?

A frown settled between his brows as he stared at the white curtains and standard issue sheets. He smoothed the material between his fingers and made a face. Maddy's floor had much nicer bedding, not to mention the surroundings. This was regular hospital issue.

"Hey, nice to see you awake." A strange nurse walked into his cubicle and pulled the curtains around his bed. She looked down at him, automatically reaching for the blood pressure cuff hanging on the side.

"How long have I been asleep?" he asked, settling back against his pillows. "What happened?"

"You had a heart attack. You're in the hospital side of The Haven." She gave him a bright professional smile that told him nothing. Typical.

"Where's Dr. Maddy?"

The nurse pursed her lips. "She's on her floor. I thought Dr. Cunningham was your physician?"

"I suppose he is." He turned away, staring at the rolling curtain at his side. So it was over. His one and only chance to save his life through Dr. Maddy was gone. The feelings of lost opportunity and sadness inside almost overwhelmed him. He was going to die soon. He'd played the last trump card and now he was out of options. Dr. Maddy hadn't wanted him there. He'd paid to get there in the first place and now, God – if there were a God – was punishing him. Whether it was because of his errant attraction or his attempt to hurt one of His angels, it no longer mattered. The hope of survival that had dangled in front of him these long months had been snatched away, leaving him bereft, lost and alone.

To his horror, tears heated the corners of his eyes. He squeezed them shut, not wanting the nurse to see. He was the doctor; he shouldn't ever be in this position. What was that saying? *Physician, heal thyself?* Well, he'd tried, and look where he was now.

He'd wagered everything on being saved by the one woman he'd tried to destroy – and he'd lost.

"How's the pain level?" A note of concern had entered the nurse's voice.

Shit. She was still there. "It's not too bad. I'm just tired."

"Then rest. You'll be feeling better in no time." With a motherly pat on his shoulder that made his skin crawl with disgust, she left. No nurse would have dared do that to him before.

He hadn't been a broken-down, useless man when he practiced medicine. He'd been a commander at the leading edge of technology. Now he was a lump for nurses to practice their skills with thermometers and blood pressure cuffs.

God, how the mighty had fallen.

Dr. Cunningham came around the still-closed curtains, his tablet in his hand. Adam waited while the doctor tapped away on his tablet. Times had certainly changed in the medical world. He loved technology, and didn't miss paper files or charts, either. Computers and tablets made a doctor's life so much easier.

"So, how's the patient this morning?" He peered over at Adam, his gaze assessing and clear.

"Waiting to die, like yesterday and the day before."

"Well, I don't know where you thought you were yesterday; however, out cold here in ICU is where I found you – not that you're going to stay here. You've stabilized and if this continues overnight, we'll make arrangements to transfer you back."

Back? Adam opened his eyes and cleared his throat, almost afraid to ask the burning question. "Am I going back to Maddy's floor?"

"I believe so, although we are having some issues with the new wing, so that may take another day or two. If that's the case, we'll put you on a different floor until your room is ready."

Dr. Cunningham starting to write down something on the tablet while Adam watched.

He was afraid to hope, afraid to believe. Desperation and fear warred together. In that moment, he saw the scales of justice as they balanced or didn't balance, regarding his life. He'd been a good doctor, a loyal partner, a fair man. Only he'd been hell on wheels to his colleagues. He'd been toughest on Dr. Maddy.

If he was clearing his chest, then he needed to come clean and tell Maddy the truth. Why he'd done what he done and how he'd changed. He needed to apologize, to ask her forgiveness and ask for her help. He'd been given a second chance and he'd do his damnedest to make the most of it.

Reaching out a shaky hand, he motioned to Dr. Cunningham just as a one of the many nurses came in to speak with him. Adam waited until they were finished. Dr. Cunningham walking closer. "What can I do for you, Adam?"

"Please tell Dr. Maddy that I need to speak with her. I have something I need to tell her. Something urgent."

The nurse bustled around getting the blood pressure cuff ready. Adam shooed her away. He might die today and that would be a shame. Maddy needed to hear what he had to say. "Just a minute – this is important."

She snagged the cuff around his arm regardless and pumped it up. Adam ignored her like she ignored him.

Dr. Cunningham raised his eyebrow. "Sure, no problem. I'll call her down in a minute."

Adam relaxed. Just another few minutes and she'd come to him. "Thank you. Just another moment, then I can tell her," he whispered to himself.

Then he could bare his soul.

And find his salvation.

Maddy leaned back in her high-backed office chair and sighed blissfully. At least her wonderful night had given her the energy to tackle anything. Good thing, as her day had been full of minor emergencies and it was only half over. Stefan had checked in to say both Doris and John had peacefully slept the night away in their own beds.

She'd heard nothing from Drew or John all morning, and Nancy had delivered a message that Dr. Lenning wanted to speak with her *now*. Nancy hadn't said it quite that way, but Maddy had gotten the gist of it.

Checking her watch, she considered when to fit in five more minutes. Blowing out a gust of breath, she decided there was no time like the present. Besides, going for a walk would help clear her head.

Maddy stood, straightened her tunic and ran down the stairs. She needed the exercise, only one floor was hardly worth the trouble. Still, the joy she felt at the endorphins rushing through her system told her just how bad her stress levels had been lately.

At the double doors, she put on her polished face, walked into the second-floor ward that led to the attached hospital unit. At the front desk, she asked for directions to Dr. Lenning's location. She frowned as she followed the corridor to a ward. She'd expected him to have a private room, not that there was any guarantee one was available. The hospital was as busy and as overcrowded as the rest of The Haven. Chances are Dr. Lenning was lucky to have any bed.

The ward was busy with nurses and visitors. The privacy curtains were pulled closed around Dr. Lenning's bed.

Standing at the outside edge, she called out, "Dr. Lenning, may I come in?"

No answer. Maddy frowned. Perhaps he'd gone back to sleep. She walked toward his bed, catching a glimpse of the window around the corner. At least he'd be able to see outside. Wards were notorious for lack of privacy and freshness.

There was still no sound. A nurse walked toward her, pushing a medication cart and holding a medication cup in the other. Maddy stepped forward to open the curtain for her. The nurse said, "Thanks, Dr. Maddy. We don't get to see you here—" Complete horror washed over her face and she screamed.

Maddy jumped forward. Dr. Lenning lay on his back, blood pouring from a knife stuck high on his chest.

"Shit."

Drew pulled into the parking lot of The Haven. After everything that had happened, he sure as hell hadn't seen this one coming. Maddy had been calm when he'd answered the call and damn near hysterical by the end. His stomach knotted. If she'd been minutes earlier, she might have been the one impaled with a fucking blade.

His hands sweated at the thought. Showing his badge, he swept through the front doors. It was easy to follow the chaos to the group of uniforms clustered outside one room. Noting the detective off to one side, he held up his own badge and motioned toward Maddy. At the detective's nod, Drew walked toward her.

Maddy sat in the hallway on a straight-backed chair, looking like a wilted celery stalk. Her face, pale, shocked. Her eyes round and glistening. His heart went out to her. "Hey, how are you holding up?"

"I've been better." Her smile wobbled. He pulled her into his arms for a comforting hug. He wasn't sure who needed the hug the most. His heart was still pounding, even though he saw she was safe.

"I'm taking you upstairs, then I have to speak with the detectives." He squeezed her gently, ending with a lingering kiss. "I don't want whoever did this to wonder if you'd had an opportunity to speak with Dr. Lenning before he went unconscious."

She shivered. "Nice thought."

Nancy waited for them at the nurses' center. "Maddy, is it true what they're saying? That Dr. Lenning was attacked?"

"Yes, he's in surgery right now. Nancy, who called you to pass on the message?"

"My friend Susie. I've known her for a while. She said Dr. Lenning had asked his doctor to send for you, but she figured he'd be too busy so she contacted me." Nancy shrugged. "She was trying to save the doctor another task and Dr. Lenning had said it was urgent."

"She didn't know what this was about?" Drew stepped in.

With a quick shake of her head, Nancy said, "She didn't say and I didn't ask."

"I'll check with her." Drew smiled, placing a hand in the small of Maddy's back and nudging her toward her office. "Maddy is going to be in her office for a while, keeping a low profile while the police try to sort out this mess."

"Good. I'm glad they're here. The floor's on lockdown, so we'll be fine up here."

Drew nodded. "Then let me out and I'll go see what I can find."

Nancy walked him to the stairwell and unlocked it.

"Make sure you lock up tight," he said.

"We will. You won't be able to get back in without someone's help. And with this mess going on, you'll only be able to go out on the first floor."

The door shut and was locked as he watched. The alarm was reset before he turned to go down the steps to what waited for him there.

***

Gerard hung up the phone, still in shock. "Dr. Lenning has been stabbed while in ICU. Unbelievable." He repeated it several times aloud, not sure when it would register. The police were all over The Haven, searching for the suspect and questioning the staff, patients and visitors. *God, what a PR mess.* This was a busy place. Surely, someone had seen something. The attacker had to be nuts. There's no way they'd get away with this.

He'd needed to call the Board. Containment was a priority.

A horrible suspicion preyed on his mind. He knew one person who was crazy. Could she have done this? No, not possible. His mother was neither mentally nor physically capable.

It made him think though. He'd hidden for so long. If there were even the slightest possibility that she was a danger to anyone – well, the new Gerard wanted to make sure he told someone so they could decide if she was dangerous or not.

Drew was the most likely person. Although finding out they were family would be a shock. Not that he thought of either John or Drew in that light. He'd removed himself as far from that family line as he could. He knew it was to time to clear the air and start fresh, without secrets.

Sandra walked into his office. "Gerard, did I hear correctly? Adam was attacked in his hospital room?"

"Stabbed in bed."

Her hands automatically covered her mouth in shock. "Oh no! That's unbelievable. Is he going to be all right?"

Gerard stood up. "He's in surgery now." He walked to the window then turned back to face her. "I have to go speak with the detective downstairs. I should have done something about this a long time ago."

She stared at him. "About what?"

"I don't have time to go into it now. I want you to stay here. Lock yourself in after I leave. I'll call when this is over."

He walked back to his desk, picked up the phone and punched in the numbers. "Hey, are you downstairs? Good, I need to speak with you. I'll be there in five minutes."

Gerard hung up. "I'll be back as soon as I can."

"You can explain afterwards. Please be careful."

"I will." A man had to stop running sometime. He walked out to face his past.

Maddy waited until Nancy completed the lockdown procedure. She couldn't get her mind wrapped around the attack on Adam. She desperately wanted to believe he'd survive. The knife had been high, but…

"All I can think about is what Dr. Lenning might have wanted to tell me."

"And there's no answer to that question for the moment. That's why you need to stay busy. Get at that paperwork on your desk. I'll head back to the nurses' station, get some of my work done, and we'll see how we're both doing in an hour or so." Nancy smiled at Maddy as she stood up. "This will work out; you'll see."

"I hope so." Maddy watched the door shut behind her friend. She hoped the police were efficient. That type of energy swirling around down there would be destructive if it made its way up here. As it was, she was certainly going to need Stefan's help to restore the balance once this was over.

Ignoring the confusion in her mind, she reached for the stack of work. An hour later, she'd worked her way through a good half of it. The stack continued to dwindle until she reached the last piece of paper. It was information that needed to be added to Jansen's file. She brought up the file on her computer. Sadness swept through her. This wasn't an easy thing to do on a day like this one. At least she wouldn't have Dr. Lenning's file to deal with. That would be Dr. Cunningham's job.

Maddy sifted through every bit of information there was. She'd had Jansen as a patient for over a year and the information was vast. Starting at the back, and slowly moving forward she read the notations, went over lab results and charts, wondering if she'd missed something.

It took an hour before she came to the night of his death. In a somber mood, Maddy realized guilt still plagued her, even though she had no idea what else she could have done.

A piece of something out of place niggled the back of her mind. Something didn't jibe. What? She wandered through the pages, looking to confirm a simple piece of information. There. In one conversation, she'd noted that Jansen had admitted to having had several affairs and quietly requested tests for STD because he hadn't wanted his wife to know. The tests had proved negative.

Except he'd had affairs. He'd been particularly worried because an old flame was on another floor and she hadn't been concerned about keeping her affairs private. Had Doris and Jansen been involved at one point? When sexual intercourse took place, energy, as well as body fluids, was exchanged. It would have been easy enough for her to recognize that energy and follow the pathway upstairs to Jansen. And with his bed shifted due to the renovations, Doris might well have had something to do with Jansen's death.

However, she wasn't getting out of her bed to walk the hallways and stab people, certainly not without someone noticing. So, just because Dr. Lenning had been on the same floor as Doris's room when he was stabbed, that didn't mean his attack had anything to do with her.

Adam had made plenty of enemies on his own over the years. She frowned. However, if he died, that did free up another bed on her floor. According to Drew and Gerard, the competition for beds could lead some people to commit murder, which meant everyone in The Haven was suspect. How many patients had applied for a transfer, and how many staff members knew someone who had put in an application form?

That included Doris again. She apparently wanted the transfer very badly. If she weren't capable of doing something like that herself, did she have someone who'd have done this for her?

Either the two crimes weren't connected and there were two perpetrators, or they were connected and Doris had someone helping her.

Yet, nothing explained why Dr. Lenning had been attacked. There'd been no attempt to suck his life force. That knife stabbed into his chest had panic written all over it.

So, why him?

How could she find out? She picked up her cell phone and called one of the nurses she knew well downstairs. "Jenny, this is Dr. Maddy. I have an unusual question. Your patient Doris – does she ever talk about her past relationships?"

Jenny laughed. "Are you kidding? I think it's those memories that are keeping her alive, maybe even healing her. She's something, that one. Now, of course, she's a bit touched in her head, so I wouldn't be listening to everything she said. Still, she apparently has a taste for men in uniform. You know, doctors, police officers, and firefighters. Men like that."

Maddy frowned. Jansen had been a shipyard worker.

"Oh, and that sailor man, apparently he'd been a hot number, too."

"She never mentioned any names, did she?"

"Well, a lot depended on her mental state on any given day. I can tell you that she's been passing around quite freely that there are several of her old flames here in the hospital with her right now."

"Really? That might be a lot of people, considering the population of The Haven."

"True enough. I can't remember any other names, though."

Maddy smiled. "Right, thanks. You've been a big help." Maddy intended to ring off, but remembered something else at the last minute. "Are the police still crawling all around the place?"

"The hallways are blue with them."

Maddy rang off and quickly called Drew. "I'm in the process of closing Jansen Svaar's file and it started me thinking. I think Doris might have been one of Jansen's lovers. And now I'm wondering if Dr. Lenning might have been one as well."

"Not likely. Adam is gay. He had a thirty-year relationship until his partner passed away five years ago. Besides, she's not up to getting out of her bed and stabbing Adam. She's just not capable of that."

Maddy blinked. *Adam was gay?* She shrugged. "So maybe not." She paused. "Not without help anyway," Maddy added as an afterthought.

"Help? As in a partner?" Drew's voice took on a brisk tone. "Let me check a couple things and call you back."

The phone went dead.

Her door opened. She looked up. "Hey, stranger. Good to see you."

FRIDAY EVENING

Drew put away his cell phone. He'd considered the concept of a partner, only hadn't been able to put one in the right place to make sense. Nothing about this case made sense.

"Damn it." Now he had to contend with Gerard. He spotted him weaving through the crowded hallway. Once Gerard saw Drew, his gaze locked on him as he made his way over.

As he approached, Drew studied him for family features. Was this man part of his family? Gerard strode determinedly forward…on a mission, a little bit like himself.

"Drew, thanks for waiting." Gerard came to a stop, his eyes a little wild and his hair presenting the opposite of his usual CEO-slick appearance.

"No problem. What did you want to talk about?" Drew crossed his arms and leaned against the wall, waiting. He'd learned a long time ago to make others speak first. Gerard took a deep breath, opened his mouth as if to speak, and then closed it again.

"I'm sorry. This is a little hard."

Drew pursed his lips. "Go ahead when you're ready."

Gerard stared past his shoulder, his eyes unfocused as if looking inward. "Well. It's just…I mean…I don't know if this is relevant or not."

"You let me decide that."

Gerard slipped his hands into his pants pocket and leaned against the wall facing Drew. "The thing is, my mom is a patient here on the second floor, and she's a little touched in the head."

"Right, my Aunt Doris."

Astonishment swept across Gerard's face. "Oh, you know already?"

Drew snorted. "I know she's your mother and my Uncle John's stepsister, making us cousins of a sort, and that there's a possibility that my uncle might even be your father." Drew watched as the information filtered through Gerard's mind.

Gerard's mouth opened. No sound came out.

"What?"

Interesting. Drew grinned. "Oh, you didn't know that part? How typical of Uncle John."

Raising his brows, Gerard calmly said, "As far as I knew, my dad was Roger Lionel, and he died over thirty years ago."

"And that may be."

Drew tossed off the information as if it were of no importance.

"I didn't know my real father, so another unknown father hardly makes any difference." Gerard stared off in the distance before continuing. "My childhood was tough. I almost died when I was nine or ten, and I spent months, even years, getting back to normal health. The thing is, back then...." He took a deep breath. "Back then, my mother kept saying some pretty creepy stuff."

Gerard searched the area to make sure no one was listening. He bent his head closer. "She kept saying that she'd sacrifice anyone and everyone if it meant I'd live."

Drew straightened, disappointed. "That's not uncommon when a parent is faced with a dying child."

"True. She used to rock back and forth, sitting cross-legged at the end of my bed and whisper stuff like that all the time. She tried everything from healers to meditation to all different kinds of weird New Age stuff. At first, I was too sick to care, but as I improved, I realized the more I healed, the worse she seemed to get. The only way I could cope was to ignore her, block out everything she said. Some of it was beyond creepy." He shuddered once before appearing to get a grip on his emotions. He continued, "Since then, she's been in and out, stable and unstable. Certain medications seemed to help her stabilize for several years. Then they'd stop working and she'd deteriorate."

He slumped against the wall and stared at Drew glumly. "I'm not proud of it, but back then I didn't want anything to do with her and her freaky statements. One phrase in particular stuck in my mind. She kept repeating in this eerie monotone voice, 'Sissy had to go' and then Sissy, a school friend of mine, died along with those other five kids."

Drew stiffened. "Sissy? She actually said that name?"

Gerard's face shadowed with the memory. "Yes. Sissy used to come to the house for piano lessons twice a week. Then I heard Sissy had died. I tell you, it freaked me out. Hell, I don't even know if all these bits are just the twisted memories of the scared, sick kid I was back then." He rubbed a hand over his face.

"Six kids died within a few months. We knew them all. At the time, I couldn't believe she'd had anything to do with their deaths. I wouldn't believe. Then I couldn't get the possibility out of my mind. I went into foster care not long after I got out of the hospital. I was terrified I'd be next." Gerard stared moodily down the hallway. "Then Dr. Miko said there was something odd recently, about Jansen's death that sounded all too familiar. Unexplained bruises at the base of the spine." Gerard came to an abrupt stop, pain crinkling his features.

That made sense. Gerard was the CEO of The Haven, so it was likely he would be in touch with Dr. Miko over this. "Okay. As an adult looking back, can you see what, if anything, your mother might have had to do with those deaths?"

"I don't know that she had anything to do with them. Just little things she said at the time made me think she had. I don't even remember exactly what she said. But..." He stopped again. "She used to say that no one would know what she'd done. That the tiny mark told no tales and soon with a little more practice, she wouldn't even leave that." He rubbed the bridge of his nose. "I don't know if that makes any sense. It certainly didn't to me."

Comprehension hit Drew. He stared down the hallway, trying to work through the information. People were coming and going with purpose all around them. As unbelievable as it sounded, Gerard had just confirmed what he and Maddy had already worked out. He just couldn't get his mind wrapped around it. Was it possible, that Gerard's mother, his Aunt Doris, could have caused all this?

"I hate to think that she hurt others to save me." Gerard stared past Drew's head toward the other end of the hall. "I don't even understand what she might have done. But then, I didn't believe in Maddy's skills before either, and look at some of the things she's achieved."

"If your mother did this and saved you back then, why wouldn't she have healed herself before now?"

A puzzled frown settled on Gerard's face. "I'm not sure. Her new medication may have been a factor. She's been much more alert this last year."

"That makes sense. And you're right, I've noticed some improvement too." Drew shrugged. "It's not easy visiting with people who don't always recognize you." He pulled out his notebook. "Who is her doctor? How long has she been in his care?"

"Dr. Cunningham is now. He's helped her a lot."

Drew wrote the name down in his booklet. "Why did she change doctors?"

"Her old doctor died...about two years ago, I think."

Drew raised his eyebrows. Another death? "There're a lot of deaths strewn around in this mess."

"This one died naturally in his sleep."

A natural death in this mess? Not likely. "I'll look into it. What was his name?"

"Dr. Michaels."

"How old was he?"

"Somewhere in his early sixties, I think. He retired. She was moved to Dr. Cunningham's care and Dr. Michaels passed on a few months later, I believe." Gerard's face twisted, as if finally comprehending Drew's train of thought. "Oh, no. She wouldn't have had anything to do with that."

"Depending on her mental state now, we may never know the answer to that question." Drew leaned back against the wall, realizing his cousin had to be a good eight or nine years older than he was. "It's so hard to contemplate this stuff. It's like the *Twilight Zone* meets the *Ghost Whisperer*."

The two men stood in silence.

"Is there anyone close enough to her they'd help her do this stuff?" Drew had a hard time seeing his aunt as Gerard's mother, let alone a murderess. When Doris entered his own life in his late teen years, he'd had a hard time calling her aunt, to begin with. He'd only done it for her sake. Since his graduation they'd gone their own ways, touching base occasionally. It's only after his uncle had fallen so sick that Drew realized he was in danger of losing both of them and had tried to reconnect with her. It had been a little too late, considering her mental state.

Gerard shook his head. "I don't think so. She doesn't have many people in her life." He half-laughed, a dry bitterness to his tone. "That's not quite true." He fisted his hands on his hips. "She's had so many men that I didn't bother to keep track of them.

"Of course, Dr. Cunningham's been there most of my life. He's been the stable uncle in the background. It's one of the reasons I offered him the job here. Then there's John. He's been even more of a background shadow."

Drew narrowed his gaze on Gerard's face. Along with an awful lot of deaths, Dr. Cunningham's name kept coming up in the conversation. "Do you know how long Dr. Cunningham has been in *her* life?"

"Oh, easily decades. If you'd told me he was my father, I would have believed you in a heartbeat. He's been around forever."

"Would he know about what she might have done for you?"

"Probably. He's been into this New Age stuff for as long as I remember. They used to get into these weird conversations and I'd walk away. It was easier not to know. Of course, that's also what made him perfect for the Maddy's Floor Project."

Drew straightened slowly. That clinched it. Of course he was. He had to have some special qualifications or interests to be part of the project with Maddy. Drew wasn't sure he'd ever seen the man. "You know, I think I'd like to speak with Dr. Cunningham."

"He spoke to the police a while ago. He's probably gone home by now."

Drew started walking toward the police who were still talking to the staff. "Why did the police want to talk to Dr. Cunningham?"

Hurrying to catch up, Gerard said, "Procedure. He was the last one to see Dr. Lenning before the attack."

"He was Dr. Lenning's doctor?"

"Sure, that was Dr. Maddy's way of getting around having Adam on her floor. Talk to Cunningham. I doubt he has anything to hide."

Drew walked up to the first uniformed officer he saw. Pulling out his own badge, he asked the officer if Dr. Cunningham had been questioned.

"Briefly. He's gone upstairs to deal with an emergency."

"You aren't looking at him for this?"

"Him? No. He had every right to be there. Besides, why would he kill anyone that way? Easier to slip them an overdose or an air bubble, and no one would ever know."

Drew thanked him and stepped back out of the way. Dr. Cunningham wouldn't stab anyone, unless he didn't want anyone to suspect him. Turning back to Gerard, he muttered. "Let's go and speak with your mother." It was easier to call his aunt Gerard's mother – it helped him dissociate from his own relationship with her. The thought of Gerard being his cousin was still something he'd have to wrap his mind around.

Gerard led the way down one of the hallways on the left. Drew had never approached his aunt's room from this direction. It was a bright, happy area, although not anywhere near as nice as on Maddy's floor.

They stopped at the bed number 232. The curtains were closed, giving her some privacy. Drawing it back, the men stepped forward. Drew's lips twitched at the knickknacks his aunt had on the night table and hanging on the wall. The full-length mirror stood as it always had, by the side of her bed. His aunt loved that mirror. It had gone everywhere with her.

"Doris, it's Gerard. How are you?"

Doris beamed at them, her face full of rosy health...and vacant eyes.

"Hi. How nice of you to visit."

Drew studied her face. There were no signs of recognition at all. She didn't know Gerard. She didn't appear to recognize him, either.

"Aunt Doris?"

His aunt's face wrinkled in confusion, her gaze going from Gerard to Drew and back again.

Gerard sighed heavily. "I'm your son, Mom, and this is your nephew, Drew. We both visit you regularly."

She beamed at him. "Such nice boys." She reached out a hand to the side. "Have you met Sissy? She's a lovely lady, isn't she?" She leaned forward and whispered. "She's getting so much better here. It's not fair." Then Doris leaned back, shot her friend a smile and turned back to face them.

It took a moment to sink in.

Then Drew didn't believe what he was seeing.

Aunt Doris was speaking to the woman in the mirror.

She was speaking to her reflection.

Sissy was her reflection.

This was one of her bad days. She'd have recognized him for sure if it had been a good day. He'd heard her say Sissy a few times over these last months, only hadn't connected the name to the first dead girl in his cold case files. Who would? Even now, it didn't make any sense.

Drew changed course. "I'm going to find Dr. Cunningham. Maybe I'll have better luck there."

They wished her a good day and closed the curtain again. Walking away, Gerard said, "Sorry, sometimes she's fine and the next, well, she's Sissy. It's like a complete split personality. I never know what to expect."

The two men walked toward the stairwell. "I haven't seen her this bad in a while myself. I stopped in to visit several times this last week, but never managed to connect for one reason or another. Is she failing or has her medication been changed?"

"I'll come up with you and we can ask Paul. He'll be more comfortable speaking if I'm around." Gerard disarmed the doors to the stairs, arming them again once they were through, then repeated the process once they stood outside Maddy's floor. The main hallway had the overhead lights turned down as if it were sleep time for patients.

Gerard walked over to the light switch and flipped it back on. Nothing happened. He frowned.

"Now this is weird."

"Nothing weird about it. Something's wrong." Drew pulled his weapon. "There are no nurses at the station, and there's nothing but silence here." He scouted the long hallway and the open patient areas. His eyes adjusted to the nighttime light settings. The small lights along the hallway at knee height were still on.

"Gerard, what's around the corner?"

"There's a nurses' supply station, lunchroom, a conference room and several clinical rooms."

"So if there's a problem here and someone has taken over the floor, where would the staff be locked up?"

Gerard blinked. "Chances are in the lunchroom or the conference room. Depends on how many staff are still on. It's not that late, so there might be visitors on the floor too. With the lockdown in effect, no one is allowed to leave."

Walking stealthily down the hallway past the nurse's station, Drew peered around the corner. Empty. He frowned. With Gerard on his heels, he walked through the main areas. Patients were in their beds. No one appeared to be bothered. Televisions were playing, radios on – only there were no nurses, orderlies, or aides. All the staff on duty for this shift were missing.

Drew considered that. Maddy's office was at one end of the floor. His uncle was at the other. Undecided, he searched from one end to the other. Then he motioned in the direction of his uncle. "Let's try the new wing."

Closer to John's bed, he heard voices. He held up a hand to stop Gerard's forward movement. "Shh."

A muffled murmur.

He moved another couple of feet and slid along the side wall. He could almost make out the words.

"You didn't think I was going to walk away from all this, did you?" The deep masculine voice destroyed the hope in Drew's heart.

***

Her world had taken a left into chaos. Dr. Cunningham held that damn gun as capably as he held a surgeon's knife. There wasn't even a tremor to indicate nervousness. He'd walked into her office and had taken control of the floor. He'd forced her staff into her office and locked it, then with the gun at her back, he'd walked through the floor checking to make sure there was no one else.

Where the hell was Drew? And Stefan? She's sent him several messages mentally, but outside of an acknowledgement from him a few seconds ago, there'd been nothing. At least, she knew the cops would be alerted.

In the meantime, she had to deal with one of the worst betrayals possible. The other person, who'd invested so much time and effort into her healing project, was...a killer. It did explain so much though. Like why she'd never noticed any sense of 'alien' energy at work. It hadn't been a stranger. Paul Cunningham had been working here since her project had started. His energy belonged here.

Somehow, she needed to buy them all more time so Drew could come rescue them. And she needed John to continue to stay calm and quiet. Not to mention her other patients. Damn Paul, anyway. How dare he put these people in danger like this?

Maddy strove to keep her voice calm and neutral. "I don't suppose so. Still, it's not as if anyone would be able to find you if you disappeared. Not with what you know how to do."

"You would."

She stalled. Of course, she would, but he didn't need to know that. "Possibly. Still that doesn't mean I'd do anything about it. You know the patients and this project mean everything to me. I'd hardly do jeopardize them."

"You wouldn't be able to help yourself. You're a sanctimonious do-gooder."

She tried for a light laugh. "I won't be able to prove anything. Just walk away." She hoped she'd injected the right amount of reasonable eagerness. She was no actress, and she'd always been a terrible poker player.

"I plan on it. Just like I plan on getting younger – no lying around waiting to die for me." Dr. Cunningham laughed. "How's that for a goal?"

"Not bad, if you can do it." She winced. Doubting him wasn't the best way to keep him amiable.

"Oh, I can, and you know it. It took me years to figure out what Doris had done, and then years of befriending that whore to figure how to get her to teach me. It took years of practicing to get to the point where I could siphon off a person's energy like she could. What wasn't fun was getting her stable enough to teach."

"I don't understand; what exactly *are* you doing? Like, what was the point of the black energy under John's bed? Why would you need that there?"

"You don't understand anything. John and Doris have been playing one-upmanship forever. Why do you think he's been sick for so long? Doris has had her hooks into John for years. It's only since we managed to get the right drugs into her and she realized how much time she'd lost that she wanted to make John pay. The hooks were already in place. The dark energy was her way of feeding off him. But it's made her crazier, too. She's getting worse. I've had to increase her medication again. Rather gross, actually."

He shrugged. "If she remains drugged, then the energy will only stay if I choose to continue to feed it. If I don't, then it will wither away. I know enough to continue my training on my own." He stared at her curiously. "She's gotten away with it for a long time."

"So she really killed this way?" Shock and pain at the terrible betrayal twisted her insides. Her brain was stuck on the fact that the man who was supposed to be making a success of Maddy's floor had been using it as a feeding ground for his evil purposes.

"Well, I can't kill anyone that way yet, but I can make them really sick while I take their energy and use it for myself."

"So was it you or Doris who killed Jansen?" Maddy couldn't believe what she was hearing. Or reconcile the woman downstairs with the killer who'd taken Jansen's life – and who knew how many others?

"That was the demonstration that went a little too far. Man, she's smooth like that. Years of practice, she said. That's how she saved her son from sure death when he was just a kid. Once he'd healed, she had to do it every few months or more, almost like a junkie needing a fix, except that engaging in that process changed her. Her mental state deteriorated. Eventually, she had trouble remembering what to do and how to do it.

"That's where I came in. I finally stabilized her medications, and when I explained to her that her old doctor was to blame, she killed him out of revenge."

He laughed, a macabre sound that made Maddy cringe inside. If Cunningham got away with the knowledge he had...well there'd be no stopping him. "She's something. She also knew things about energy that most of us would never imagine. The combination was deadly."

Maddy said, "Except for one slight problem. She's a mental case from hell due to that knowledge...that's all." Her sarcasm was lost on him. The things these two people had done made her want to vomit.

He shrugged. "She was on the delicate side to begin with."

"Do you know who she killed years ago to save her son?"

"Ask that detective friend of yours. He'd be able to look it up. She picked on children back then because they were so innocent and open. That made it easier for her. Besides, children's energy is healthier and stronger than adult energy. She wasted much of it because she didn't really know what she was doing.

"She believed that children's energy was better to heal a child. Something about being a better match, like blood types. Once her mental state started to slide, she wasn't capable of doing that anymore. She said it had something to do with a healthy person's energy being able to block hers. The healthy energy would see her energy as abnormal – parasitic. For those here on Maddy's floor, their energy systems are compromised already, making them easier targets." He laughed. "Thanks for giving us this wonderful opportunity."

So it wasn't a feeding ground, at least not for him. Instead, her floor had been his training field.

He walked around Maddy, keeping the gun trained on her and John, who'd stayed still.

He slipped his hand in his pocket. He pulled a small blue book out of his pocket and waved it around. "Talk about coincidence. I had an old guy come into the ER. He'd gotten into an argument with another old fart about this diary. Seems his kid was murdered years ago and this is the diary his wife kept at the time. She listed all the people and places the kid had been in contact with – to help the police find his killer. All these years, the diary had been lost in the house.

"I grabbed it out of curiosity, thinking to accidentally 'find' it and return it later. Only it actually lists Doris in here several times, so I couldn't hand it over." His face twisted with satisfaction. "After all these years, she was finally going to be caught. I wasn't going to hang around to wait for that. Who knows what she'd end up saying."

Like a crazy man who'd pulled off something everyone else said couldn't be done, he was proud of himself. His work.

Maddy stood in shocked disbelief.

"Doris might still say something." Maddy didn't want to put Doris in any danger, yet she needed to keep Dr. Cunningham talking.

"No, she won't. I've changed her medication. She'll be a blathering idiot by now."

Nice. Use her mental illness to make her a non-suspect. Maddy tossed her head. "So much for being a doctor and caring about your patients."

"I've been a great doctor. When have I ever done a patient wrong? And no, Doris doesn't come into this. She's a bloody murderer. You should be thanking me for taking care of the problem. She won't be able to kill any more people now. Too bad you didn't realize she was hurting and killing people right under your nose." His voice changed to mimic a woman's high voice, his hand wafting in front of him. "Oh no, not Dr. Maddy – she's so perfect."

Maddy winced. That sounded horrible coming from him. "I've never professed to be perfect."

"Maybe not, but you've been blind to her murderous tricks. She's killed at least two men that I know of, one young and one old, and that's just in the last two weeks. She told me about them. She'd known the one since forever and the young one since he was a kid. Said she couldn't resist. Even then, her grasp on reality wasn't very good. The more she did, the worse she got. She hadn't gone after those two with the intent to kill, but hadn't been able to stop herself. She's losing control. I had to stop her. I couldn't trust her anymore." Something about the look on his face – it had turned analytical – gave Maddy the impression he wanted to experience the same sensations Doris had.

Maddy shuddered. Two? Eric and Jansen? One young and one old. And maybe more that she didn't know about. They'd have to go back to the date of Doris's arrival and check. She'd heard a whisper in her mind during her mad flight to Eric's bed that day. Could that have been Doris?

Paul continued to talk. "Adam told me how much he needed to see you, to tell you the truth. I had no idea what he'd planned to tell you, although the odds were good that it wasn't in my favor. He'd overheard me on the phone one day when I thought he'd been sleeping. I'd been confirming my travel plans to the Canary Islands. I didn't dare let him tell anyone.

"I panicked actually. With Doris done and out of the picture, I'd planned to leave this weekend anyway." He snorted. "But how the hell you got the message I don't know. No one was supposed to find him that fast. Had to have been that nurse. Because there you were...again." He glared at her. "Made me move my schedule up."

Maddy's jaw dropped. "You stabbed Adam just because he *might* have overheard a phone call of yours? A call that in no way connected you to any murders or attacks...yet you stabbed him for that?" The more she studied his face and his aura, the more she realized how unstable *he* was. "You've been practicing the techniques Doris has shown you, haven't you?"

"Of course." He glared at her. "I'm over sixty, Maddy. I have no intention of waiting until I'm dying before I start availing myself of all that glorious energy. That would be stupid."

"Stupid or not, you've made the same mistake she did. You've been collecting bits and pieces of other people around you. See Doris, the way she is? That's your future."

He rolled his eyes. "Nonsense. I've perfected her technique. She's the nutcase. I'm careful. I have a beautiful future ahead of me. No one is going to mess that up." His head cocked to one side. A calculating look came over his face.

"Don't make a sound," he whispered, his gaze sweeping over John huddled under his covers and the rest of the empty room.

Maddy had been harboring a snake in her own space and hadn't known it. He'd used her and her project. Unforgivable. She thought he'd been such a stalwart supporter, a hard worker and a good friend. Instead, that shell harbored a hardened, callous animal.

An odd sound whispered from behind her.

Dr. Cunningham motioned to something behind Maddy. "Welcome to the party. But throw your gun to the ground."

Maddy spun around.

Drew and Gerard walked into the open.

Drew glared, steely eyed at Dr. Cunningham, the gun steady in his hand.

"Do it. Or Maddy gets the first bullet."

The gun dropped from Drew's hand. Drew kicked it off to the side. A muscle in his jaw pulsed, but he never dropped his gaze from Dr. Cunningham.

Crap. The right man was here to help her – the wrong man was holding the gun.

Drew's face bolstered her courage. Pissed, his eyes held a cold, hard edge. Damn, the man looked good. And damn, she had it bad, if she could stand here with a crazed killer and think how wonderful Drew looked.

"Maddy, are you okay?" Drew's eyes were still trained on the gun.

"Why don't you ask me how I'm doing?" John's querulous voice quavered from the direction of the bed. His small, shrunken frame hard to see under the blankets. "I'm fine, thank you. Almost dead because of him and his damn mother. I could hardly believe all he was saying." He pointed at Drew. "Now, what the hell are you going to do about this mess?"

Dr. Cunningham snorted. "As if he's in a position to do anything."

"He's my nephew and he's a cop, so he'd damn well better do something."

Maddy winced. Just what she needed – a fight between a patient and a killer. "Everything is going to be fine, John."

"Sorry, Maddy, you're not going to be able to fix everything this time," Dr. Cunningham said, moving the gun between the four of them. "So who wants to go first?"

Without warning, Drew jumped him. The gun went off as Drew kicked it out of Dr. Cunningham's hands. The two men went down in a flurry of arms and legs. Gerard rushed in to help. Maddy snagged up the gun as it skidded across the floor, then waded into the fight to hold the gun to her colleague's head.

"Stop right there, or I'll shoot."

The men froze, their chests heaving. Dr. Cunningham laughed and snatched at the gun. In the fight to keep it, somehow the gun was fired again. She couldn't see if it did any damage as Dr. Cunningham wrenched it from her hands. "You won't kill me. You're too damn soft."

A third gunshot sounded.

Maddy jumped back. The first gun dropped to the floor as Dr. Cunningham fell, groaning. Everyone turned to John, who held himself up on one elbow, shaky but defiant, a small revolver in his hand.

"Like I'm going to let some asshole like him kill me."

Gerard walked over and plucked that gun from his uncle's hand. "You don't need that anymore."

Maddy dropped to the floor, her instincts taking over. John had shot true. Dr. Cunningham was dead.

With his cell phone Gerard called for security and emergency assistance.

Maddy looked at Drew. "I can't believe it was him. He was actually using my project to hurt people." The whole concept bewildered her. "He stabbed Adam. I passed him in the hallway on my way to Adam's room. I didn't think anything of it at the time." She shivered. "He had such an odd look on his face."

"Maddy, where are the staff?"

The color drained from her face. "Oh my God, I forgot about them. They're locked in my office."

"I'll go get them." Gerard ran down the hallway as security opened the locked doors. Police flooded the area. She was so going to need Stefan's help to rid the floor of these negative energies, to restore the healing balance here – but not tonight.

Maddy stepped back, turning to look at Drew and gasped in shock. "Damn it, Drew, why didn't you tell me you'd been hurt?" Maddy reached his side, her hand slapping down on his chest.

He tried to brush her hands away. "No, I'm fine."

Only he wasn't. Maddy gaped at her hand. Fresh blood dripped from her fingers. As Maddy watched, the color drained from his face and he leaned on her slightly before collapsing. She slid her arms around him and tried to support his weight as two officers raced over to help.

Maddy dropped to her knees by his side. "Oh, God." She slid her hand underneath. There was no exit hole. "Call emergency, he's been shot in the chest." A nurse ran toward her. Maddy snapped, "Get a stretcher. We have to get him downstairs. Now!"

Organized chaos ensued when Maddy's training and the training of those around her kicked in.

***

Maddy had trouble remembering the sequence of events or the people involved after that. The next thing she knew, she was staring at the closed surgery doors. She'd been stopped from entering as Drew was rushed inside.

Firmly, the surgical nurse turned her around and pushed her in the direction of the waiting room.

Maddy paced for the first hour, then sat for the next. She'd been pouring energy into the operating room since she'd been kicked out. She'd tried to direct it into him, but there'd been so many people clogging the path, she hadn't been able to do that. She should have left her body and gone in to help heal him, but she'd been so distraught she couldn't function on that level now. Stefan was in there funneling energy, but he wasn't the healer – she was.

What was taking them so long? When no one came out after a reasonable time, she knew in her heart it was bad. Why hadn't she checked Drew first? Because she hadn't known he'd been hurt. He'd acted so normal and she'd been so numbed by the shooting of Dr. Cunningham, and what she'd learned…she hadn't realized exactly what had happened.

He'd been in there a long time. Too long. Nancy had even come to check on her, handing her a hot coffee. Maddy had phoned John to update him. Now everyone had to wait. Currently, Gerard sat beside her. The CEO had never looked so haggard.

Maddy sympathized. Her world centered on what was going on in the surgical room. She was locked in by her fear. In a place of no return. She should be helping them. She had skills that could help – if she were calm enough.

She needed to find her center of balance. He needed her. She shuddered. He had the best team possible working on him. They'd save him. They had to.

Maddy. Stefan's voice in her mind stopped her in her tracks. *Stop and calm down. He needs your help. Our help. It's bad. You have to pull back. You're needed but you can't help him like this.*

Just then, the door opened and Dr. Samson, a physician she knew slightly, came out. The blood drained from her face at the look on his.

Drew hadn't made it.

He didn't want to meet her gaze. She ran up to him. "Dr. Maddy, we tried. Honest. He'd lost too much blood. The tears on the inside..." Dr. Samson shook his head. "I'm sorry, but the bullet nicked an artery—"

Maddy was no longer listening. She bolted through the double doors and into the OR. Drew was still on the operating table, a sheet over his head, blood coating – well, everything. They'd tried. She got that. Only they didn't know what she did.

She might be able to save him. There was one more thing she could do. She'd never tried on someone this far gone, but...

Once she saw his cord, threadlike and wispy and still attached, she knew for sure. She flipped the sheet back to see his face. As Maddy pulled up a high stool from against the wall, the operating nurses withdrew, leaving her alone.

Stefan... Help.

Maddy closed her eyes and slipped out of her body.

And slipped into Drew's.

It took a long scary minute to find his consciousness.

Maddy? What the hell?

Hush. You're hurt. I have to heal you. Don't waste your energy. Think about life, living and loving. Especially about loving. And Maddy had to do the same. To take her abilities to this level, with this deadly level of damage, she had to let go. Of her fears, her doubts, her emotions. She had to be one with him, no walls, no hesitation, no holding back – *she had to be him.*

Maddy poured her energy into his damaged body, filling his heart with life, his veins with the blood and his body with healing energy. She knitted the artery closed, repaired torn tissues and damaged muscle.

The whole time she sensed Stefan's protective energy around her, funneling love, caring and energy her way. To heal like this took strength. It took acceptance. It took surrender. To herself. To Drew. To what could have been. To what could be.

She didn't know how long she was in there. She didn't care. She wouldn't leave until it was done. Seconds ticked by, then minutes. Vaguely, she heard noises going on behind her. She knew the OR staff watched her. She thought someone wanted to move her, but heard Nancy stopped stop them before making the attempt. She didn't worry. Stefan would take care of them. Right now, she was caught in an energy frenzy that filled the room with heavy pulsing vibrations.

Static buzzed and the air moved on its own. No one there could misunderstand that something major was stirring in the ethers.

Maddy's space. That was her domain.

The OR belonged to the medical world. The ethers belonged to her. She intensified her efforts. She had to save Drew. He'd become too important to let go. She wasn't even sure if she could anymore. If he died, he might take her with him at this point.

Dimly, she heard a series of beeps, followed by yelling and the sound of rushing footsteps. Maddy shoved everything out of her mind. The waves pulsed from her fingers, her heart and her soul.

More. Stronger energy, whiter energy. Everything she had, everything she'd been, everything she was – poured into his soul.

"Maddy?"

"Maddy. Stop. We can take it from here."

Let go, Maddy. He's back. Stefan's warm, loving voice slipped deeper into her subconscious, pulling her back, helping her return home. Finally, other voices penetrated the fog she'd buried herself in. Maddy slowly sensed other people in the room. She saw the matrix of other energies working at her side, working to save Drew.

"He's back. We've got him. It's okay. Let go now before you collapse."

"Dr. Maddy, stop!"

Maddy heard something else too. *Maddy, I love you. Let go, sweetheart. I'm fine.*

Love you, too. Sorry, I couldn't let you go. Then she did let go and crumpled to the floor, unconscious.

SATURDAY

Drew woke up feeling like shit. He groaned and tried to roll over. Pain stabbed at his chest and radiated outward. A cry wrenched free. Christ, he hurt.

"Don't move, you've been shot and you've had surgery. You're going to be fine. However, you're going to feel terrible for a while."

Duh.

He opened his eyes. A very tired looking, breathtakingly lovely Maddy sat on the edge of his hospital bed, smiling at him. His first attempt to speak was a little weak, a little thin. "Does this mean I get to move to Maddy's floor?"

"Hell no. You won't be here for longer than a day or two at the most. Just long enough to regain your strength. And if you behave, they might release you early for good behavior." When she smiled down at him Drew thought he'd never seen anything so beautiful as his beloved Maddy.

Memories filtered back into his mind. A sporadic image. The odd word.

"Did you have a hand in my recovery?" Drew studied the weariness on her face. Had she slept at all? He glanced over at the chair beside his bed. Sure enough, her purse and what looked to be several discarded coffee cups sat on the floor beside it.

The room around him came into clearer view. His surroundings were nowhere near as nice as Maddy's floor. Still, like she said, he wouldn't be here long enough to care. As a matter of fact, he wasn't feeling too bad at all.

"Maybe. How are you feeling?"

"I feel good. How about you? Did you sit in that chair all night? Have you no sense at all?" he teased.

"I'm fine." She snickered. "I'm not the one who walked into a bullet."

He closed his eyes at the reminder. "Right. I'm willing to forget that part. It couldn't have been that bad. I'm here, aren't I?"

Dr. Samson walked into the room in time to hear that last part. "And that part is a miracle. I'm going to tell you, young man, you shouldn't be here at all. You took a bullet to the chest that nicked a main artery of your heart. You bled out on us and for all our best efforts, we lost you. We gave up." He tapped on his stylus for a moment then looked up to run a professional eye over Drew.

Drew started. What? "I died?" His gaze encompassed Dr. Samson and Maddy, her lips quirking at his question.

Dr. Samson nodded. His years of medical experience showed in the pure white hair and wrinkles, but his face was animated. "Not only died, but we couldn't revive you. And we tried hard." He walked over to where Maddy sat. "I went out, told this young lady, and she bolted into the operating room and refused to let you go."

Maddy patted Drew's hand, her warm eyes smiling down at him.

The doctor studied her, a light in his eyes, wonder in his voice. "I've got to tell you, I've seen a lot of things in my life, including many miracles, but I've never ever seen anything like what I saw her do to you. She healed the hole in your artery, made your heart beat again, filled your veins with blood, and did too many other things to mention. I stood in the back of that room with my colleagues and watched in awe while the room pulsed and glowed as she put you back together."

He shoved his hands in his pockets and rocked back on his heels. "Somehow, she did what shouldn't have been possible to do – she brought you back to life." With an apologetic glance at

Maddy, he explained, "I only stepped in to help because she appeared to be on the point of collapse. We stitched you closed and that's about it."

He patted Maddy's shoulder. "Now that I have some idea of what goes on in the special project of yours, young lady, I've got to admit, I'd like to learn a whole lot more."

Maddy looked up at him, a small smile playing at the corner of her lips. "Anytime."

"It obviously takes a toll on you, and I can see why you don't want to advertise your abilities. So make sure you rest for a couple of days yourself. Okay?"

"I will," she promised and watched him leave the room.

Turning back to face Drew, she found him studying her speculatively. "What's that look for?"

"You can do that? Bring people back from the dead?"

She frowned, shook her head, stared down at the sheets, her hands instinctively smoothing the wrinkles away. "You mean the others I've helped? There are a lot of factors that go into it, and then sometimes, if everything goes well, I might stop some of them from dying. Not always and not everyone, but sometimes...I can save one."

"And that makes it all worthwhile," he said, instinctively knowing the answer to his question. Because he had died. And she had brought him back.

She gazed down at him, her eyes so warm and loving.

He knew he was blessed.

"And that makes it all worthwhile."

"Speaking of people dying, how are Dr. Lenning and my uncle?"

"Your uncle is raising hell on my floor, and soon Dr. Lenning will be returning to help him." She grinned in delight. "Those two are going to get along wonderfully. Stefan says 'hi' and to stop doing things like catching bullets or you'll give *him* a heart attack."

"Well, you can tell him that I don't plan on ever going through that again."

She laughed. "I'm sure he knows already."

Drew studied her face. "I also remember something else while I was under."

Maddy gazed at him quizzically. "Really? What was that?"

"I remember a certain doctor telling me that she loved me."

A rosy flush rolled across her cheeks. She gave him a knowing smile. "That's okay – you said it first."

"Did not," he protested.

"Did too." They grinned at each other.

"Mean it?" he asked, studying her face intently.

She studied his features, her insides melting. "Absolutely. Did you?"

"Oh yes." He tugged her toward him, and kissed her thoroughly. So thoroughly, she didn't think he'd be in the hospital for more than a day – if that. "I feel great. It must be that extra dose of Maddy energy."

She grimaced. "There might be a few side effects of that, by the way."

"Like a more intimate knowledge of what you're thinking and feeling?" he murmured, tugging her back down to nestle against his good side. "Yes, I'm healing very rapidly, thank you."

She chuckled. "Yes, something like that. Of course, it works both ways, and just to inform you, the hospital bed is not the place to make love – you're not that healthy."

Surprise lit the depths of his eyes and he chuckled. "This will take some getting used to. We have a fun journey ahead of us."

"That it will be," she whispered against his lips. "Scared yet?"

"No way. Interested. Intrigued. In love. And looking forward to seeing how well this works out for both of us." Laughter colored his voice.

Sounds good to me, she whispered in her mind.

And to me, too. Did I tell you I love you, Dr. Maddy?

Not recently.

Well, I do. Now and forever.

DALE MAYER

Garden of Sorrow

Book 4 of Psychic Visions Series

Her world is in chaos. His world is in order. She wants to help the innocent. He wants to catch the guilty. But someone is trying to make sure that neither gets what they want.

Alexis Gordon has spent the last year trying to get over the loss of her sister. Then she goes to work on a normal day...and reality as she knows it...disappears.

Detective Kevin Sutherland, armed with his own psychic abilities, recognizes her gift and calls in his friend Stefan Kronos, a psychic artist and law enforcement consultant, to help her develop her skills. But Kevin has never seen anything like this case - a killer with a personal vendetta to stop Alexis from finding out more about him...and his long dead victims.

The killer can be stopped. He must be stopped. But he's planning on surviving...even after death.

About the author:

Dale Mayer is a prolific multi-published writer. She's best known for her Psychic Visions series. Besides her romantic suspense/thrillers, Dale also writes paranormal romance and crossover young adult books in several different genres. To go with her fiction, she also writes nonfiction in many different fields with books available on resume writing, companion gardening and the US mortgage system. She has recently published her Career Essentials Series. All her books are available in digital and print formats.

Books by Dale Mayer

Psychic Vision Series
Tuesday's Child
Hide'n Go Seek
Maddy's Floor
Garden of Sorrow
Knock, knock...

Death Series – romantic thriller
Touched by Death
Haunted by Death - (Fall 2013)

Novellas/short stories
It's a Dog's Life- romantic comedy
Sian's Solution – part of Family Blood Ties
Riana's Revenge – Fantasy short story

Second Chances...at Love
Second Chances - out now
Book 2 - Winter 2013/2014

Young Adult Books
In Cassie's Corner
Gem Stone (A Gemma Stone Mystery)

Design Series
Dangerous Designs
Deadly Designs
Deceptive Designs – fall 2013

Family Blood Ties Series
Vampire in Denial
Vampire in Distress
Vampire in Design - out now!
Vampire InDecision – coming soon!

Non-Fiction Books
Career Essentials: The Resume
Career Essentials: The Cover Letter
Career Essentials: The Interview
Career Essentials: 3 in 1

Connect with Dale Mayer Online:
Dale's Website – www.dalemayer.com
Twitter – http://twitter.com/#!/DaleMayer
Facebook – http://www.facebook.com/DaleMayer.author

CPSIA information can be obtained
at www.ICGtesting.com
Printed in the USA
LVOW10s1332080218
565801LV00020B/481/P